DEAD BESIDE THE THAMES

THE CASEBOOK OF BARNABY ADAIR: VOLUME 9

STEPHANIE LAURENS

ABOUT DEAD BESIDE THE THAMES

THE NINTH VOLUME IN THE CASEBOOK OF BARNABY ADAIR NOVELS

#1 NYT-bestselling author Stephanie Laurens returns with a confounding case that sees her favorite sleuths acting to save a friend wrongly accused of murder.

When a detested viscount is found murdered by the banks of the Thames and Charlie Hastings becomes the prime suspect, Barnaby and Penelope Adair join forces with Stokes to discover the real story behind the unexpected killing.

Charlie Hastings is astonished to find himself accused of murdering Viscount Sedbury. Admittedly, Charlie had two heated altercations with Sedbury in the hours preceding the man's death, but as Charlie is quick to point out to Stokes – and to Barnaby and Penelope – there are a multitude of others in the ton who will be delighted to learn of Sedbury's demise.

As Penelope, Barnaby, and Stokes start assembling a suspect list, Charlie's prediction proves only too accurate. Yet the most puzzling aspect is who on earth managed to kill Sedbury. The man was a hulking brute, large, very strong, and known as a vicious brawler. Who managed to subdue him enough to strangle him?

As the number of suspects steadily increases, the investigators are forced to ask if, perhaps, one of their suspects hired a killer capable of taking Sedbury down. With that possibility thrown into the calculations, narrowing their suspect list becomes a futile exercise.

Their pursuit of the truth leads them to investigate the many shady avenues of Sedbury's life, much to the consternation of Sedbury's father, the Marquess of Rattenby. Rattenby does not want Sedbury's distasteful proclivities exposed for all the world to see, further harming the other family members who Sedbury has taken great delight in tormenting for most of his life.

In the end, the resolution of the crime lies in old-fashioned policing coupled with the fresh twists Barnaby and Penelope bring to Scotland Yard's efforts.

And when the truth is finally revealed, it raises questions that strike to the very heart of justice and what, with such a victim and such a murderer, true justice actually means.

A historical novel of 62,500 words interweaving mystery and murder with a touch of romance.

PRAISE FOR THE WORKS OF
STEPHANIE LAURENS

"Stephanie Laurens' heroines are marvelous tributes to Georgette Heyer: feisty and strong." *Cathy Kelly*

"Stephanie Laurens never fails to entertain and charm her readers with vibrant plots, snappy dialogue, and unforgettable characters." *Historical Romance Reviews*

"Stephanie Laurens plays into readers' fantasies like a master and claims their hearts time and again." *Romantic Times Magazine*

Praise for Dead Beside The Thames

"When Charlie Hastings becomes a suspect in the murder of Viscount Sedbury, he turns to high-society investigators Penelope and Barnaby Adair to clear his name. Navigating the haut ton alongside Inspector Stokes, the sleuths peek at the darker side of some noble families, where greed, jealousy, and depravity weave a tangled web among supposedly proper gentlefolk." *Kim H., Copyeditor, Red Adept Editing*

"When Viscount Sedbury, one of the most loathed men in London, is found murdered next to the Thames, it's up to husband-and-wife team Barnaby and Penelope Adair to help the police find the killer. The clever duo uses their social connections to track down a murderer in this suspenseful mystery where no one is free from suspicion." *Brittany M., Proofreader, Red Adept Editing*

"Readers will love the engaging characters and unexpected twists of this mystery set in the deceptive elegance of London's haut ton." *Irene S., Proofreader, Red Adept Editing*

OTHER TITLES BY STEPHANIE LAURENS

Cynster Novels

Devil's Bride

A Rake's Vow

Scandal's Bride

A Rogue's Proposal

A Secret Love

All About Love

All About Passion

On A Wild Night

On A Wicked Dawn

The Perfect Lover

The Ideal Bride

The Truth About Love

What Price Love?

The Taste of Innocence

Temptation and Surrender

Cynster Sisters Trilogy

Viscount Breckenridge to the Rescue

In Pursuit of Eliza Cynster

The Capture of the Earl of Glencrae

Cynster Sisters Duo

And Then She Fell

The Taming of Ryder Cavanaugh

Cynster Specials

The Promise in a Kiss

By Winter's Light

Cynster Next Generation Novels

The Tempting of Thomas Carrick

A Match for Marcus Cynster

The Lady By His Side

An Irresistible Alliance

The Greatest Challenge of Them All

A Conquest Impossible to Resist

The Inevitable Fall of Christopher Cynster

The Games Lovers Play

The Secrets of Lord Grayson Child

Foes, Friends and Lovers

The Time for Love

The Barbarian and Miss Flibbertigibbet

Miss Prim and the Duke of Wilde

A Family Of His Own

Lady Osbaldestone's Christmas Chronicles

Lady Osbaldestone's Christmas Goose

Lady Osbaldestone and the Missing Christmas Carols

Lady Osbaldestone's Plum Puddings

Lady Osbaldestone's Christmas Intrigue

The Meaning of Love

The Casebook of Barnaby Adair Novels

Where the Heart Leads

The Peculiar Case of Lord Finsbury's Diamonds

The Masterful Mr. Montague

The Curious Case of Lady Latimer's Shoes

Loving Rose: The Redemption of Malcolm Sinclair

The Confounding Case of the Carisbrook Emeralds

The Murder at Mandeville Hall

The Meriwell Legacy

Dead Beside the Thames

Marriage and Murfer (March 2025)

Bastion Club Novels
Captain Jack's Woman (Prequel)

The Lady Chosen

A Gentleman's Honor

A Lady of His Own

A Fine Passion

To Distraction

Beyond Seduction

The Edge of Desire

Mastered by Love

Black Cobra Quartet
The Untamed Bride

The Elusive Bride

The Brazen Bride

The Reckless Bride

The Adventurers Quartet
The Lady's Command

A Buccaneer at Heart

The Daredevil Snared

Lord of the Privateers

The Cavanaughs
The Designs of Lord Randolph Cavanaugh

The Pursuits of Lord Kit Cavanaugh

The Beguilement of Lady Eustacia Cavanaugh

The Obsessions of Lord Godfrey Cavanaugh

Other Novels
The Lady Risks All

The Legend of Nimway Hall – 1750: Jacqueline

Medieval (As M.S.Laurens)
Desire's Prize

Novellas
Melting Ice – from the anthologies *Rough Around the Edges* and *Scandalous Brides*

Rose in Bloom – from the anthology *Scottish Brides*

Scandalous Lord Dere – from the anthology *Secrets of a Perfect Night*

Lost and Found – from the anthology *Hero, Come Back*

The Fall of Rogue Gerrard – from the anthology *It Happened One Night*

The Seduction of Sebastian Trantor – from the anthology *It Happened One Season*

Short Stories
The Wedding Planner – from the anthology *Royal Weddings*

A Return Engagement – from the anthology *Royal Bridesmaids*

UK-Style Regency Romances
Tangled Reins

Four in Hand

Impetuous Innocent

Fair Juno

The Reasons for Marriage

A Lady of Expectations An Unwilling Conquest

A Comfortable Wife

DEAD BESIDE THE THAMES

DEAD BESIDE THE THAMES

Copyright © 2024 by Savdek Management Proprietary Limited

ISBN: 978-1-925559-72-9

Cover design by Savdek Management Pty. Ltd.

Cover couple photography by Period Images © 2024

First print publication: October, 2024

Savdek Management Proprietary Limited, Melbourne, Australia.

www.stephanielaurens.com

Email: admin@stephanielaurens.com

The names Stephanie Laurens and the Cynsters and the SL Logo are registered trademarks of Savdek Management Proprietary Ltd.

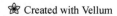 Created with Vellum

CHAPTER 1

SEPTEMBER 7, 1840. JERMYN STREET,
LONDON.

Charlie Hastings sank deeper into his favorite armchair beside the hearth in his Jermyn Street house and turned the first page in that morning's news sheet. To Charlie's mind, this was the very best time of his day, when, while digesting the excellent breakfast his housekeeper, Mrs. Swann, had provided, he could sit in peace and comfort and indulge his curiosity over what his fellow men were doing with their lives.

Inevitably, the answer was more exciting than what he was doing with his life, a situation that routinely left him feeling quietly smug. He infinitely preferred the calm and orderly peace of "nothing happening" to the alternative.

Reaching for the corner of the next page, he paused as a niggle, a small one, wormed its way through his brain. There were times when he wondered if being cocooned in such untrammeled comfort while life passed him by was truly as pleasant as he told himself it was. That perhaps "nothing happening"—at all, ever—was just a trifle dull. Boring, even.

He contemplated that question for all of a minute, then quashed it deep.

Comfort and "nothing happening" was his cup of tea.

Determinedly, he gripped the next page and was about to turn it when a sharp *rat-a-tat-tat* fell on his front door.

Charlie frowned, wondering who on earth would call at such an early hour; a quick glance at the mantelpiece clock confirmed it was barely nine o'clock. He wasn't surprised to hear his man, Garvey, hurry up the front hall. There was something about the solid, deliberate nature of that summons that demanded an immediate response.

Garvey opened the door and, faintly breathless, inquired, "Yes?"

Charlie heard a deep voice rumble a from-this-distance-incomprehensible yet somehow ominous reply.

Apparently, Garvey recognized the visitor's claim to entry and admitted him.

After trying and failing to identify the man's voice, Charlie folded the news sheet and set the paper aside. He heard heavy footsteps approaching the parlor door and got to his feet, schooling his expression to one of mildly curious civility as the door opened and Garvey ushered in the visitor.

"Inspector Stokes of Scotland Yard to see you, sir," Garvey intoned.

Charlie felt his expression blank, then his eyes widened as they landed on the man who followed Garvey into the parlor. "Stokes?"

Detective Inspector Basil Stokes halted and nodded in greeting. "Hastings."

Stokes's expression was unreadable, yet Charlie couldn't imagine this was a social call. His curiosity morphed into puzzlement, tinged with confusion and a touch of apprehension.

Charlie had always considered Stokes an unexpected policeman. Tall, well built, and broad shouldered, with steely gray eyes, dark-brown hair, and a face that appeared hewn from granite, Stokes effortlessly projected an imposing and faintly menacing presence, but unlike the vast majority of the force, he was gentry born and grammar school educated. While most policemen struggled to navigate the upper echelons of society, Stokes possessed the background, insight, and experience to do so. His success in solving several high-profile cases involving the aristocracy had seen him rise through the ranks to his present position as one of the more senior inspectors at Scotland Yard.

Over the years, Charlie and Stokes had crossed paths several times when Charlie had been assisting his good friend, the Honorable Barnaby Adair, with solving some mystery or crime. Charlie was aware that Barnaby—now joined by his wife, Penelope—continued to assist Stokes in cases involving the ton; he'd heard that Barnaby and Penelope were now called on in an official capacity as consultants to the Metropolitan Police, of which institution Barnaby's father, a close friend of Charlie's father, was one of the overseeing peers.

Despite all those connections, Charlie couldn't imagine what had brought Stokes directly to his door. He drew in a breath and asked, "Is there something I can help you with?"

Smoothly, Stokes replied, "A situation has arisen on which, I believe, you might be able to shed some light." Stokes's gray gaze cut to Garvey, who was hovering behind him.

Charlie took the hint and nodded a dismissal to Garvey, then waved Stokes to the second armchair, which was angled to face Charlie's favored seat. "Of course. I'm happy to assist in any way I can."

Charlie waited until Stokes sat, then resumed his seat, crossed his legs, clasped his hands loosely in his lap, and bent an inquiring expression on Stokes.

Stokes studied him for a moment, then grimaced. He drew out a small black book and a pencil from his coat pocket and, finally, volunteered, "A body was hauled from the Thames yesterday, and items found on the corpse suggest the dead man is Viscount Sedbury."

Charlie's eyes flew wide. "Sedbury?" After a moment of stunned stupefaction, he repeated with more force, *"Sedbury?"*

When Stokes did nothing but watch him closely, Charlie blustered, "But good God, man! Sedbury was a great hulking fellow. How on earth did someone kill him?"

Stokes mildly replied, "I don't have any details as yet, but currently, we're working on the hypothesis that he was attacked and killed or stunned on one of the bridges and tipped into the river."

"Good Lord!" Charlie just stared.

After scribbling some note, Stokes searched Charlie's face, then on an exhalation that was close to a sigh, Stokes went on, "The reason I'm here is that while investigating Sedbury's recent movements, I learned of an altercation between you and the viscount that occurred at White's on Saturday evening. I was told that Sedbury bailed you up in the card room, and you responded to his statements with some degree of heat, the subject under discussion being a previous encounter between you and Sedbury earlier in the day." Stokes trapped Charlie's gaze. "Would you care to elaborate on that earlier encounter?"

Charlie met Stokes's scrutiny with his best blank expression while his wits whirled. Sedbury dead? After...

It took less than a minute for Charlie to conclude that he would rather be talking to Stokes than being interrogated by anyone else. He huffed out a breath and considered giving the man a less-than-full account. Regretfully jettisoning that notion as a recipe for misunderstanding, he reluctantly accepted the inevitable, filled his lungs, fixed his gaze on the far wall, and admitted, "I was strolling in Long Acre at about eleven o'clock on Saturday morning, intending to look in at several establishments to see whether anything caught my eye. People were gathering on the pavement just ahead, and when I reached the edge of the crowd, I saw that everyone was watching Sedbury, who had a young lad—a street sweeper—by the scruff of the neck and was shaking the boy like a rat. Sedbury was furious —red-faced and spewing threats the like of which were enough to chill anyone's blood. Then he hauled the boy into the street and reached for his whip."

"Whip?" Stokes looked up from his notebook.

"Sedbury carried a short-handled horsewhip in the same manner other gentlemen carry swordsticks." Charlie shook his head. "An affectation, true enough, but Sedbury definitely knew how to wield that whip. He was famous for it."

Frowning, Stokes nodded. "Go on."

Charlie blew out a breath. "Well, it was clear Sedbury was going to whip the tyke, and in the mood he was in, he would have flayed the skin from the boy's back. Then I heard a cry, and I saw a girl of maybe thirteen or fourteen screaming for the boy, and I—well, we, the whole crowd —realized that the boy had only been trying to protect his sister from Sedbury's unwanted attentions." Charlie huffed. "Well, I could hardly stand by and let Sedbury whip the lad for that. I couldn't hope to physically overcome Sedbury, so I waited until he raised his whip, and I stepped in and filched it from his grasp." Charlie smiled cynically. "I might not be up to meeting the man at Gentleman Jackson's, but I do know whips." He shifted his gaze to Stokes's face. "As I'd expected, Sedbury rounded on me—and the boy seized the chance to wrench free. I walked steadily backward, and predictably, Sedbury stalked toward me, scowling and swearing, and meanwhile, the boy and his sister vanished down an alley." Reliving the moment, Charlie acknowledged, "Mind you, by then, the crowd had definitely taken against Sedbury. Not that he paid them any heed." After a second, Charlie focused on Stokes and concluded, "Once the boy and girl were well away, I halted and handed Sedbury his whip."

"You didn't fear he'd use it on you?"

"He certainly threatened to," Charlie admitted with a reminiscing smile, "but there are some lines even Sedbury knew he couldn't cross."

Holding Stokes's gaze, Charlie added, "I don't regret my actions, Stokes —not that morning or that evening, either. If Sedbury went and got himself killed later, well, I doubt you'll find anyone evincing any degree of surprise. He was a nasty piece of work—the absolute antithesis of a credit to the ton."

Stokes grunted and scribbled several lines, then met Charlie's gaze. "So, to the incident at White's."

Involuntarily, Charlie grimaced. He saw Stokes take note and felt a faint blush rise in his cheeks. "That was...uncalled for and...quite unseemly. I had no idea Sedbury was in the club until he bowled up, brash and bold as only he could be, and interrupted our game. He started flinging insults and followed up with threats. I can't say that it was an edifying moment for any of us forced to hear him."

Consulting his notebook, Stokes said, "I understand that at the table with you were Viscount Mollison, Mr. Carruthers, and Lord Abercrombie."

Charlie nodded. "Quite. And there were others about—the room was rather crowded—and the longer Sedbury ranted, more wandered in to see what the commotion was about."

"Was Sedbury with anyone? Any friends?"

"No." Considering the point, Charlie frowned. "I don't think he has any. Friends, I mean, as distinct from mere acquaintances. He is—was—a loner, was Sedbury. Very much one who preferred his own company."

Stokes continued busily scribbling. "So, what happened to make Sedbury leave?"

Charlie huffed contemptuously. "I might not be top-o'-the-trees, but I am reasonably well-connected and well-known within the ton. The family is, too. Sedbury was loud and getting louder by the second, and the others who had gathered around started to object. Increasingly forcefully. In his inimitable fashion, Sedbury sneered at us all, then flung an order at me to stay out of his path or else and spun on his heel and stalked out." Charlie looked at Stokes. "That was the last I saw of him."

Stokes came to the end of his jotting and looked up. "Thus far, the last time for which we have witnesses to Sedbury being alive was when he quit White's."

Stokes studied the man before him. He'd met Charlie Hastings several times over the years, and his reading of the man was of a quiet gentleman who liked and, indeed, preferred the simple pleasures of tonnish life. However, behind the well-cut blond hair, the rather kindly brown eyes, and the pleasant features almost perennially set in a genial, easygoing expression was a steady solidity that spoke of principles and sound character. While intellectually, Charlie might be a lightweight compared to his good friends Barnaby and Penelope, the very fact that they'd remained close friends for decades spoke volumes.

Mentally reviewing his previous encounters with Charlie, Stokes acknowledged that the man before him had matured—physically, emotionally, and almost certainly socially. Hastings was a little over average height, lean rather than heavy, and cut an unobtrusively elegant figure. Stokes pegged him as a gentleman who would rather inhabit the background than take center stage.

Evenly, Stokes observed, "I understand that you left White's soon after. Alone."

Charlie looked faintly uncomfortable. "Well, my evening had gone downhill, thanks to Sedbury." He met Stokes's eyes. "But you can't have found anyone to say I went after Sedbury because I didn't. I came home —here."

Stokes inclined his head. "I admit that we have no witnesses who saw you and Sedbury together after you both left the club."

"That's because we *weren't* together later." Charlie flung up his hands. "Just think of it—at that time, Sedbury was literally the last man in London I would seek out, much less look to spend more time with!"

Stokes studied Charlie. "I can certainly see how that might be. However, we also have it on good authority that you and Sedbury are rivals of sorts in the matter of collecting whips." Stokes trapped Charlie's gaze. "That was why, in Long Acre, you were confident in your ability to take the whip from him."

Stokes hadn't previously heard of gentlemen collecting whips, but given the time and attention gentlemen of the ton paid to all things to do with horses, he couldn't say he was surprised that such a fraternity existed.

Charlie frowned, but readily admitted, "Yes, that's true, but I can't see what that has to say to anything. There are several whip collectors in London, and we don't go around murdering each other over whips." He spread his hands. "What would be the point?"

Stokes had to admit that was a reasonable question; men with collections of any stripe liked to display their acquisitions to others.

He was aware that Charlie was studying his face and knew there was nothing to be read there; he was long past the stage of allowing his thoughts to show.

Eventually, Charlie shifted, then stated, "I say, Stokes—I didn't murder Sedbury, and I have absolutely no idea who did."

Stokes believed him, not least because Charlie's emotions were easy to discern; he was somewhat affronted to find himself considered a suspect in a murder, but at the same time, he understood what had brought Stokes to his door and was trying to be reasonable and helpful without in any way incriminating himself. There was also, Stokes judged, the early stirrings of curiosity over how and why Sedbury had been killed. Yet the critical point in stamping Charlie as highly unlikely to be Sedbury's murderer was the disparity in size, weight, and strength.

Stokes had never encountered Sedbury, but the initial description of the corpse from the Thames River Police was of a great hulking brute of a man in excellent physical shape, with no obvious injuries—not shot, not stabbed. Charlie's comments had only added to the picture of Sedbury's strength. Consequently, while Charlie was hardly a stripling or a weakling, it was seriously difficult to imagine how he could have overcome a man of Sedbury's stature.

Still studying Stokes's unrevealing face, Charlie frowned. "Here, I say, this is truly serious, isn't it? I mean, Sedbury is Rattenby's heir, so there's bound to be a huge ruckus over his murder even if no one's all that surprised."

That was the second time Charlie had referred to people not being surprised to learn of Sedbury's murder. Before Stokes could ask for clarification, Charlie straightened and went on, "Perhaps involving Barnaby and Penelope might be wise. I've heard that you're now working with them on a more formal basis, and clearly, this case qualifies as one in which their input would help."

With a quick smile, Stokes shut his notebook. "I agree." He paused, then added, "I need to get permission from the commissioner to bring them in as consultants." He met Charlie's gaze. "While I head back to the Yard for that, why don't you go to Albemarle Street? At this hour, Barnaby and Penelope should both be at home, and you can bring them up to date with what I've told you and your recent interactions with the man." Stokes paused, then rose and added, "And you can ask for their help in ensuring you're not taken up for the crime."

"Here, I say!" Charlie got to his feet. "I'm not truly a suspect, am I?"

Stokes smiled more definitely, headed for the door, and didn't reply.

Behind him, Charlie huffed, then followed him into the hall. Stokes quit the house, leaving Charlie shrugging on his coat and instructing Garvey to fetch his hat.

~

Barnaby sat on one of the sofas in the garden parlor and laughed at the sight of his wife and two sons rolling on the rug before the hearth while the family's new addition—a puppy named Roger—gamboled about the three, yipping and darting in to playfully tug on any available clothing.

The puppy had been a gift from Barnaby's father, the Earl of Cothelstone. Roger was a spaniel puppy of prestigious lineage, a product of the earl's kennels, which were renowned for producing excellent gun dogs. Barnaby was looking forward to taking Roger, once he was old enough, out with the pack when they visited Cothelstone.

Meanwhile, Roger was proving an excellent source of distraction for the entire household; the pup had quickly ingratiated himself with Mostyn, their majordomo, and, of course, Cook.

A smile wreathing his face, Barnaby watched Penelope encourage their younger son, Pip, just eight months old, to sit up so he could grip the end of the rope that Roger had between his jaws and tug.

Pip tugged, then chortled happily when Roger obligingly tugged back. Meanwhile, Oliver, now nearly four years old, gathered up and made a pile of the soft toys the boys had donated to the puppy.

Barnaby felt a definite inner glow as he watched the three most important people in his life laugh and have fun. He and Penelope had vowed to make a conscious effort to spend at least a little time each day with the boys—just him, her, and their sons.

And now, the puppy. Barnaby seriously doubted Oliver and Pip would willingly be parted from the small black-and-white dog, and as young children and pets went, that was how things ought to be.

Today, they'd come to the parlor directly after breakfast and had been there for more than half an hour. Focusing on Penelope, he caught her eye and asked, "What are you planning on doing today?"

She glanced at the boys, then left them to their game of tug and swung to face Barnaby. "I have that translation for the museum in Sheffield. It's only half done, and I suppose I should get back to it while I can. That said, there's no rush." From behind her spectacles, she opened her eyes wide at him. "You?"

He confessed, "I have to admit I'm at loose ends."

"Good gracious!" the wife of his heart riposted. "How has *that* come about?"

He grinned. "I'm not quite sure."

Their banter was interrupted by the pealing of the new front doorbell.

Barnaby blinked, then met Penelope's gaze. As the pealing continued in what could only be termed an agitated manner, he arched his brows in surprise.

Even the boys and the dog registered the implication and stopped their game to look at the door in expectation.

Distantly, Barnaby caught the sound of voices—Mostyn's and another male's—then footsteps approached in rapid and determined fashion.

Penelope caught Barnaby's gaze and tipped her head toward the bellpull. "Hettie?"

Barnaby was already rising; Hettie was the boys' nursemaid. "An excellent idea."

He tugged the bellpull, then turned as the door opened and Mostyn ushered Charlie Hastings into the room.

One look at his old friend, and Barnaby could tell he was seriously unsettled.

Penelope was every bit as observant as Barnaby. She got to her feet and, with a welcoming smile, went forward to take Charlie's hands. "Charlie—how lovely to see you. Do come in."

Charlie grasped her fingers and half bowed over them, mumbling his thanks for the welcome and, with a glance at Barnaby, added that he was relieved to find them at home.

If Barnaby and Penelope had needed any further hint that something was drastically wrong, that "relieved" provided it.

Penelope turned and beamed at the boys. "We were just playing with these two." She bent and hoisted Pip to her hip. "Oliver—come and make your bow to Uncle Charlie."

Oliver was delighted to front up and do so.

Charlie smiled and duly offered his hand for Oliver to shake, which the boy did with gusto.

"Er…" Charlie cast a helpless glance at Barnaby.

Understanding the look, Penelope stated, "The boys were about to go upstairs."

On cue, Hettie appeared in the doorway. She'd heard Penelope's dictum, saw the way Oliver's face fell, and, reaching for Pip, brightly said, "Cook has, just this minute, taken a sheet of shortbread biscuits from the oven." She smiled at Oliver, then at Pip. "Shall we go to the kitchen and see?"

Shortbread biscuits trumped adult conversation every time. "Yes!" Oliver paused only long enough to command, "Come along, Roger!" then, with the dog at his heels, hurried off with Hettie.

Smiling benignly, Mostyn followed the small procession from the room and closed the door behind him.

Immediately, Penelope tugged Charlie to the sofa, sat, and waved him to the place beside her.

Charlie dropped onto the pale-green silk, and Barnaby sat opposite as Penelope directed, "Tell us what's wrong."

Charlie looked from her to Barnaby. "I'm a whisker away from being charged with murder, that's what!"

"Murder!" Penelope exclaimed.

Frowning, Barnaby asked, "Whose?"

"Sedbury's!" Needing no further urging, Charlie poured out the somewhat amazing tale of Stokes's morning visit to Jermyn Street and what Stokes had revealed. "In the end, Stokes and I agreed that this was one case where your assistance was most definitely required, and he went off to ask the commissioner for approval." Charlie glanced toward the door. "He said he would join us here."

"Sedbury." Frowning, Penelope glanced at Barnaby. "I can't remember ever meeting the man. Are we sure he's of the ton?"

Barnaby grimly nodded. "Most definitely. He's Rattenby's eldest child and heir, the only child of his first marriage."

"Then that I've never met him is even more strange," Penelope pointed out. "I've met the marquess and the current marchioness several times, and I've met their children. All of them." She widened her eyes at Barnaby. "Why have I never met the oldest son?" She blinked, then added, "Until now, I didn't even know there *was* an older son."

Barnaby met her gaze. "The reason for that very likely feeds into the motive for his murder."

"Indeed," Charlie averred. "Sedbury was a rum 'un and rarely appeared in wider society. The clubs, hells, and so on, yes. Racing tracks and the like. But generally speaking, you wouldn't expect to find him in the ballrooms."

"That said," Barnaby concluded, "given Sedbury's status, Stokes was entirely correct in thinking that we need to be involved in this case."

On the words, the front doorbell rang, and a minute later, Stokes walked into the room.

He smiled at Barnaby and Penelope, who eagerly welcomed him and waved him to join them. Claiming the place on the sofa next to Barnaby, Stokes inquired, "Did Hastings here fill you in?"

"He did," Penelope replied. "So are we now officially on the case?"

Stokes grinned at her. "If you're willing."

Penelope huffed. "Of course we are, on Charlie's account if for no other reason. Now, is there anything more you can tell us?"

"Such as," Barnaby put in, "what information led you to Charlie's door this morning."

Charlie looked much struck. "I hadn't thought to ask." He looked at Stokes.

Smiling faintly, Stokes obliged. "After being informed that the body hauled from the river was presumed to be Sedbury's—a card in a card case found on the body carried the name and an address—I headed for Sedbury's rooms and thought to call in at White's on the way, hoping someone there could give me a decent description of the man. As it happened, the porters gave me an excellent picture and a great deal more. Enough that instead of going to Sedbury's rooms, I diverted to Jermyn Street and Hastings's abode." Stokes glanced at Charlie. "Have you told them of your two run-ins with Sedbury on Saturday?"

Charlie nodded.

"But," Penelope said, swiveling on the sofa to fix her dark gaze on Charlie, "you didn't really give us the details. So…"

Stokes watched and listened as she and Barnaby led Charlie through more or less every minute of both altercations in an inquisition of mind-numbing exactitude. Courtesy of Penelope's connection with the Foundling House and the children of the lower classes she interacted with there, she had incisive insight into the incident in Long Acre, while Barnaby, with his knowledge of White's and those who inhabited its halls, knew what questions to ask to draw Charlie into giving a much more complete account of the clash there.

Quietly listening without interrupting, Stokes added to his notes. This was precisely why he—and Scotland Yard—needed the help of this pair of consultants.

When it seemed that Barnaby and Penelope had extracted every last detail of Charlie's recent encounters with Sedbury, Stokes turned to another issue of which he didn't as yet feel sufficiently informed. "This business of whip collecting." He looked at Charlie. "You mentioned there are other whip collectors in London. Who are they?"

"Well." Charlie blew out a breath. "There are six others, including me. The other five are Crookshank, Quisley, Ellerton, Napier, and Hoskings."

"And you each have a collection?"

"Yes, although mine, Quisley's, and Napier's are the best known." Charlie frowned. "I knew Sedbury was a collector because he would occasionally outbid one of us when a notable whip was auctioned, but I've never heard anyone describe his collection." He tipped his head, considering. "In fact, I couldn't tell you how extensive Sedbury's collection is. It might be quite sizeable."

Stokes grunted. He looked over his earlier notes, then said, "The way you spoke of the whip Sedbury was carrying in Long Acre, it sounded as if it was a specific whip. You called it 'his whip' as if it was a particular one." He raised his gaze to Charlie's face. "Was it?"

Charlie nodded emphatically. "He had a favorite whip—a particular type of horse whip known as a Duckleberry Longe—that he carried most frequently. That was the whip he had in Long Acre."

"I see." Stokes added the name to his jottings.

Penelope fixed her gaze on him. "You must know more about how Sedbury—his body—was found."

That wasn't a question. Stokes faintly smiled. "All I've heard thus far is that two boatmen pulled the body from the river about noon on Sunday and ferried it to the River Police. They found a card case in his jacket pocket and made out enough to guess his identity and notify the Yard. The commissioner dumped the investigation in my lap first thing this morning, and that sent me to White's and, subsequently, to Hastings's door. When I went back to get permission to call you in, there was a note from the sergeant at the River Police office, saying that the postmortem will be carried out sometime today, and they'll send word so I can speak with the examiner. The only other tidbit the sergeant imparted was that when the examiner came in, he glanced at the body and declared that Sedbury had been strangled and, either dead or unconscious, was then tipped into the river. They'll have more details when I get there later."

Barnaby pulled a face. "That's really not a lot of information regarding the actual killing."

"It isn't," Stokes agreed. "We'll have to wait for the postmortem and hope the examiner can tell us more."

"All right," Barnaby said. "So what do we actually know to this point?" He glanced at Charlie. "Sedbury was known to be an aggressive, belligerent, pugilistically inclined brawler. He was larger and significantly heavier and stronger than most gentlemen and was widely known as a bully of the worst sort."

Barnaby transferred his gaze to Stokes. "I have to say that, all things considered, it's really not credible to assert that Charlie strangled Sedbury, then heaved the body into the river."

Penelope put in, "Certainly not without sustaining some degree of damage himself, of which there appears to be precisely none."

Stokes and Barnaby obediently looked at Charlie, who stared innocently back, his face and hands entirely free of marks, scrapes, cuts, or bruises.

"Right," Stokes said. "I believe we can all agree that Hastings does not fit the bill for our murderer." Stokes flashed them all a sardonic smile. "I confess that I wasn't enthralled by the notion of Hastings as murderer, but given the situation as it currently stands, that only underscores the urgent need to find the real murderer."

Barnaby blinked as the situation—the one Stokes had already seen—blossomed in his mind. "Ah. Yes. I hadn't thought that far ahead."

For a moment, Penelope regarded him in mystification, then understanding lit her features. "Oh, good heavens! Yes, of course."

Proving that he was not as slow-witted as he sometimes appeared, Charlie somewhat waspishly retorted, "While I'm delighted at no longer being the prime suspect, we all know what the ton is like, and with Stokes having already interviewed various staff at White's, some version of my altercation with Sedbury immediately before his death will already be doing the rounds, and ton gossip being what it is, my name and reputation will be mud—besmirched beyond repair—unless the real murderer is laid by the heels, and quickly, too!"

Penelope grimaced. "Unfortunately, you are one hundred percent correct. Just the weight of mere suspicion will be a cloud over your name."

Barnaby glanced around the circle. "I believe we're all on the same page. We need to find Sedbury's murderer with all speed."

"And then there's the complication of Sedbury's family." Penelope looked at Stokes. "Has the next of kin been informed?"

Stokes stirred. "The commissioner has taken on that task. However, he didn't mention who the next of kin actually was." He looked inquiringly at the others.

Barnaby replied, "That would be Sedbury's father, the Marquess of Rattenby."

Stokes groaned. "I knew he was a viscount, but a marquess's heir?"

Penelope tried not to smile. "Late heir."

Stokes grumbled, "So I can expect a visit from the marquess, breathing fire and demanding an immediate arrest, at any moment."

Penelope tipped her head. "Actually, you'll most likely be spared such a meeting for at least a few days. If I'm remembering correctly, Rattenby prefers to remain in the country at his principal seat in Gloucestershire. I know that he and the marchioness are not in London at present."

Stokes reached for his notebook. "What do you know of the family?"

"Well, I know the marquess and his current marchioness have five children. The eldest is a daughter, Claudia, who must be about twenty-eight by now." Penelope frowned slightly. "She's of similar age to me. It's odd that she hasn't married, yet I'm sure she hasn't. Next in line is a son, Jonathon, who must be twenty-six or so, followed by another son, Bryan, who I think is about twenty-two, and a daughter, Margot, who is eighteen and due to make her come-out next year, and last, another son, Conrad, who must be just fifteen."

Still frowning, Penelope shook her head. "I must admit that with the marquess and marchioness rarely being in town, I'm not as up to date with the latest regarding their family as I would like to be."

Charlie gently scoffed, "You still know more than the rest of us combined."

"Regardless," Barnaby said, addressing Stokes, who was busy scribbling, "you won't have Rattenby breathing down your neck just yet."

Stokes grunted. "A small mercy, but I'll take it."

"Actually..." Penelope caught Stokes's eye and lightly grimaced. "There's a paternal aunt, Lady Selborough, who lives in town, and her husband is quite influential politically, and I believe Sedbury's older three half siblings—Claudia, Jonathon, and Bryan—are also currently in town. I'm not sure how close any of them were to Sedbury, much less how they'll react to the news of his death."

Stokes softly groaned and wrote some more.

Penelope frowned more definitely. "It's annoying that I know so little about the Hales—that's the marquess's family name—but I will rectify that situation as soon as possible. Meanwhile, to confirm, Lord Jonathon

Hale, being Sedbury's oldest half brother, is the next in line to the marquessate and, therefore, is now Rattenby's heir."

Stokes looked up from his notes. "Well, that's something—someone I'll need to check on." He closed his notebook and tucked it away. "And while it's a minor relief to know that I won't immediately be hauled before the marquess to face demands for definitive and conclusive answers, given those involved, the commissioner himself will be demanding answers all too soon. Members of the nobility being murdered tends to make everyone in the force extra nervous."

His expression sympathetic, Barnaby suggested, "We should plan what next we need to do." He glanced at the others. "We know what facts we have thus far. Working from those, what do we most urgently need to learn?"

They cogitated for a moment, then Charlie offered, "Stokes said that Sedbury walking out of White's was the last time he was seen alive, but someone must have seen him after that." Charlie looked around the circle. "Sedbury walked out onto St. James Street at a quarter to midnight or thereabouts on a Saturday night. Quite aside from members of the ton, there would have been jarveys and street lads about, and one thing you have to say of Sedbury, he cut a figure that was hard to miss. Someone had to have seen him."

Stokes slowly nodded. "You're right. And yes, we should follow that up and see what we can find."

"By the same token," Penelope said, "we should seek witnesses who saw Charlie leave White's and walk home to Jermyn Street."

Barnaby nodded. "And check with Garvey for the time Charlie arrived home."

Charlie looked happier.

"And top of my list," Stokes said, "is finding anyone who witnessed a meeting between Sedbury and someone else on one of the bridges later that night. Jarvey, boatman, passerby—someone must have seen him or heard an argument or fight."

Barnaby said, "Given the victim was Sedbury, who loved to brawl, then any fight that resulted in him being overcome and tipped off a bridge had to have been noticeable." He paused, then added, "Sedbury wasn't the sort of man who would have been taken unawares."

Stokes humphed. "We'll see what the postmortem tells us. Perhaps someone slipped a knife between his ribs, but from what you and the coroner have already said, that seems unlikely."

"In essence," Penelope said, "we need to gather all the information we can on Sedbury's last hours. He left White's at a little before midnight—where did he go next?"

Stokes nodded. "That's our most obvious avenue to pursue."

"And while you and Barnaby and Charlie are looking into that," Penelope said, "I'll see what I can learn about the Hale family members currently in town."

The sound of the doorbell reached them, and they paused expectantly.

Moments later, Mostyn appeared and announced, "Sergeant O'Donnell has arrived, Inspector. He says you've been summoned to the morgue of the River Police. Apparently, the medical examiner has completed his task and says there's information you need to hear."

"Well!" Stokes uncrossed his legs and rose. "That sounds promising." He glanced at the others. "I'll return here with whatever insights the examiner has to share—"

"And while you're gone," Barnaby said, "we'll put our heads together and work out how to learn all we need to know."

Stokes grinned, saluted the company, and strode for the door.

CHAPTER 2

Stokes had been to the Thames River Police's morgue multiple times before, and it was never a pleasant duty. The River Police's headquarters was a gloomy gray-stone building that squatted in the shadows of the Tower. Stokes made his presence known to the sergeant at the front desk and was promptly waved toward the narrow corridor that led to the even narrower stairs that gave access to the building's basement, in which the morgue was housed.

Stokes glanced at O'Donnell.

Immediately, the experienced sergeant said, "I'll wait here."

Stokes snorted and left him, knowing O'Donnell would use the time to see what he could learn from the other sergeant.

On his way down the stairs, Stokes felt a damp chill envelop him. This close to the river, any subfloor level was inevitably dank and cold, a fitting place to store the remains of the dead pulled from the river's embrace.

Steeling himself against what he would see and smell, Stokes pushed through the morgue's door. A quick scan of the three steel tables revealed that only one—the last in the row—was occupied. He'd been told that Findlay was the examiner on duty, which was something of a relief.

At the sound of Stokes's steps, the grizzled veteran medical examiner looked up from where he sat at a desk in one corner, then lumbered to his feet. "Stokes." Findlay nodded a greeting, but didn't offer to shake hands;

few medical examiners did. Findlay tipped his head toward the shrouded form occupying the third table. "Heard you'd been given this one."

"Unfortunately for me," Stokes said. "It seems he's a marquess's heir."

"Oh-ho!" Findlay, whose girth was considerable, waddled to the table. "The plot is therefore thick to begin with."

Stokes had to smile. "So, what can you tell me? Dare I hope for an open-and-shut case?"

Findlay snorted. "With the nobs involved, what's the likelihood, heh?" He lifted the sheet and gently drew it all the way back to reveal the naked form of a very large and powerfully built man.

Taking in the full measure of the victim, Stokes silently whistled. "You said he was strangled. How the devil did anyone manage to strangle him?"

"That's the mystery, heh?"

Studying the corpse, Stokes moved to stand at its feet. He shook his head. "If it wasn't for the haircut and perhaps the features, I'd peg him for a Limehouse brawler."

Findlay grunted. "And I wouldn't argue. But the cards in his card case, which were wet but printed, so the ink didn't run, say otherwise."

Stokes glanced up. "Anything else in his pockets?"

"Two letters, which were sodden and useless, and several pounds' worth of coins." Findlay tipped his head toward the desk. "They're ready for you to take." When Stokes continued to frown at the dead man, Findlay added, "Given the way his clothes and boots fitted, they were made for him and by the best makers in town. If he isn't this viscount, he's nevertheless someone from that level of society."

Stokes grimaced. "The description I have of Viscount Sedbury is of a great hulking brute of a man."

Findlay waved at the table. "They don't come much more hulking than this. Sounds like Sedbury is, indeed, your victim. That said, we'll need formal identification by a family member."

Stokes sighed and nodded. "I'll have someone arrange it." He glanced at Findlay. "So, what can you tell me about how he died?"

Findlay tugged one earlobe. "Well, he was definitely dead before he hit the water—no trace of the river in his lungs. And if you look here"—Findlay pointed to marks about the corpse's neck—"you can see that he was strangled. The hyoid bone is broken, which would have required considerable force. Given the victim's size, musculature, and rude health, that suggests that, realistically, the murderer must be equally large, at least as tall, and at least as strong. In my opinion, you're looking for someone even stronger. It would have taken enormous strength to manage this man's weight while actively strangling him."

Stokes tried to imagine that. "Could he—our victim—have been subdued before being strangled? I mean by being knocked over the head or drugged or rendered unconscious in some way?"

Findlay nodded approvingly. "An excellent question, but the answer is no, or rather, not exactly. I've made a thorough examination and can find no hint whatsoever of inebriation or injury that might have rendered him unconscious. However"—he pointed to a large bruise darkening the bridge of the corpse's nose and one cheekbone—"that was done close to the time of death. I seriously doubt it knocked him out, but likely it would have stunned him for an instant. But nothing more. I say that because of the bruises and abrasions on his knuckles and the scrapes on his neck." Findlay picked up one flaccid hand and pointed at the damage. "Both hands. See? The marks are consistent with him putting up a fight. Quite a fight. And here"—Findlay set down the hand and pointed to marks scored in the skin of the corpse's neck—"he scrabbled desperately hard at the noose, as it were. He didn't die easily." He looked at Stokes. "If I had to guess, I would say your murderer should be sporting bruises at least and perhaps scrapes on his face and hands."

Stokes tried to imagine the scene. "So our murderer and Sedbury meet and…"

Findlay accepted the invitation to hypothesize. "At some point in the ensuing discussion, our murderer hits Sedbury in the face, stunning him for just long enough to loop a piece of leather around his neck. Sedbury struggles and fights, yet is nevertheless strangled."

Stokes frowned. "Piece of leather?" He'd never heard of a leather garrote.

Findlay beamed. "Yes! That's the single most interesting feature of this death. Look here." Findlay pointed to the strap-like mark that crossed Sedbury's thick neck. "I'd swear the man was strangled with a length of finished leather—either a whip or a rein. If you look closely, you can see that whatever it was had smoothed edges, and given the slight tapering in the width of the mark, my money's on the thong of a whip as the murder weapon."

Stokes peered at the mark on Sedbury's neck and couldn't fault Findlay's reasoning.

"Mind you," Findlay said, "that's even more remarkable because leather has at least a little give. Strangling someone with a leather strap would take even greater strength than doing the same with a rope or cord."

Stokes straightened. "So our murderer is remarkably strong."

Findlay nodded. "It might seem bizarre, but I truly believe you have a whip as your murder weapon."

Stokes grunted. "Sedbury was a whip collector."

"Was he?" Findlay looked at the corpse anew. "The odd choice of weapon might be relevant, then."

"It might, indeed." Stokes glanced at Findlay. "I take it no whip has been found?"

Findlay shrugged. "No telling where it might be now. The killer might even have taken it with him."

Stokes grimaced. "Time of death?"

Findlay regarded the corpse. "Judging from when he was found and the state of the body, I'd say between midnight Saturday to three o'clock on Sunday morning. I'll testify that he hadn't been in the water for more than twelve hours."

Stokes nodded. He stepped back from the table and surveyed the corpse again, weighing the possibilities. While a whip as the likely murder weapon and Charlie also being a whip collector suggested Charlie as a suspect, given Sedbury's size and weight versus Charlie's, and that Sedbury had fought yet Charlie had no mark on his face or hands, Stokes still couldn't see Charlie as Sedbury's murderer. The scenario was simply too implausible—too much of a stretch of the imagination.

"Oh—one last thing." Findlay flicked out the sheet, preparing to shroud the corpse once more. "Where he went into the river. It wasn't off any of the bridges, if that's what you were thinking."

"It wasn't?" Stokes perked up. "Where, then?"

"We can't say exactly, but the body fetched up in the marshes on the south bank near Cuckold's Point. I spoke to the rivermen, and in light of the conditions on the river and the tides on Saturday and Sunday, the consensus is that the body was put into the water from the north bank, somewhere between the Tower and the Duke Stairs. If I had to guess, then based on the time I believe he was in the river, I'd put the entry point farther to the west along that stretch."

This was why Stokes appreciated working with the more experienced examiners; they thought of asking the right questions of those around them. "Thank you. That will be a great help. We'd assumed a bridge because we were imagining an altercation between gentlemen." Stokes paused, eyes narrowing. "But if he died near where he was put into the river..."

Findlay nodded sagely. "Indeed. Rather more likely he was involved in some nefarious doings, and something went wrong. He wouldn't be the first lordling who bit off more than he could chew." He drew the sheet over Sedbury's body, then stepped back and looked at Stokes. "That's about all I can tell you." He clapped his hands together. "Right! You've got a murderer to chase, and I've got two floaters arriving any minute."

Stokes held up a hand in thanks and turned toward the door. "I'll leave you to it." He was infinitely grateful that the other two corpses hadn't been brought in while he was there.

As Stokes reached the door, Findlay called after him, "Don't forget the formal identification!"

Stokes waved in acknowledgment, but didn't stop.

He walked quickly up the stairs, down the corridor, and through the foyer, collecting O'Donnell with a glance. Once outside on the pavement, Stokes paused to finally fill his lungs. The aroma of the river wasn't the sweetest, but it was a definite improvement over the scents of the dead.

O'Donnell halted beside Stokes, and he swiftly filled the sergeant in on the information regarding where the body had entered the river.

O'Donnell frowned. "That's quite a stretch."

"It is, and until we know more, we have to assume that the murder site lies somewhere close to the river in that area." Stokes looked at O'Donnell. "You're in charge of the search, with Morgan assisting. Pull in as many constables as you can and see what you can learn. Start with any informants in the area, but ultimately, we're going to need witnesses."

O'Donnell nodded. "In that area on a Saturday night, someone must have seen something."

~

Stokes walked into the front hall just as Penelope was leading Barnaby and Charlie from the garden parlor to the dining room.

"Perfect timing!" She linked her arm in Stokes's. "You can join us for luncheon and tell us what you discovered at the morgue."

Stokes had to laugh. "Only you would look forward with such open expectation to news from that quarter delivered over the dining table."

Penelope opened her mouth to refute that statement, then shut her lips on a "Hmm."

They settled about the table, which Mostyn had already laid for four. The majordomo and the footman, Connor, brought in the platters, then retreated, leaving them to serve themselves.

Once they had, Barnaby said, "First, let me reiterate what we believe should be our next steps, then we can see how your latest information affects our thinking."

With a mouthful of ham, Stokes nodded agreement, and Barnaby quickly listed their agreed next steps, namely to learn more about Sedbury and his family, the Hales, to search for witnesses to Sedbury's movements after he left White's, and lastly, to find witnesses to Charlie's journey from White's to Jermyn Street.

"We know who to ask for the first and the third," Barnaby concluded, "but depending on where Sedbury went, his movements might prove more difficult to investigate. Not impossible, but it might take time."

"However," Penelope chimed in, "as there was little we could achieve during what remained of the morning, we delayed any decisions until after you returned and we heard what you'd discovered at the morgue."

Taking that as his cue, Stokes revealed, "In truth, I learned more than I'd expected, largely thanks to Findlay, the medical examiner who did the postmortem. He's an old hand with years of experience. Nothing much slips past him, and he's quick to put two and two together."

"That's convenient for us." Penelope folded her hands on the table. "So what had he deduced?"

"First, Sedbury was already dead when he entered the water, so it was, indeed, strangulation rather than death by drowning."

"Given Sedbury's physique," Barnaby said, "that's a clue to his murderer in and of itself."

Stokes nodded. "Findlay thought so, too, and I have to admit that, now I've laid eyes on Sedbury, I comprehend the situation rather better. More, there were indications that Sedbury had put up a significant fight. Findlay is of the opinion that Sedbury would have marked his killer—a scratch, a bruise, something like that. On face or hands or both."

Penelope looked at Charlie. "So definitely not Charlie."

Stokes smiled faintly. "Definitely not Hastings, but it'll take more than that to exonerate him in the eyes of the ton."

Penelope heaved a sigh. "Sadly, that's all too true. So what else did you learn?"

"The next point of note was that Sedbury went into the river from the north bank, and the experts—meaning the rivermen—say he went in somewhere between the Tower and the Duke Stairs."

Penelope's eyes flew wide. "Really? That's a rather rough area."

Barnaby frowned. "That's not the sort of place a gentleman would choose for a meeting."

"No, indeed." Stokes set down his cutlery. "And even more unfortunately, that location throws our list of suspects wide open. In that area, there's always willing hands to do a gentleman's dirty work for the right price."

Penelope huffed in disgust, but then canted her head. "Regardless, one has to wonder why Sedbury would go there." She widened her eyes at Stokes. "Perhaps he was killed somewhere else and brought to the river?"

Stokes pulled a face. "Until we learn where he went and why, we won't be able to formulate any reasonable list of suspects. As things stand, we don't even know what sort of man we might be after."

"Well," Charlie said, "other than that the murderer has to be someone who could take down a man like Sedbury."

Stokes nodded. "Sedbury was the very definition of a big, heavy bruiser."

"Mean with it, too," Charlie added.

"Findlay was very clear that we're looking for a man at least as large and at least as strong," Stokes stated.

"Sometimes," Barnaby said, "surprise might overcome a physical disadvantage, but I have to admit that seems unlikely with Sedbury. He always seemed highly alert and aware of his surroundings."

Charlie concurred. "Not the sort you expect to easily sneak up on."

"However," Barnaby went on, "if there was more than one attacker, even three, that might have tipped the scales."

"True." Stokes pushed away his empty plate and dabbed his lips with his napkin. "Regardless, the most notable insight Findlay shared was that he believes Sedbury was strangled with a whip. With the thong, not even the handle."

Barnaby and Penelope stared at Stokes in open surprise.

"Was he, indeed?" Charlie exclaimed, then added, "I wonder if it was his whip. How ironic if that were true."

Faintly puzzled, Stokes looked at Charlie. "I know you said that he carried his whip like other gentlemen carry swordsticks, but surely, he wouldn't have had it with him then? Not after visiting White's?"

To Stokes's surprise, Charlie nodded emphatically. "I told you—it was his favorite whip, and he carried it damned near everywhere he went."

Stokes looked incredulous. "Even inside White's?"

"No, not inside," Charlie admitted, "but only because the committee wouldn't allow it. Too outré for them. They made him leave it at the door with the porter, so the porter on duty that evening should be able to confirm if Sedbury had the whip when he left."

"If Sedbury headed for the docks that night, after he left White's, then I can't believe he wouldn't have taken his whip with him." Barnaby tipped his head toward Charlie. "As Charlie said, it was Sedbury's favorite accoutrement, and he carried it whenever he could."

"Wait!" Penelope held up a hand. "We've been assuming Sedbury was killed that night, sometime after he left White's." Lowering her hand, she looked at Stokes. "Do we have any grounds for thinking that?"

"We do," Stokes said. "Findlay placed the time of death—or at least, the time Sedbury's dead body was put into the water—as between midnight and three o'clock on Sunday morning."

Barnaby nodded. "So he was killed sometime in the window between him leaving White's and three o'clock in the morning."

"Exactly," Stokes said. "Returning to the whip—now the likely murder weapon—I'll get the word out to see if we can find it. It might be lying on the bottom of the Thames or…"

"Or it might be found somewhere that will help us identify the site of the murder," Penelope offered.

"Or," Barnaby more grimly added, "it might be in someone else's possession and lead us to the murderer."

"All good reasons to hunt for it," Stokes said. "I've already got a team under O'Donnell and Morgan searching for signs of the murder site. I'll ask them to keep their eyes peeled for any sign of the whip."

Penelope caught Barnaby's eye. "This might be a good case on which to enlist the help of your new network."

In unison, Charlie and Stokes asked, "What network?"

"It occurred to me," Barnaby explained, "that there are a lot of young lads who, for various reasons to do with their employment—or sometimes, lack of it—are out and about all over London."

"They see and hear and take notice far more than adults do," Penelope stated.

Barnaby threw her a fond smile. "We started with some of those who have passed through the Foundling House and expanded from there. They've proved surprisingly useful in gathering information whenever we've had cause to use them."

Penelope met Barnaby's gaze. "Aside from anything else, we should see if they can find someone who saw Charlie after he left White's."

Barnaby dipped his head in agreement. "Around St. James at that hour, it's even possible some of them saw him themselves." He smiled at Charlie. "To tick every box, we should also get Garvey's testimony."

"I'll leave all that to you," Stokes said. "And if your network stretches to the riverbank east of the Tower, you could get your lads asking around there, too. From the Tower to the Duke Stairs is a fair stretch to search, and if we do find where Sedbury was put into the water, we'll need to determine if he was killed nearby or elsewhere and brought to the spot already dead."

"Ultimately," Penelope stated, "we'll need to learn why Sedbury went to wherever it was he was killed."

No one argued. Stokes looked around the table. "Any other pertinent information?"

"Actually," Penelope said, "while I'm not up with the latest regarding any Hale family issues, when I wracked my brain, I recalled hearing some rather vague rumors about Sedbury looking to marry the Ellis girl, but she's barely out, and from all I've heard of Sedbury thus far, she doesn't seem the sort one would imagine would catch his eye. She's very much a sweet innocent, so I suspect the rumors are mistaken, but it's an oddity—one I'll clarify."

Barnaby said, "Earlier, Charlie and I were going over what we know of Sedbury's half brothers—the older two, Jonathon and Bryan."

"They're much younger than us," Charlie put in, "and so don't move in the same circles, so we don't know them well."

"True," Barnaby concurred. "Nevertheless, from what we do know, both live entirely unremarkable lives and have done nothing that would strike one as out of the ordinary."

"Out of the ordinary, and we would have heard of it," Charlie explained. "But in that family, as far as the menfolk go, it was always Sedbury who grabbed all attention."

"Albeit very much on the male side of the ton." Barnaby smiled at Penelope. "He was rarely seen in the ballrooms or drawing rooms."

Penelope wrinkled her nose. "It sounds as if I'll have to focus my inquiries on the other members of the Hale family and leave Sedbury himself to you and Charlie."

"On that point"—Charlie looked at Stokes—"if you wish, I could ask around the other whip collectors—put out feelers, so to speak—to see if any of them have heard of a Duckleberry Longe coming up for sale."

Eagerly, Stokes nodded. "That's an excellent point. For all we know, it could already be out there in some shop."

"Not necessarily in the hands of the murderer," Barnaby said. "Even if he took it, he would know it was the murder weapon and would pass it on as quickly as he could."

Stokes had pulled out his notebook and was jotting. "Indeed."

"I'll contact my usual sources," Penelope said, "and see what they can tell me about those rumors concerning the Ellis chit and also what they know about the other members of the Hale family and about any known tensions between them and Sedbury." She arched her brows. "Or for that matter, any known tensions between Sedbury and anyone else in the ton."

"That would be extremely useful." Stokes grimaced. "Especially as I will doubtless find myself answering to the marquess at some point. However"—he shut his notebook and pushed back his chair—"before we do anything else, you two and I need to search Sedbury's rooms and question his staff."

Barnaby readily pushed back from the table. "Where are Sedbury's rooms?"

"Number fifteen, Duke Street. First floor."

Penelope stood, bringing the men to their feet. "Right, then." She bustled around the table. "We each have work to do." Watching her fondly, Barnaby saw her eyes gleam behind her spectacles as she enthused, "Let's get to it!"

Stokes smiled and followed Penelope from the room, leaving Barnaby and Charlie bringing up the rear.

"Must say," Charlie murmured as they headed for the front hall, "I can see why you two get drawn into these investigations. Now that I know I'm free of official suspicion at least, I can see the attraction of puzzling out who actually did the deed."

Barnaby smiled. "Exactly."

CHAPTER 3

$\mathcal{B}$arnaby, Stokes, and Penelope elected to walk the few blocks from the house in Albemarle Street to Duke Street, one of the most favored locations for the residences of wealthy and, generally, titled bachelors.

On reaching that street, flanked by Barnaby and Stokes, Penelope paused on the pavement opposite Number 15 and surveyed their destination. The redbrick building was in an older style, with a high-pitched roof, ornate cream-stone window and door surrounds, and leaded diamond-paned windows. A short flight of stone steps led up to a brown-painted front door.

Penelope looked up at the first-floor apartment, which sported a bow window that overlooked the street.

Behind the glass, a figure moved, unidentifiable but definitely there.

"Someone's at home," Stokes said. "Let's see who it is, shall we?"

Penelope had no argument with that course of action, and their party swiftly crossed the street. As they ascended the steps to the front door, she noticed a small black town carriage drawn up to the curb outside the house next door. The driver, a large individual wearing a dun-colored driving cloak, sat on the box, holding the reins loosely and, she would swear, observing them intently.

Pausing on the porch behind Stokes, she inwardly frowned.

Without knocking, Stokes opened the front door, which gave access to multiple apartments and, at this hour, was left unlocked.

Penelope felt Barnaby's hand at her back, urging her on, and she dismissed the strangely watchful coachman in favor of more interesting sights.

A set of narrow but elegant stairs faced them. Ignoring the corridor that led to the rear of the ground floor and a door that must open to the ground-floor rooms, they started up the two flights to the first floor. About them, the building was quiet, and courtesy of the thickness of the stair runner, they made little sound. Expensive patterned paper covered the stairwell walls, and the banister was polished oak, cool and smooth under their hands. The stairwell was dim, but a skylight far above shed enough light for them to see their way.

They stepped onto the first-floor landing. The stairs turned and continued to the upper floors, while directly ahead of them stood a solid oak door, presumably the entry to Sedbury's rooms.

Stokes raised his hand to knock, then paused and, instead, tried the doorknob. It turned, and he eased the door slowly and silently open. He paused on the threshold, cast a swift glance at Penelope and Barnaby, then faced forward and quietly walked in.

Penelope followed, equally silently, at Stokes's heels.

The small front hall opened onto one end of a decent-sized parlor well-lit by light slanting in through the front bow window. To their right, at the far end of the room, two doors, both closed, bracketed a fireplace, while another door, also closed, was in the side wall immediately on their left. Several large studded-leather armchairs and a matching couch were arranged before the hearth and, together with several low tables, took up much of the floor space, along with a large rolltop desk positioned against the inner wall, halfway down the room directly opposite the bow window.

One swift glance informed Penelope that the room was very much lived in, with several editions of sporting magazines, all appearing well-thumbed through, tossed on various tables. Riding gloves and a quirt rested on a side table, and several invitations were stuck in the ornate frame of the mirror above the mantelpiece.

All well and good, but what riveted her attention was the lady standing facing the desk. The top of the desk was rolled back, revealing a mélange of papers pushed into the pigeonholes and haphazardly stacked before them, virtually covering the desk itself.

The woman was garbed in an expensive coat of recent style, and her wavy brown-blond hair was caught up in a fashionable topknot. She was of average height and curvaceous build and held a paper in one hand. Her eyes were glued to the sheet, and her delicate features were contorted in a frown of patent puzzlement.

Whatever she was reading was so engrossing that she hadn't heard them enter.

Stokes cleared his throat, and the lady startled, and with one hand rising to her throat, whirled to face them.

When she simply stared, wide-eyed, Stokes calmly said, "I'm Inspector Stokes of Scotland Yard. And you are?"

The lady's gaze had shifted from Stokes to take in Barnaby and Penelope, who had moved to stand alongside Stokes. A flicker of recognition passed through the lady's large blue eyes, but after a second of silence, she returned her gaze to Stokes, tipped up her chin, and haughtily replied, "Lady Claudia Hale." Deftly, her fingers folded the sheet. "These are my brother's rooms. Why are you here?"

Under cover of her words, she smoothly slipped the folded paper into her pocket.

Stokes walked forward. "I'm here because I'm in charge of the investigation into Viscount Sedbury's murder, so if you don't mind, I'll have that note." He held out his hand. "And my associates, who you might recognize, are the Honorable Mr. Barnaby Adair and his wife."

Penelope came forward. "I believe when you and I were first introduced, I would have been Penelope Ashford."

She halted beside Stokes, and Claudia Hale politely inclined her head. "I know who you are, but why are you here?"

"Mr. and Mrs. Adair act as official consultants to Scotland Yard in cases involving the ton," Stokes informed her, "as this case clearly does." He hadn't lowered his hand. "That letter, if you please."

Claudia didn't want to hand over the note—that much was clear in the set of her jaw and the suspicion in her gaze—but Stokes had put enough steel behind his words that, after a long-drawn moment, with obvious reluctance, she withdrew her hand from her pocket and placed the paper in Stokes's palm.

"Thank you." Stokes unfolded the sheet and briefly scanned it, then tucked it into his pocket.

Claudia had been looking from Penelope to Barnaby. "So Sedbury was definitely murdered?"

"It seems he was," Penelope replied. "But how did you learn of his death?"

Claudia was fast losing her starchiness and looked increasingly puzzled and more than a little worried. "The police commissioner called at my aunt's house—Selborough House, which is where I'm staying—to confirm that Papa is at Rattenby Grange, and he—the commissioner—told us that Sedbury's body had been pulled from the Thames." She looked at Barnaby, then at Stokes. "He didn't say Sedbury was murdered."

"The cause of death was unclear at that time," Stokes said. "But I regret to inform you that subsequent evidence is quite conclusive. Sedbury was murdered, and his body was dumped into the river." Stokes glanced at the desk beside him, at the disarranged stack through which Claudia had clearly been searching. "But you suspected that, didn't you?"

Claudia's frown deepened, and her lips compressed, but she made no reply.

Penelope said, "You're Sedbury's half sister, I believe."

Claudia returned her attention to Penelope. "Yes. The current marchioness—Papa's second wife—is my mother."

"And," Penelope blithely went on, intent on holding Claudia's attention while Stokes and Barnaby looked through the papers in the desk and examined the items scattered through the room, "I understand you have several younger brothers."

Grudgingly, Claudia volunteered, "Sedbury was the only child of Papa's first marriage. I'm Papa's second oldest child, and then come my brothers, Jonathon and Bryan, and our sister, Margot, and the youngest is Conrad."

"How old was Sedbury?" Penelope asked.

"Gordon—Sedbury—was thirty-six." Guessing Penelope's next question, Claudia went on, "I'm twenty-eight, and Jonathon is twenty-six. Bryan is twenty-two, Margot eighteen, and Conrad has just turned fifteen."

Penelope smiled encouragingly. "Thank you. Now, am I correct in thinking that Jonathon and Bryan are currently residing in town?"

Claudia grimaced. "Yes." Reluctantly, she added, "They both have lodgings—Jonathon in Jermyn Street and Bryan shares lodgings in Bury Street with three of his friends." Lips tight, she glanced at Stokes and Barnaby, who were both busily searching. "And before you ask, I haven't as yet seen Jonathon or Bryan today. I doubt they know that Sedbury's dead."

Barnaby glanced at Claudia. "You didn't send word?"

Claudia shook her head. "Selborough—my aunt's husband, Lord

Selborough—said that we should wait to hear more details before troubling people with incomplete information." She gestured at the desk. "I came here to see—"

When she pressed her lips tight and didn't continue, Penelope, with wide-eyed innocence, supplied, "If there was anything incriminating lying about?"

Claudia eyed Penelope with suppressed irritation, then huffed and folded her arms. "If you must know, I had no idea what I might find. I wasn't looking for anything specific—anything I knew to search for—but we've lived in fear for the past decade that Sedbury would one day land the entire family in some almighty scandal. And him getting murdered would be merely the start of it. That's why I came." She looked at Stokes, who was steadily working through Sedbury's correspondence, and pointedly stated, "To remove anything the police do not need to see."

Stokes cast Claudia a sidelong glance, then went back to his search.

Barnaby, who had been systematically going through the drawers of tables, coolly replied, "Admirable though such a sentiment might be when viewed through the prism of familial devotion, I assure you the police are not interested in anything that doesn't pertain to your half brother's murder."

Clutching her elbows, Claudia muttered, "That's likely to prove scandal enough."

Stokes set down a handful of letters and, with a frown, turned to Claudia. "I assume Sedbury had staff?"

Claudia nodded. "A gentleman's gentleman—Duggan. He let me in. I've called before with my aunt or brothers, so he knows who I am." She hesitated, then went on, "Duggan told me Sedbury hadn't returned here since Saturday evening, but Duggan didn't seem perturbed by that. He said he didn't know when Sedbury would be back—he clearly didn't know Sedbury was dead—but he needed to fetch supplies from the market. I said I'd wait, and Duggan left. That was about five minutes before you arrived."

Penelope, Stokes, and Barnaby shared a glance, then Barnaby looked at Claudia. "So Duggan didn't know Sedbury had died."

"No," Claudia stated. "I'm sure he didn't, and I saw no reason to tell him." After a second, she added, "I know nothing about Sedbury's relationship with Duggan, so I didn't know how he might react."

Penelope interpreted that as meaning that Claudia hadn't known if Duggan might get in the way of her search. Penelope was itching to read the note that was now in Stokes's pocket. "It's unlikely, therefore," she concluded, "that Duggan was in any way involved in Sedbury's murder."

Deciding that she'd learned everything Claudia was likely to tell her —at least for now—and that it was time to join in the search, Penelope stepped past the other woman and walked to the door beside the fireplace and closest to the outer wall. The knob turned freely, and she set the door wide and walked through.

"Oh!" She halted just over the threshold, her eyes widening as she took in the contents of the small room—really more an antechamber to the parlor. A window in the outer wall admitted enough light to make out the whips arrayed around the room. There must have been thirty or so whips displayed in glass cases and on pegs attached to all four walls. Other than the whips, the room held only one armchair that was set beneath the window, facing into the room. "Ah-ha!" Penelope walked farther into the chamber. "I take it this is Sedbury's whip collection."

Claudia had followed her and stood in the doorway. "Collecting whips was his hobby. He was obsessed with owning certain whips. I have no idea why or if they're of any value."

"There are no empty spots." Penelope glanced at Claudia. "So it seems none are missing."

In the parlor, Stokes said, "There are several letters here that might mean something."

That was a request for Barnaby's help. Penelope saw Barnaby come up behind Claudia. Over her head, he glanced around the room, then turned and went to assist Stokes.

Somewhat grumpily and clearly still worried, Claudia retreated to stand before the bow window and watch Stokes and Barnaby as they examined Sedbury's correspondence. After a last glance at the whip display, Penelope followed and halted before the whip room door.

Studying several letters, Barnaby observed, "On the surface, some of these appear to be the usual things—letters from acquaintances—but there's a tone to them that suggests some underlying communication that's not explicitly stated."

Stokes grunted. "Meanwhile, these—which appear to be copies of Sedbury's letters to such acquaintances—have a distinctly belligerent style, but again, seem to skate around whatever the point of the exchange actually was."

Claudia stated, "Belligerence was Sedbury's default. He was…a diffi-cult man to like." When Stokes glanced her way, she caught his eye. "The commissioner mentioned some gentleman who had a falling-out with Sedbury on the day before he died. Shouldn't you be looking for him?"

A brief smile lifted Stokes's lips. "We've already spoken with that gentleman, and it's unlikely he had anything to do with Sedbury's death." He tipped his head to the letters and notes he and Barnaby held. "These, however, offer us a wealth of possible suspects."

Setting down the letters, Stokes turned to Claudia and, reaching into his pocket, drew out the note she'd been staring at when they'd arrived. "And then there's this. A letter in Sedbury's hand, started on Saturday morning, but left unfinished." Stokes flicked the sheet open and read, "'Dear Jonno.'" He looked at Claudia. "I assume that's your brother, Jonathon Hale?"

Claudia's features tightened. "I don't know, but I assume so."

Stokes nodded and continued to read, "'I thought you'd like to know that a few months ago, I ran into that little maid you used to be so fond of. You know the one—pretty as a picture with rosy cheeks and long blond pigtails. I could see what caught your eye. I have to confess that I had my wicked way with her.'" Stokes looked up. "The letter ends there. Unfinished, presumably intended to be finished later and, subsequently, sent." He focused on Claudia. "Do you have any idea to what this refers?"

She frowned and shook her head. "I have no notion at all."

Penelope put in, "That's hardly surprising. Brothers don't tell sisters what they get up to, much less upon whom their fancy alights." Penelope studied Claudia. "However, the tone suggests a certain rivalry between Sedbury and Jonathon."

Claudia returned Penelope's regard, then closed her eyes and sighed. Opening her eyes, she admitted, "Sedbury lived to undermine Jonathon whenever and by whatever means he could." She watched Stokes pocket the letter again, along with several other communications, then went on, "Sedbury resented all of us—Mama, me, and my siblings. He has since Mama married Papa, and his resentment grew as each of us were born. But his worst was always reserved for Jonathon."

"Jonathon," Barnaby said, "who, on Sedbury's death, becomes your father's heir."

Claudia gave vent to a strained laugh. "The irony is that Sedbury never imagined he would be the one to die, thus ceding that position to Jonathon. Quite the opposite. He—Sedbury—told us, to our faces, multiple times, that the instant Papa died, we would all be cast out. That he would make sure of it—more, that he would relish and glory in the act.

Of course, he never uttered such words in Papa's hearing, but still." She visibly bristled. "Telling eight-year-old Conrad that he best study hard because, one day, he would have to make his way in the world with not a farthing to his name is little short of despicable and an example of Sedbury's barbs."

Penelope asked, "What was your father's reaction to Sedbury's threats? Does he know of them?"

"He knows," Claudia said, "and he does not approve and supports and reassures and comforts the rest of us as best he can, but Sedbury is—" She broke off, then amended, "*Was* his heir, and there was little Papa could do to effectively refute Sedbury's declarations."

Claudia studied Penelope, then went on, "You'll ask around and no doubt hear the stories, so I may as well tell you. If Papa and Sedbury are in the same house for more than an hour, there'll be an almighty row because Sedbury will deliberately say something to provoke Papa. And when Papa tries to counter him, Sedbury dwells on what he might do to bring scandal down on the whole family, then smugly walks out." Disgust dripped from her words.

"So," Barnaby concluded, "Sedbury had your father over a proverbial barrel in terms of the future of the family."

Claudia faintly shrugged. "That's the situation, more or less."

Penelope frowned. "Although until today, I wasn't aware of Sedbury's existence, that only underscores that he has never made any attempt to find a bride, and consequently, he's never loomed on my horizon."

Claudia scoffed. "Even if he had thought to marry, no family of suitable standing would countenance a match between him and their daughter."

Penelope widened her eyes. "Is that so? Because I believe there have recently been rumors of him showing an interest in pursuing an alliance with the Ellises. With Rosalind Ellis."

Claudia's face darkened. She stared at Penelope and transparently wrestled with her conscience, then her features firmed with resolution. "I've heard too much of your reputation to believe you won't learn the truth, so for what it's worth, Sedbury pursuing Rosalind was another example of his family-directed cruelty. The Ellises are our nearest neighbors in Gloucestershire, and Rosalind and Bryan are childhood sweethearts. They've always and forever had eyes only for each other. The Ellises have consistently encouraged the match, as have our parents—it would be an excellent outcome all around. But Sedbury hated—viscerally hated—the prospect of seeing any of us happy, and he's been pressuring the Ellises to allow him to marry Rosalind. Of course, Rosalind knows Sedbury well enough not to want to have anything to do with him. However, with Sedbury in line to inherit Rattenby and the power he will then wield as the largest and most influential landholder in the district, I have heard that the Ellises—well, Mr. Ellis—has been wavering. I don't know what threats Sedbury made regarding his actions once he succeeded to the title and estates, but you can easily imagine the sort of things he might have said."

Penelope didn't like the sound of any of that at all, and she was unsurprised to find her estimation of Sedbury—hardly high to begin with—sinking even lower.

Stokes and Barnaby digested the information, then Stokes crossed to the anteroom and looked inside. He turned to Claudia. "Do you know if Sedbury's favorite whip—a Duckleberry Longe, apparently—is in there?"

She frowned. "The whip he always carried with him?"

"So we're told," Penelope replied.

Claudia made a disgusted sound. "Such an affectation! But no, Inspector. Sedbury usually kept that whip with him. I never saw him put it in that room." She waved toward the still-closed door at the other end of the room. "You should check in his bedroom. It might be there."

Barnaby turned and went to the bedroom. He opened the door and passed through. Stokes followed.

They returned within a few minutes, shaking their heads.

"Nothing useful," Barnaby reported.

"Let me take a look," Penelope said. "I might see something you two have missed."

Stokes and Barnaby waved her on. Leaving Claudia in their care, Penelope went into the bedroom. It contained a bed, a wardrobe, and a dresser. She made short work of searching everywhere but discovered nothing of interest. "Just what you'd expect to find in a bachelor gentleman's bedroom."

She returned to the parlor, where Stokes was asking Claudia more about her family, especially those currently in town, with Barnaby listening and taking mental notes. Penelope left them to it and went to the last unopened door—the one on the other side of the fireplace. Through it lay an intimate dining room, from which another door led to a small kitchen. Beyond the kitchen was a large pantry and a small room which, judging by the narrow bed and unvarnished chest of drawers, was Duggan's.

Penelope set about searching the rooms. In truth, there was little in the cupboards or drawers in the kitchen, dining room, and pantry, just the basic pots, pans, and utensils. Duggan owned two sets of clothes in addition to those he must be wearing and one other pair of boots, a comb, and not much else.

On returning to the parlor and meeting Stokes's and Barnaby's questioning looks, she shook her head. "Nothing of note, other than that the cupboards are bare, and Duggan did, indeed, need to go shopping."

"Right, then." Stokes waved them toward the exit. "We're finished here for now."

Somewhat reluctantly, Claudia gave in to Penelope's urging and accompanied her into the front hall and out of the apartment. Penelope started down the stairs, and Claudia trailed after her.

Barnaby and Stokes followed. Stokes closed the apartment door, and he and Barnaby caught up with the ladies on the front porch.

Stokes dipped his head to Claudia. "Lady Claudia. You might mention to your aunt that I will be calling on her in due course. Your brothers as well."

Claudia grimaced, but replied, "I'll warn them." She nodded to Stokes. "Inspector." Then she turned to Penelope and Barnaby and inclined her head. "Mr. and Mrs. Adair."

They nodded back and watched as Claudia went down the steps and walked briskly to the waiting carriage.

The large, heavyset coachman swung down from the box and opened the carriage door for Claudia. After she'd entered, he shut the door, climbed back up, and picked up the reins. Seconds later, the coach drew out from the curb and rattled down the street toward Mayfair.

Penelope linked her arm in Barnaby's, and they joined Stokes in descending to the pavement and strolling in the same direction. "Did you happen to notice," Penelope said, "that Claudia's very large and strong-looking coachman has a nasty cut over his left eye?"

Barnaby glanced down at her and smiled. "I did, as it happens."

"Hmm," Penelope mused. "I wonder if he's a family retainer. Perhaps a very loyal one."

Stokes grunted. "If he is, I'll leave him to you. On the face of the information now in our hands, it seems that several family members, including Sedbury's sire, had good reason to wish the man dead."

"Possibly," Barnaby allowed. "However, while I can imagine Claudia, her sister, or her mother, and given his age, even the marquess, using a hireling—or a trusted retainer—to accomplish such an end, I can't see Jonathon or Bryan, both of whom have the strongest motives at this point, doing so. Or, for that matter, agreeing to meet Sedbury down by the docks or, alternatively, choosing the docks for any meeting with him." He paused, then added, "In fact, I can't see any retainer or hireling choosing that area, either. They would have needed to entice Sedbury down there with some quite potent lure."

"Ah, but we don't yet know where he was killed," Stokes said. "It might have been in Mayfair, and while Jonathon might not have got that letter, he's the one in line for the title."

Barnaby dipped his head in acknowledgment. "True. We need to locate the site of the murder sooner rather than later. Wherever it is will tell us quite a bit about the murderer—about who the murderer might be."

Stokes nodded. They'd reached Piccadilly, and he halted on the pavement. "I'm off to confer with O'Donnell and Morgan to see if they've turned up anything useful."

Barnaby looked at Penelope. "I'll see you home, then go on and find my lads and set them on Sedbury's and Charlie's Saturday-night trails."

Penelope consulted her lapel watch and softly humphed. "Sadly, it's too late to catch up with my usual sources today." She looked at Stokes. "I'll have to leave it until tomorrow, but I'm sure I'll be able to learn a lot more about the Hales and Sedbury from them."

Stokes grinned. "Better you than either of us." He glanced at Barnaby. "But before you and I part ways, I've just remembered that there's another venue of interest that we need to investigate."

~

Stokes's venue of interest proved to be White's Gentlemen's Club.

After escorting Penelope home, Barnaby walked with Stokes to St. James Street and the front door of the venerable institution. As Barnaby —and his father and brothers—were well-known members, he led the way in asking the porter, Harry, who was in his cubicle just inside the porch, whether he'd been on duty on the previous Saturday, late in the evening.

"No, sir," Harry answered readily. "The evening porter last Saturday was Jenkinson."

Barnaby glanced at Stokes, then looked back at Harry. "In that case, the inspector and I will need to speak with Jenkinson."

"About this strange business with Viscount Sedbury?" Harry guessed, already beckoning to a hovering page. "At this hour, Jenkinson will be in his room. I'll just send for him. I'm sure he'll be down quick as a wink."

Stokes and Barnaby waited in the recess of the deep porch, and neither was surprised when, only a handful of minutes later, a stout man still tugging the club's livery into place hurried out and presented himself. "Jenkinson, evening porter, sirs. How can I help?"

It was obvious that the news of Stokes's earlier visit had done the rounds of the club's staff, and Jenkinson was only too thrilled to have his moment in the limelight.

Barnaby knew what Stokes needed to know, and in short order, Jenkinson confirmed that he had been the porter on duty between eight in the evening and two o'clock in the morning the previous Saturday into Sunday. "It's a prime time for tips, you know, when I hail carriages and help gentlemen who are a bit wobbly-like into them."

"So," Barnaby said, "on the Saturday night just past, you were in your cubicle when Viscount Sedbury entered the club and also when he left."

"That's correct," Jenkinson replied. "He's one as is hard to miss."

"Indeed. Did he have his whip with him?" Barnaby asked.

Without hesitation, Jenkinson nodded. "Always carried that thing, but the committee decreed he couldn't take it inside, so he always left it with the porter, and he left it with me on Saturday night."

"Did he fetch it when he left?" Stokes asked.

"He did, indeed, sir." Jenkinson preened. "Handed it to him myself."

Stokes smiled faintly. "Excellent. And he walked off with it in his hand?"

"Well, as far as I could see." Jenkinson frowned. "Which, I admit, is not all that far." He brightened. "But he definitely had it in his hand when he stepped onto the pavement in front of the club."

"Thank you," Barnaby said. "That's very clear. Did you happen to notice if he summoned a hackney or got into a carriage?"

"Not as I saw, sir," Jenkinson replied. He shifted and pointed toward the street. "He walked out, stepped onto the pavement, and headed toward Pall Mall."

"Definitely Pall Mall?" Stokes asked.

Jenkinson nodded. "Can see it now, in my mind's eye. He definitely went that way."

With all sincerity, they thanked Jenkinson and quit the porch.

They stepped into the weak, late-afternoon sunshine and halted.

"All right," Stokes said. "So Sedbury left here carrying his favorite whip, and it's possible that same whip was used to strangle him."

"Assuming he still had it with him when he met his murderer," Barnaby said, "that raises the question of who in their right mind would have taken on a brute like Sedbury." He glanced at Stokes. "Sedbury wasn't just large and extremely strong, he was also armed with his weapon of choice and known to be dangerous."

Stokes grunted. "I've a feeling the whip is going to prove pivotal to solving this case." He met Barnaby's eyes. "Best we get on finding the damned thing."

"And locating the murder site." Barnaby glanced at the sky. "We've still got a few hours to set searches in motion."

After a short discussion of plans, they hailed a hackney and rattled off eastward.

Stokes let Barnaby off at Holborn and continued on his way to the docks.

Left on the bustling pavement, Barnaby sank his hands into his pockets and looked around. At this time of day, he could usually count on finding one of his older, more experienced lads somewhere around there.

CHAPTER 4

*M*idmorning of the following day saw Penelope tugging on the bellpull that hung beside the front door of St. Ives House in Grosvenor Square.

The time was precisely correct for attending a fashionable at-home, and for Penelope, the venue offered the certain prospect of hosting all her "usual sources" gathered together under one roof. While there were doubtless many other tonnish at-homes occurring at that hour elsewhere in Mayfair, the Cynster ladies and their close connections who resided in London had long deemed Tuesday mornings as the time to congregate more or less en famille to exchange the latest gossip and rumors without the bother of wider society and concerns over who might overhear shared secrets.

For learning about the Hale family and Viscount Sedbury, Penelope knew she would not find a more useful group from whom to inquire.

Besides, she always enjoyed chatting with her favorite group of older ladies, and they, in turn, delighted in trolling their memories for snippets that would enlighten her.

After a minute, in response to her summons, the door swung open to reveal a rigidly proper butler.

On seeing her, Hamilton's features softened, and his lips curved upward. "Mrs. Adair. It's been several weeks. The ladies will be delighted to see you."

"Thank you, Hamilton." Penelope stepped over the threshold. "The back parlor as usual?"

"Indeed, ma'am."

She allowed Hamilton to relieve her of her bonnet and coat, then waved airily. "I know my way."

Hamilton smiled in avuncular fashion and bowed, and she walked to the rear of the front hall and on down the long corridor that led to the ducal family's back parlor, a room that had always been the family's private gathering place.

The back parlor overlooked the mansion's rear gardens, and when Penelope walked into the room, the light from the windows softly illuminated the ladies settled on the long sofas and the many armchairs arranged in the center of the space. She was pleased to see that her favorite grandes dames were in attendance, along with a full complement of the middle-aged Cynster matrons.

She was also reassured to note that no one who was not considered "a part of the family" was present. Although she herself wasn't a Cynster by either birth or marriage, as she had two Cynster sisters-in-law and a Cynster brother-in-law, she had for many years been considered "one of the tribe."

The ladies noticed a newcomer and, as a group, broke off their conversations to look questioningly in her direction. Their eyes lit as they recognized who had come calling.

"Penelope!" Honoria, Duchess of St. Ives, their hostess and the natural leader of the middle-aged contingent, smiled in welcome and waved her forward. "How lovely to see you. Come in, my dear."

"Is this a social call?" Patience Cynster archly inquired. "Or do you have questions for our collective mind?"

Penelope grinned as she joined them. She knew they all delighted in her inquiries, which they took as a challenge to their knowledge of the ton. "The latter," she confirmed, much to the group's obvious pleasure.

She spent several minutes greeting and being greeted by those present, which included three of the ton's more ancient grandes dames—Helena, Dowager Duchess of St. Ives, Lady Horatia Cynster, and the redoubtable Lady Osbaldestone.

With the formalities of her children's health and most recent accomplishments and the well-being of her family duly reported, Penelope subsided onto a large ottoman that placed her more or less at the focal point of the gathering.

"So!" Lady Celia Cynster regarded her with open anticipation. "What's your question for us?"

Lady Osbaldestone snorted and tapped her cane on the floor. "In my opinion, we're in dire need of some meaty puzzle with which to invigorate our brains."

"Do say you have one," Honoria advised. "Ton-wise, it's been rather dreary of late."

Penelope grinned. "I do have such a query, and the case it's connected to is liable to cause quite a social brouhaha."

"Excellent!" Helena declared. "Those are the puzzles we like best."

"So, dear," Celia instructed, "start at the beginning. Who's dead?"

"I suspect you might not yet have heard, but Viscount Sedbury's body was pulled from the Thames on Sunday. He'd been strangled."

"About time!" and "What a relief!" and similar reactions echoed through the room. Penelope heard not one single expression of sorrow or even regret. She waited silently for the furor to abate, and her assumption that she wouldn't need to say anything else to learn more was soon borne out.

"Sedbury, heh?" Honoria exchanged a meaningful glance with Patience. "How telling that I feel so much relief and not a shred of grief on learning that a member of the nobility—a marquess's heir, no less—was murdered."

"Indeed." Patience looked around the gathering. "I don't know about anyone else, but I find myself quite in charity with whoever managed to bump Sedbury off. He was an out-and-out bad 'un, and the world is a better place without him in it." Patience met Penelope's eyes. "I doubt you'll find anyone in the ton who will mourn his passing."

Penelope grimaced. "I never met the man, which I find decidedly odd."

"Consider yourself lucky," Horatia advised. "But given your age, you never having crossed his path socially is understandable."

Honoria explained, "All the hostesses ceased sending him invitations within two years of him coming on the town. He was an arrogant bore and, indeed, a dangerous case. No one wanted to be responsible for introducing him to innocents, male or female, that he might subsequently corrupt."

Lady Osbaldestone nodded sagely. "From the first, there was something exceedingly 'off' about him."

"His death is truly the best thing that could happen to his family." Helena glanced at Honoria. "Do remind me to send Georgina a note."

"The marchioness?" Penelope guessed.

Helena nodded. "She's younger than us, of course"—with a wave, she included Lady Osbaldestone, Horatia, Celia, and Louise, the older generation present that day—"but older than our children's generation. That said, we—the grandes dames and our peers—have always known what a cross Sedbury was for Georgina and her children, and Rattenby, too, to bear."

Celia nodded gravely. "Horrible to say it, but Sedbury's death will be a huge weight off their shoulders. Rattenby's especially, even though Sedbury was his heir."

"Indeed," Lady Osbaldestone put in. "The prospect Rattenby was facing, even if from the other side of the grave, was enough to curdle anyone's liver."

Penelope asked, "So it's true that Sedbury intended to turn his stepmother and her family into the street?"

Horatia nodded. "That's certainly what we've heard." She looked around the circle. "Although I suspect none of us have heard that directly from Sedbury's lips."

"Well," Honoria admitted, "as none of us invite him to cross our thresholds, I'm sure that's true."

Penelope reflected that given Sedbury had been the heir to a senior title and significant wealth, that situation spoke volumes. "Hmm." She frowned. "Do we have any confirmation from someone not a Hale that Sedbury had, indeed, vowed to disown his father's second family?"

"Oh, most definitely," Alathea said. "Alasdair once heard Sedbury swear that was his intent. As I gather the occasion occurred at some fashionable gaming hell, it's possible Sedbury was in his cups, but still."

"Gerrard also reported hearing Sedbury say the same while at some Bohemian event," Patience said. "I gather quite loudly."

"So," Penelope said, "we can say it was common knowledge among the ton that Sedbury was intent on beggaring his remaining family once he succeeded to the title." She looked around the faces. "From that, can I infer that the rest of the Hale family had reason to wish Sedbury dead?"

The ladies exchanged glances, wordlessly trading opinions as only those who knew each other well could.

Eventually, Lady Osbaldestone put the silent consensus into words. "Each member of the family might have had sound reason to wish

Sedbury dead, but wishing and hoping and even praying are not the same as doing."

All the others were nodding.

"Quite frankly," Honoria added, "if the murderer does lie within the family, I would be wondering why they've waited this long to remove the thorn from their collective side."

Murmurs of agreement came from all quarters.

"For instance," Helena said, "ask yourself why it is that Lady Claudia Hale, an attractive lady of impeccable birth and standing, is as yet unwed."

Penelope frowned. "Because of Sedbury?"

"Who would want a man like Sedbury as an in-law?" Louise delicately shuddered. "Just the thought."

"Exactly," Alathea said. "Quite literally no family in the ton would want to brave the prospect."

"Actually," Penelope said, "there might be an answer to the question of why someone in the family might have felt compelled to finally act. There was a letter Sedbury was writing and left unfinished on his desk." She recited the contents of the letter, concluding with, "So it's possible, even likely, that Sedbury was actively goading Jonathon with both words and deeds. And also, there's the situation with Bryan Hale and the Ellises' daughter, Rosalind. Sedbury appears to have been set on interfering there as well."

As she'd hoped, the assembled ladies had insights to offer on both counts.

Lady Osbaldestone opined, "I don't know how much weight you should attach to Sedbury's letter to Jonathon, but I know for a fact that Georgina has been seriously exercised over how Jonathon might find a bride, not only because of the same situation that has smothered Claudia's prospects, but also because any young lady at whom Jonathon might cast his eye—or who dared to cast her eye at him—would instantly become a target for Sedbury and his particular vileness. The brute literally had no bounds—or at least no decent ones."

"In case you're wondering why Rattenby doesn't exercise more control over Sedbury and rein in his outrageous behavior," Horatia said, "it's because Rattenby lost the usual financial hold over Sedbury when, at quite a young age, Sedbury inherited a tidy sum from a misguided great-uncle."

"The inheritance wasn't that much," Celia added, "not weighed against the Rattenby estate, but the sum was sufficient to free Sedbury of his father's control."

"More's the pity," Honoria put in. "Although Rattenby's rarely in town and, of course, of the older generation, I've always found him to be a sound, steady man."

The others all agreed.

"As for the Ellis chit," Helena said, "my understanding is that no matter what pressure Sedbury has brought to bear on Mr. Ellis, both Mrs. Ellis and Rosalind are holding firm. The family would not have accepted Sedbury's suit for Rosalind's hand." Helena smiled gently at Penelope. "I'm acquainted with Mrs. Ellis, and I do not believe she would have bowed to Sedbury's demands."

"I second that assessment," Honoria put in. "Rosamund Ellis is a sound sort and not one to be pushed around, much less browbeaten."

"So," Patience summarized, "it's difficult to say how much real motive was generated by Sedbury's play for the girl."

Penelope forbore from pointing out that the degree of motive would very much depend on how Bryan Hale viewed the matter, and young gentlemen threatened with having their lady love stolen away could not be said to be the most calm and logical of creatures. Penelope doubted that any of the ladies present could, of their own knowledge, shed light on Bryan Hale's state of mind, but given that some had sons of similar age, she thought it prudent to ask if any had greater insight into Bryan's condition via said sons.

But Honoria shook her head. "Bryan is a full year older than Sebastian, so older than the others by several years, and Bryan's much quieter, too. They don't move in the same circles."

"In terms of having a motive to murder Sedbury, however," Lady Osbaldestone stated, "I fear you have no shortage of candidates. Starting with Lord Ferrier." She looked at Helena and Horatia. "Remember that scandal?"

"Lord, yes," Horatia said. "Ferrier never really recovered from that." For the younger crew, Horatia explained, "Ferrier was hard-pressed but hiding it well and thought to improve his position by rigging a race at Doncaster. But the scheme fell apart and came to nothing, and Ferrier was severely reprimanded and banned from the race meets, but otherwise, the matter was hushed up."

"Until Sedbury somehow found out," Lady Osbaldestone said, "and when he realized Ferrier couldn't pay to keep him silent, Sedbury set about destroying Ferrier's standing in the gentleman's clubs."

"Mind you, I gather that Sedbury only has entrée to the better clubs because of his father's title," Alathea said.

"Oh, and then there's Minchinham!" Bright-eyed, Celia looked around the circle. "Do you remember that kerfuffle?"

Penelope sat back, amazed and increasingly dismayed as her trusty sources presented her with an astonishingly long list of ton personages, all of whom, on the basis of the company's collective memory, Sedbury had threatened and subsequently damaged, via either possessions or their good name, to an extent sufficient to ensure those affected had sound motive to strike back, even to the extent of murder.

Her head reeled trying to keep track of all the names.

Eventually, she expostulated, "Are you seriously telling me that, had the opportunity presented itself, a good fifth of the ton might have killed Sedbury? Or at least might have arranged for him to be murdered?"

Her trusty sources looked around the circle, meeting each other's eyes, then they all looked at her and nodded.

"You need to remember," Lady Osbaldestone told her, "that Sedbury came on the town more than fifteen years ago. Unlike the majority of souls, a gentleman with a personality like his appears to delight in going around gathering enemies."

"Moreover," Helena advised, "just because some of the incidents we've described occurred years ago, and it might be hoped that the wounds inflicted would have healed or at least scabbed over, there's no telling if some more recent happening ripped off the scab and reopened the wound."

"And given circumstances would have changed over the years, this time, the one affected might have reacted much more strongly." Patience met Penelope's gaze. "I fear that in Sedbury's case, identifying his murderer might be more akin to finding a particular needle in a stack of similar needles."

Penelope grimaced feelingly.

"While I hesitate to mention it," Horatia put in, "a huge number of people will happily dance on Sedbury's grave, and those are just the ones we know about."

Alathea nodded. "We can't even be sure we know of all those within the ton who considered Sedbury an enemy, but even less can we guess who beyond our circles had even more reason to kill him." She glanced at the others. "I do know that he wasn't any kinder to those of lesser station."

"Indeed not." Honoria looked severe. "I once saw him bullying a hackney driver, threatening to beat the man to within an inch of his life, all because the driver had swerved—to miss a child, no less—too close to where Sedbury was walking and splattered the man's boots with mud." She sounded utterly disgusted. "I was passing and would have instructed Finch to intervene, but other jarveys and drivers came to the maligned driver's aid, and Sedbury was forced to back down." She humphed. "Not that he did that with any grace at all."

Penelope looked around the company, then heaved a heavy sigh. From their information, she'd hoped to identify a single good suspect, but instead, she'd landed in a mire of possibilities.

Helena caught her eye, smiled understandingly, and asked, "Now, what can you tell us about Amelia and Luc and Amanda and Martin and their broods?"

Penelope settled more comfortably on the ottoman and obliged her listeners with the latest news from Calverton Chase, Luc and Amelia's home, and from Hathersage, Martin and Amanda's estate. This was the unvoiced contract—her way of repaying the ladies for their help in the coin they valued most, namely, news of her wider family. She spent some time dwelling on the various children and their recent exploits, knowing that was gold to her listeners.

"And your mama is still well?" Helena asked.

"Yes, quite well," Penelope replied. "Although she can't come to town anymore—the air here isn't good for her at all—she still moves among the others' houses. At the moment, she's with Portia and Simon in Somerset."

Eventually, the gathering broke up with the various members heading to this luncheon or that. Penelope took her leave of the group and climbed into her waiting carriage. She sat back and mentally catalogued all she'd learned while the carriage rolled around Grosvenor Square and on toward Albemarle Street.

She'd just set her hat on the hall table when the front door opened again, and Barnaby strolled in.

He saw her and smiled in the particular way that still made her pulse race. "Hello. Finished with your meeting with your 'usual sources'?"

"Indeed." She raised her face for his kiss, then waited while he shrugged off his coat and handed his cane to Mostyn to tell the major-domo, "We'll have luncheon in half an hour, Mostyn."

"Very good, ma'am."

Then she looped her arm in Barnaby's, and together, they ambled toward the garden parlor.

Barnaby smiled, she suspected at her managing ways. "So," he asked, "what did you learn?"

They entered the parlor, presently free of small people, and he steered her to her favorite chair. She settled and, as he sat in the chair opposite, replied, "I learned a lot—indeed, far too much—about Sedbury. It seems there's a small army of ton persons who had motive to murder the man. His family possibly led the pack, but there are so many others." She flung up her hands. "Just memorizing all the names gave me a headache. There are at least twenty-three good prospects. How good is anyone's guess."

He grimaced sympathetically. "I asked—very quietly—around the clubs and came away with much the same impression. I knew Sedbury was not well liked, but I had no idea he was so universally loathed."

"And, apparently, with good reason! He seems to have gone out of his way to make himself the object of people's hate."

After a moment, Barnaby said, "Or of their fear." He met her questioning gaze. "Insecure men—those who, due to some personality defect, are unable to make friends in the normal way—sometimes resort to instilling fear into others to make themselves feel powerful."

Penelope studied him for a moment, then sat upright. "That's it! That's exactly what Sedbury was doing." She met Barnaby's eyes, her own alive. "Not one person has mentioned a friend—not a single friend—and they most certainly would have if one had existed."

Barnaby dipped his head. "I've heard of no one said to be or claiming to be Sedbury's friend." He thought, then concluded, "Your information means that, motive wise, we're looking at a potentially open-ended list of suspects."

She nodded. "There's no telling who he made an enemy of or when or over what." She paused, then added, "In the matter of suspects, the trick will be to winnow the list."

"I'm not sure how much winnowing we'll be able to do, not with Sedbury," Barnaby observed. "Perhaps we should concentrate on getting some idea of who had the most urgent and compelling motive last Saturday night."

After a moment of considering that, Penelope offered, "Approaching solving this murder in our customary way—through investigating and weighing suspects—simply isn't going to work. As my sources observed, just because some had a reason to do away with Sedbury doesn't mean they did. And obviously, a large number didn't act on their motive. So motive alone is of little help, and realistically, the only viable way forward lies in the actual action surrounding the murder—we need to identify who had the necessary opportunity for that."

Barnaby nodded. "And the ability. Don't forget that. The ability to strangle Sedbury isn't something many possess."

"Indeed. But to assess all of that, we need to know exactly how and where Sedbury was strangled." Penelope met Barnaby's gaze. "We need to identify the murder site and search for witnesses to the killing."

"Yes, that's right. Apropos of finding the site, I checked with the lads, but as yet, they haven't found any sighting of Sedbury after he left White's." Barnaby lightly grimaced. "I went past the docks and spoke with Stokes. He and his men haven't found anything helpful yet, either."

Barnaby paused, then went on, "On a more positive note, the lads have found witnesses who can place Charlie on his way home on Jermyn Street, which is something of a feat given the short distance between his house and White's."

Penelope said, "That's something, at least. Not that I ever thought Charlie was involved, but proving it might have been more difficult."

"So, with Charlie more definitely out of the picture, we need to learn everything we can about the murder itself." Lightly, Barnaby drummed his fingers on the chair's arm. "The murder site, the weapon—was it Sedbury's whip?—and most importantly, we need to find some witnesses who can shed light on who we need to investigate further."

Penelope put a finger to the center of her glasses frame, the action one of habit rather than necessity; she'd recently got a new pair of spectacles, and they didn't slide down her nose as the previous pair had. "In reality, investigating the murder itself—the actual killing—is our only sure way forward."

Barnaby met her gaze, then smoothly rose and extended his hand to her. "I wish I could argue." She gave him her hand, and he gripped it and helped her to her feet. "However," he continued, setting her hand in the crook of his arm and turning toward the doorway, "I fear you're one hundred percent correct."

∼

Two hours later, Charlie was comfortably ensconced in his favorite armchair in his parlor, a thick slice of fruitcake in one hand and a cup of tea brewed just as he liked it on the table beside him, when a single commanding rap fell on his front door.

He froze, wondering. He listened with mounting wariness as Garvey's footsteps approached the front door. Garvey opened the door and spoke with someone, then Charlie heard the door close and breathed more easily.

He refocused on the slice of cake, but before he could take a bite, Garvey entered with a note on his silver salver.

Garvey presented the salver. "For you, sir. Delivered by a boy. He didn't know anything about it—he was just the courier."

"I see." Charlie regarded the simple folded note with mixed feelings. After yesterday's adventures with Stokes and Barnaby and Penelope, he had wondered what the future would bring.

The note looked like it might hold the answer, but did he want to know what it said?

After a prolonged moment of indecisiveness, he fortified himself with a large bite of cake, then set it aside on its plate and reached for the note.

He unfolded it and read, then stared at the sheet. "Bless me! Fancy that."

Garvey was hovering. "Sir?"

Charlie didn't keep many secrets from his longtime gentleman's gentleman. "It's a note from Lord Jonathon Hale, most politely and deferentially asking me for any assistance I might care to give regarding Sedbury's whip collection." Charlie regarded the note with a degree of fascination. "I hardly expected that. I only vaguely know Jonathon through a mutual friend."

"Well, sir, you are one of the foremost authorities on whips, after all," Garvey loyally stated. "Not surprising that Lord Jonathon might think to ask you about the viscount's collection."

"Yes, but"—Charlie flicked the note with a finger—"this suggests that Jonathon doesn't realize that I was in any way a suspect in Sedbury's murder."

Garvey considered that, then offered, "Perhaps he does know and also knows you've been cleared of suspicion, so to his mind, you're safe to ask."

"Hmm." Charlie wasn't convinced, but... "Well." He picked up his coffee cup and took a healthy swallow, then set the cup aside and rose. "I have to admit that I'm beyond eager to get a look at Sedbury's collection."

"Then clearly," Garvey said, collecting the coffee cup and half-eaten cake, "this is your opportunity."

"And I'd be a fool to pass it up, especially if the Hales decide to sell Sedbury's whips." Charlie headed for the hall, and Garvey followed.

Within minutes, Charlie was coated, hatted, and out of his door and striding the short distance to Sedbury's address, which Jonathon had given as Number 15, Duke Street.

Reaching the building, as instructed, Charlie climbed to the first floor. Faced with a single oak door, he knocked a sharp *rat-a-tat-tat* on the panel.

A few seconds passed, then the door opened, revealing Lord Jonathon Hale. On seeing Charlie, relief lit the younger man's features. "Thank you for coming." Jonathon waved Charlie inside. "Do come in. I take it you've heard that Sedbury's dead?"

"I had heard, yes." Although no report had as yet appeared in the news sheets, in the way of such happenings, whispers of the event had spread like wildfire through the ton, so Charlie knowing of it meant nothing. He halted just beyond the short entrance hall and turned to his host. As Jonathon halted beside him, Charlie's gaze was drawn to a livid scrape that slashed across Jonathon's left cheek. "I say, that looks nasty."

Jonathon blinked, then grimaced and raised his fingers to gingerly touch the wound. "I went riding yesterday morning and wasn't looking ahead well enough. I rode straight into a branch. It nearly took my head off."

With another quirk of his lips, Jonathon held out his hand. "But thank you for coming. Bryan and I have been tasked with seeing to Sedbury's things, and neither of us have any idea about his whips other than the lot were said to be something of a collection."

Jonathon turned as another gentleman—another Hale by his features and size; all the Hale men were tall, large, and solid—came out of a room to their left. "Ah, Bryan—this is Charlie Hastings. He's the whip collector I told you I'd asked for assistance."

Bryan Hale hesitated, then held out his hand and gave Charlie a careful nod. "Hastings."

Charlie returned the nod and shook Bryan's hand, but it was obvious Bryan had heard about Charlie's altercations with Sedbury.

Bryan confirmed that by asking, "Forgive me, but aren't you the gentleman Sedbury bailed up in White's card room on Saturday night?"

"I am," Charlie admitted. "And I believe I was the first gentleman the police inspector investigating the case questioned, but he—Inspector Stokes—has accepted that I had nothing to do with Sedbury's murder."

That might have been stating matters in a somewhat more definite light than, currently, was warranted, but Charlie knew he was innocent, and he was confident that Barnaby and Penelope would ensure he was fully exonerated by finding Sedbury's murderer.

Jonathon and Bryan studied Charlie. The pair were a good head taller than he was and half again as wide, and Sedbury had been even larger and heavier and arguably stronger. After only a moment of consideration, the brothers nodded in ready acceptance of Charlie's innocence.

Jonathon shared a grimacing look with Bryan. "We both know what a ferocious brawler Sedbury was, and if you'll excuse the observation, it's difficult to see how you might have bested him."

Charlie waved the apology aside. "Believe me, I've never been so glad to be average-sized before."

Jonathon and Bryan smiled, and Jonathon waved toward an open door at the far end of the room. "So, to the whips. They're through there—"

He broke off as, behind Charlie, the front door opened.

Charlie swung around as a fashionably dressed lady—he was in two minds as to whether to label her a young lady as she clearly wasn't that young—swept inside. Long, wavy, brown-blonde hair, caught up and anchored beneath her elegant hat, large, thickly lashed brilliant-blue eyes, an oval face blessed with a straight nose, perfectly arched brown eyebrows, and a pair of lush lips all combined to render the lady quite striking, at least to Charlie's eyes.

The lady's gaze landed first on the Hales, then moved to Charlie, and she halted. "Oh!" Her eyes widened.

He met her bright-blue gaze and was instantly seized by countervailing impulses—to step back and fade into the background, as he normally would in the presence of a beautiful and eligible female, or stand his ground in the hope of appeasing his unexpectedly flaring curiosity regarding her.

Despite her scrutiny, he remained where he was and waited...

Jonathon broke the momentary hiatus. He waved at Charlie. "Claude, this is Mr. Charles Hastings, who is a renowned whip collector." To Charlie, he said, "My sister, Lady Claudia Hale." Returning his gaze to Claudia, Jonathon explained, "I invited Charlie to call, hoping to pick his brains over Sedbury's whips."

Bryan leapt in to reassure her, "Charlie was the gentleman who had a run-in with Sedbury at White's on Saturday evening, but that inspector you met has already spoken with him, and Hastings is no longer a suspect."

"I see." Claudia's clear blue gaze returned to Charlie's face.

It was a shock to realize that he found her quite dazzling, even though she was plainly in two minds about whether to accept his exoneration or treat him with suspicion. He couldn't really see why he was drawn to her. She appeared to be a managing sort of female, and he'd never been fond of those.

Claudia was, indeed, sizing up Charlie Hastings and mentally cursing her brothers' readiness to acknowledge him free of suspicion. Didn't they realize that this was a case of the more the better, and other gentlemen being suspected of Sedbury's murder would help deflect attention from them?

She had no doubt that, all too soon, the investigators' attention would turn her brothers' way. Aside from all else, Penelope Adair knew far too much of the ways of the ton to overlook two such prime suspects.

Still, perhaps this was an opportunity to learn more about Hastings and his association with Sedbury. Fashionably attired in a unostentatious way, with his neat fair hair and kind brown eyes, Hastings looked to be the quiet sort of gentleman who saw and knew far more than anyone expected. Even if he himself was entirely innocent of the crime, he might know more than he realized, enough to point the finger at someone else.

Claudia held out her hand. "Mr. Hastings."

He clasped her fingers and half bowed. "Lady Claudia."

Retrieving her hand, she studied him intently. He really didn't seem the sort to put himself in Sedbury's way. "If I may ask, what was the substance of Sedbury's quarrel with you, sir?"

"Oh, well..." Hastings appeared uncomfortable, but he couldn't politely deny her. "He and I crossed paths, quite by accident, in Long Acre earlier in the day, and I was compelled to intercede when Sedbury... er." Hastings cast an imploring look her brothers' way.

Bryan obligingly supplied, "As I heard it, our dear half brother had decided to accost some poor flower seller and took umbrage—as was his wont—when her street sweeper brother tried to defend her, and Sedbury threatened to flay the lad." Bryan went on, admiration coloring his tone, "And he would have, but Hastings here stepped in and filched the bastard's whip from his hand and put an end to it."

Claudia turned a wide-eyed gaze on Charlie Hastings. Sedbury had been huge, belligerently minded, and physically intimidating. That Hastings, significantly shorter and slighter, had had the courage to intervene, let alone been able to prevail, spoke volumes. "How on earth did you manage it?" The words had slipped from her before she realized how they might sound.

Hastings blushed faintly, but answered, "I know whips, so I knew just when he would ease his grip to adjust the angle, and I grabbed the handle then."

"He would have been *furious*." Claudia could imagine the scene all too readily.

"Well, yes, but I backed away, and he followed—stalking me, you might say—and that gave the brother and sister a chance to vanish, and once they had, I halted and handed Sedbury back his whip." Hastings shrugged. "He growled, but there was really nothing he could do, and by then, the crowd that had gathered had turned rather ugly for him, so…" Hastings shrugged again. "That was it. He stalked off, and I continued on my way."

"And it was about that encounter that he bailed you up in White's?" Jonathon shook his head. "No matter what else you can say about Sedbury, the man never lacked for sheer hide."

"He was a bully through and through," Claudia declared. "But someone has relieved us of his presence, for which, I might add, I'm truly grateful." She smiled at Charlie and advanced, drawing the men with her into the parlor proper. She'd revised her first impression of Charlie; his mild-mannered exterior obviously cloaked a man of principle and significant courage. Also quick wits; he'd seen how to disarm Sedbury and had done so expeditiously and in a way that had defused the situation.

Even though having Charlie continue to be a suspect would have increased the ranks and possibly helped muddy suspicion directed toward her brothers, in light of his actions, Claudia was content to have Charlie absolved of the murder. In truth, she would have loved to have witnessed that scene in Long Acre.

Furthermore, that Charlie was no longer a suspect freed her to make use of him in other ways. She bent a reassuring smile on her brothers. "It was an excellent notion to invite Mr. Hastings to view Sedbury's collection." To Charlie, she continued, "We really have no idea of the significance of what might be there."

"Well"—Charlie straightened—"I should be able to clarify that much at least."

With a wave, she invited him to continue to the relevant doorway. "Are there many collectors in town?"

"Several in London." Charlie fell in beside her as she led him to the anteroom door. "Five others as well as myself. It's quite a serious endeavor."

"Have you viewed Sedbury's collection previously?" Bryan asked. Claudia's brothers were trailing her and Charlie.

"No," Charlie replied. "In fact, I haven't heard of anyone whom Sedbury allowed to view his collection. Certainly, none of the acknowledged collectors."

"I always thought of it as Sedbury's strange hobby," Claudia admitted, "but I see I misjudged the male interest in whips."

From behind her, Jonathon snorted.

They reached the open doorway, and Claudia waved Charlie inside. "Please, satisfy your curiosity and ours as well."

He took her at her word and entered the room, swiftly scanning the displays on the walls before approaching more closely to examine individual whips.

Claudia waited with Jonathon and Bryan just inside the door. When Charlie paused, staring frowningly at one particular whip, she said, "We know that Sedbury had a favorite whip, but we don't think that's it."

"It's not." Briefly, Charlie glanced around the room again. "That whip is a Duckleberry Longe, and it isn't here."

He reached up and lifted down the whip that had captured his attention. He turned it over in his hands, examining the handle and the braiding closely, then he straightened and, with a perplexed look on his face, said, "But I certainly didn't expect to find *this* particular whip in Sedbury's possession."

"Why?" Jonathon asked.

"Because the last time I saw it was at the meeting of the Four-in-Hand Club a week ago, and then, it was in Lord Napier's hand." Charlie glanced at the siblings. "Napier's another of the collectors, and this is definitely his whip. There's no other like it."

Claudia stared at the innocent-looking whip. To her, it was still just a whip. "Is it valuable?"

"Yes. Quite valuable," Charlie replied. "It's a rare specimen and, therefore, hard to put a price on." He stared at the whip and shook his head. "I'm flabbergasted that Napier let it out of his hands."

Charlie looked up and caught the glance Jonathon and Bryan exchanged.

Then Jonathon looked at Charlie. "Perhaps Napier didn't surrender the whip willingly."

Charlie frowned, but it was Claudia who leapt on the point.

"You think," she said, searching her brothers' faces, "that Sedbury forced Napier to give him the whip?"

Bryan shrugged. "Who can say, but given all we know of Sedbury's ways, it's likely, isn't it? We know how he operated. He saw something someone else valued and moved heaven and earth to take it from them."

Charlie noted the underlying bitterness in Bryan's tone. The younger Hale was obviously speaking from experience, and judging by the looks on Claudia's and Jonathon's faces, both his siblings possessed similar insights.

Claudia also heard the emotion in Bryan's voice and knew exactly what had put it there. She wished her brothers would not go out of their way to paint themselves as the prime suspects in Sedbury's murder—Jonathon because of that odd letter Sedbury had never finished coupled with the damage to his face, and Bryan because of Sedbury's efforts to steal Rosalind from him.

Luckily, she was there, and as a devoted sister, she was ready and willing to seize the prospect Napier's whip being discovered in Sedbury's collection offered. It seemed likely that Lord Napier, too, might have had reason to wish Sedbury ill. To her mind, the more suspects, the better.

Someone needed to establish Napier's link to Sedbury, but that shouldn't involve either of her brothers. She cast the pair a stern glance. "You two need to finish sorting through Sedbury's things and set aside for the inspector and the Adairs anything that might point to a motive to kill Sedbury." She glanced around at the display of whips. "Leave the whips for now." She smiled at Charlie. "I'm sure Mr. Hastings will be able to advise us as to their disposal later."

Charlie brightened, and she fought to keep her smile from deepening.

"Now, however," she rolled on, her gaze fixed on him, "I hope I can prevail upon you, Mr. Hastings, to accompany me to Napier House." She nodded at the whip still in his hands. "I suggest we call on Lord Napier on the pretext of returning his whip and see what we can learn regarding how it came to be in Sedbury's collection."

Charlie kept his expression as bland as he could manage. The notion of bailing up Napier at his home and attempting to elicit some explanation of how Sedbury had come to possess Napier's prize whip in no way appealed, but he could see the determination in Claudia's eyes, and the truth was, if she was to broach that subject with Napier, it would be sensible for Charlie to be with her rather than one of her brothers, neither of whom knew anything about whips.

"Yes," he said in response to the look of polite inquiry Claudia was directing at him. "All right."

He walked forward, and as he joined her, Claudia confidently took his arm. "Do you know where Lord Napier lives?" she asked.

Charlie noted that Jonathon and Bryan were clearly used to taking direction from their older sister as both meekly returned to the parlor and resumed their sorting of Sedbury's belongings. "I do. He has a house in Brook Street."

Charlie paused to exchange farewells with Jonathon and Bryan, then Claudia steered him toward the front door. "We can take my carriage. It's waiting outside."

While she didn't exactly tow him along, Charlie felt that he'd been swept up by some irresistible force.

The carriage proved to be a small, unmarked black town carriage, with a groom-cum-coachman who was every bit as large and intimidating as Sedbury had been. Even more discombobulating was the long and plainly recent gash that ran above the coachman's left eyebrow.

Claudia addressed the looming giant. "Fosdyke, this is Mr. Hastings. He's helping us with this business about Sedbury. He and I need to go to Brook Street."

Rather numbly, Charlie added, "Napier House."

The giant tipped his head and rumbled, "I know it." He held the door as Charlie handed Claudia inside, then quickly followed.

Once Fosdyke had shut the door and climbed back onto the box, Charlie glanced at the lady beside him. "Is Fosdyke just your coachman?" The man seemed far too alert and aware and, indeed, menacing for that.

"Oh, no." Claudia peered out of the window as Fosdyke turned the coach. "He was originally Mama's groom, but over the years, he's come to fill a role more in the nature of a coachman-cum-bodyguard, not just for Mama but for all her children."

Charlie sat back and listened to the wheels rattle over the cobbles and wondered just how far a devoted coachman-cum-bodyguard might go in protecting those he deemed in his care.

CHAPTER 5

*A*t much the same time that Claudia's coach left the curb in Duke Street, Barnaby was making his way along the north bank of the Thames. He'd found the police wagon on Narrow Street and, assuming that Stokes had elected to start his search around the Duke Stairs—according to the River Police, the most easterly point from which Sedbury's body might have entered the water—had descended from the hackney, told the jarvey to wait, and set off, walking eastward on the path beside the stone embankment.

The weather was gloomy, the sky overcast and gray, and the breeze off the water carried a damp chill. The slap of waves against the stone edging the bank was a counterpoint to Barnaby's footsteps as he strode along the narrow path between the buildings and the river.

He found Stokes, as gloomy as the day, watching his men as they canvassed the area, asking literally everyone they could find if they'd been in the vicinity on Saturday night and, if so, what they recalled and whether they'd noticed anything untoward.

Barnaby spotted another group of constables carefully examining the stone embankment and the adjacent area, presumably searching for any sign of a recent struggle.

He halted beside Stokes, who stood with his hands sunk in his greatcoat pockets and his shoulders slightly hunched against the breeze. "Anything yet?" Barnaby asked.

Stokes grunted and looked to where a young constable was interviewing a brawny stevedore. "In this area, people have very short memories." He swung his gaze to the searchers combing the embankment itself. "That said, I'm fairly certain we haven't missed anything from the Duke Stairs to this point. We actually started a little farther east, at the entrance to Limehouse Dock. I spoke to the River Police again, and they swear that, given the relevant tides, Sedbury's body couldn't have been put into the river farther east than that."

Barnaby nodded. "Being thorough might be slow, but you can't afford to miss the spot."

"And sadly, given we're working westward into the heart of the docks, our progress is only going to get slower." Stokes sighed. "I wish there was some faster way to find the site, but if there is, I can't think of it."

"Neither Penelope nor I can, either."

"At least with Sedbury hailing from a noble house, the commissioner has all but given me carte blanche with respect to calling in extra men. I've already taken advantage of that, but even if I had yet more men, I don't think we could go much faster. We still have to wait for people to appear before we can question them."

Barnaby pulled a face. "Frustratingly slow it might be, but at this point, steady and certain is what we need. Speed would be nice, but we can't risk missing the site. Knowing where it is and what we can deduce from that is likely to prove crucial."

"I'm not looking forward to explaining our progress to the marquess."

"As I recall," Barnaby said, "he's not such a bad egg. I crossed paths with my father this morning, and he considers Rattenby a reasonable man."

Stokes didn't look convinced. "Until we know how he views the murder of his heir, I'm not sure we can predict how he'll behave." He turned to regard Barnaby. "How's your lads' network doing?"

Barnaby smiled with almost paternal pride. "They've found witnesses enough to exonerate Charlie, even without Garvey's testimony. Not that we truly suspected Charlie, but still, it's nice to have solid evidence to support our assertions."

Stokes grunted in agreement.

"And," Barnaby went on, "I'm delighted to report that they've picked up Sedbury's trail. That's what I came here to tell you. He left White's and walked to Pall Mall, where he hailed a hackney and directed the jarvey to drive in this direction, meaning eastward. At present, the lads are working on locating the jarvey."

"More power to them," Stokes said. "Learning exactly where Sedbury went next—where he left the hackney—would be a boon." His expression was approving as he looked at Barnaby. "That was an inspired notion of yours, to put all those idle eyes and brains to good use."

Barnaby laughed. "You won't be surprised to learn that it was Penelope who first thought of it. She came up with the notion out of her work finding jobs for the Foundling House graduates."

Stokes fell silent for a moment, then said, "I should speak with her about recruiting some of her brighter lads into the force. We could do with more who have their roots in the areas we're trying to police."

Barnaby clapped him on the shoulder. "You should definitely mention that. I predict the patronesses will leap on the idea—it's precisely the sort of employment that appeals to them, a job helping society, which, after all, is their founding principle."

"Hmm. I will, then." Stokes straightened as Constable Morgan approached.

The baby-faced Morgan looked abnormally serious as he snapped off a salute. "We've done with that street, guv. No news there, so we're on to the next."

Stokes nodded. "All we can do is keep at it."

Morgan dipped his head to Barnaby, who he knew well, then turned and went back to the group of younger constables he was overseeing.

Stokes sighed. "As I said, this will take time. I just hope we learn something useful from the exercise."

"We will." Barnaby watched Morgan reassign the young constables. "I think that once we get some idea of why Sedbury was down here—or wherever it was that he went after leaving Pall Mall and that hackney— we'll have a much better feeling for who might have killed him."

"I certainly hope so," Stokes replied. "If it transpires that he wasn't killed elsewhere and his body carted down to the river, but was, indeed, killed around here, somewhere by the bank, that implies he came here of his own accord, and that widens the suspect list considerably."

Barnaby grimaced. "True. However, given the victim is Sedbury, in terms of suspects, I greatly fear that we're going to have far more than is helpful. Far more than we can manage."

Stokes made a distinctly sour sound.

Barnaby glanced around. "Can you leave O'Donnell and Morgan in charge of the search?"

Stokes met his gaze. "Yes."

"Good. Because we should head back to Albemarle Street. Penelope has information gleaned from her usual sources to impart, and Charlie might have news as well."

Stokes readily gave his men orders to continue their endeavors until five o'clock, then he joined Barnaby, and they walked back to where Barnaby had left the hackney.

~

With Claudia beside him, her hand on his arm and Napier's whip in her other hand, Charlie mentally girded his loins and knocked on the door of Napier House.

Napier's butler opened the door, and Charlie promptly handed him a card. "Mr. Charlie Hastings and Lady Claudia Hale to see his lordship."

The butler's assessing gaze passed over them, then he bowed, stepped back, and waved them inside. "If you will wait in the drawing room, sir, my lady"—he gestured to a door on the left—"I will inform his lordship of your presence."

"We would like just a moment of his time," Claudia informed the butler and led the way into the drawing room.

Charlie followed her, and the butler closed the door behind him.

Claudia sat on the sofa, then frowning slightly, looked at Charlie. "I wondered if Napier would be at home, but it sounds as if he is."

Charlie had already considered that issue. "It's unlikely he'd be anywhere else at this hour." He walked to the armchair opposite Claudia and sat. "It's too early for dinner and too late for the usual afternoon pursuits of a gentleman of his age."

The door opened, and the butler came in and bowed. "If you will follow me, sir, my lady, his lordship will see you in his study."

They rose and followed the man along a corridor that led toward the rear of the house.

Charlie wondered at Napier's choice of room. If it had been Charlie alone, seeing him in the study would have been normal enough, but to receive a marquess's daughter, one with whom Napier wasn't on familiar terms, in his study? Charlie suspected that Napier had already heard of

Sedbury's death and felt the need of the more private setting for the upcoming interview.

The butler halted before a door at the end of the corridor, opened it, announced them, and ushered them into a decent-sized room lined with bookcases.

Napier rose from behind a large desk placed before a pair of long windows that overlooked the rear garden. He half bowed to Claudia. "Lady Claudia. A pleasure." More familiarly, Napier exchanged nods with Charlie. "Hastings."

With the formalities observed, Napier waved them to two armchairs facing the desk. "Now, what can I do for you?"

Claudia had carried Napier's whip down by her side, and the whip had largely been concealed by her skirts. As she sat, she placed the whip on her lap, and instantly, Napier's gaze locked on it.

Studying the man's reaction, Charlie had absolutely no doubt that he'd been correct in identifying the whip as Napier's.

Napier was having difficulty dragging his gaze from the whip, but eventually, he managed it and looked at Claudia. "Lady Claudia, I understand that Viscount Sedbury has died. Permit me to offer my condolences to you and your family."

"Thank you, my lord," Claudia smoothly replied, "but the truth of the matter is that none of the family were close to Sedbury, and he will not be deeply mourned."

"Ah. I see." Napier looked a trifle less uneasy, and his gaze lowered again to the whip.

Claudia went on, "In dealing with Sedbury's possessions, we came upon his collection of whips, and as none of the family are knowledge-able about such items, we asked Mr. Hastings to assist us. On viewing Sedbury's whips, Mr. Hastings identified this one"—briefly, she lifted the whip, breaking the hold it had on Napier—"as recently belonging to you." When Napier raised his gaze to her face, she smiled and asked, "We wondered if you would explain the circumstances that led to your whip being in Sedbury's hands."

Napier returned Claudia's regard with a steady gaze, plainly weighing what he should say.

Mildly, Charlie said, "I remember you had the whip at the last club meet and was surprised to find it in Sedbury's rooms."

Napier's gaze deflected to Charlie, and he studied him for a moment, then Napier returned his gaze to Claudia and said, "My son, Percy, has only recently come on the town, and he was unwise enough to fall in with a crowd that frequented a particular hell in Pall Mall. By the time I learned of it, Percy had lost…quite a sum. That was bad enough, but not impossible to rectify. However, unfortunately, his debts in the form of notes of hand had somehow ended in Sedbury's pocket."

"Ah." Charlie nodded understandingly. "And Sedbury demanded the whip in settlement."

Napier snorted. "You plainly didn't know Sedbury well." Napier looked at Claudia. "Sedbury demanded that I cover the debts and, in addition, surrender the whip to him by way of interest." Napier's lips tightened. "Initially, I refused, but cool as you please, Sedbury threatened to blacken Percy's name throughout the clubs and ensure that he was never admitted to any of them." Napier's gaze remained steady on Claudia's face, as if he was intent on ensuring she understood. "No matter that most of us couldn't abide the man, as Rattenby's heir, at some point, Sedbury would have been in a position to wield considerable power and influence." Napier paused, then sat back and admitted, "In the end, I gave him the whip as well as the money." He shook his head. "To be rid of the threat Sedbury posed, it was worth it. My son's future was more valuable to me."

Claudia smothered a sigh. "I feel I should apologize for Sedbury and his crass behavior, yet the truth is that he was as bad to us as he was to everyone else."

Napier dipped his head, acknowledging her words. "In turn, I'm sorry to hear that."

Charlie cleared his throat and asked, "When did you last see Sedbury?"

Napier readily replied, "He came here last Tuesday evening. I'd sent around a note to say I was willing to meet his demands."

Claudia asked, "You didn't see him after that?"

Napier shook his head. "And before you—or the police—ask, I sent Percy off to visit his aunt in Northumberland on Tuesday morning. He won't be returning for at least a month."

Charlie inclined his head. "Thank you for being so forthcoming. As you've no doubt guessed, we're trying to establish Sedbury's movements around the time of his death for the investigators."

"Indeed." Claudia rose, bringing both men to their feet. "Thank you for your time, my lord." She held out the whip. "Please, take this back, in recompense as it were." She met Napier's gaze. "I assure you the rest of the Hales are nothing like Sedbury."

Napier hesitated for only a second, then reached across the desk and took the whip. "Thank you, Lady Claudia." He inclined his head to Charlie. "Hastings."

Napier rang for the butler, and with genial farewells, they left Napier in his study, smiling at his whip, and quit the house.

Charlie paused on the pavement outside, and Claudia halted beside him and quietly said, "He might have considered protecting his son worth handing over that whip, but..."

Charlie grimaced. "Handing Sedbury that particular whip definitely hurt."

"So Napier remains on the suspect list?"

Charlie met her gaze. "In the circumstances, we have to let Stokes—and Barnaby and Penelope—know what we've learned. We can leave it to them to decide what weight to attach to the information."

Claudia inclined her head in agreement. She wanted as many names on the suspect list as possible, and while she doubted Napier had had any hand in Sedbury's murder, she was content that he remained in contention. "In that case"—she placed her hand on Charlie's sleeve and turned to where Fosdyke was waiting with the carriage—"we had better go and report our findings." That would also bring her up to date with anything the investigation had uncovered. She glanced at Charlie. "Where to?"

Obligingly, he steered her to the carriage. "Barnaby and Penelope's house in Albemarle Street."

～

Penelope was standing at the drawing-room window, idly looking out at the street, when a small unmarked black town carriage driven by an exceedingly large and burly coachman drew up outside their door.

Eagerness seized her; at last, some news!

As she watched, the coachman climbed down to the pavement and opened the carriage door, and the last of the waning afternoon light fell on his face and illuminated the gash above his eyebrow. She was making a mental note not to forget to investigate the large, strong coachman with the damaged face when, to her considerable surprise, Charlie descended from the carriage and handed Claudia down.

Penelope stepped away from the window. "I didn't know they knew each other."

The doorbell pealed, and she heard Mostyn open the door, and seconds later, Claudia came into the room with Charlie in her wake.

Penelope's mind seethed with possibilities as she smiled in welcome. "I'm glad you could join us." She touched fingers with Claudia, nodded to Charlie, then waved them to seats. "Barnaby said he'd fetch Stokes. They should be here soon." Resuming her customary place on one of the two long sofas, the instant her guests had settled—Claudia on the sofa opposite and Charlie in an armchair—she asked, "Am I to take it you have fresh information?"

Charlie exchanged a glance with Claudia. "We've learned a thing or two," he said, "and we thought we should come and report."

Penelope was about to encourage them to tell her all—and by all, she meant *all*—but just at that moment, they heard the front door open and the rumble of familiar voices as Barnaby and Stokes entered the house.

A minute later, after divesting themselves of coats and hats, the pair strolled into the drawing room.

Stokes surveyed the company, then nodded to Claudia. "Lady Claudia. I hadn't expected to see you so soon."

Claudia smiled. "Please, just Claudia. And I came upon Mr. Hastings, who was helping my brothers sort through Sedbury's things, and he discovered an anomaly in Sedbury's whip collection that he and I subsequently followed up."

"We thought we should let you know what we found," Charlie put in.

"Good." Stokes sank into the armchair beside the one Charlie occupied.

Penelope suspected Stokes was a trifle leery of Claudia's unexpected presence, yet at the same time, he wanted to hear any information she was willing to share.

After exchanging polite nods with Claudia, Barnaby sat on the sofa beside Penelope.

The instant he did, she opened her lips to start questioning Claudia only to hear Stokes declare, "A round of reports seems in order." His gray gaze fixed on Penelope. "You first, I think. I'm keen to hear what your usual sources had to say."

She inwardly heaved a put-upon sigh but, deciding that the fastest way to learning everyone else's news was to share her own, she marshalled her thoughts, then looked at Claudia. "Claudia, I apologize in advance for any aspersions implied by what I have to report, but at this stage of an investigation, it's imperative that everyone who could possibly have a motive is identified."

Claudia's faint grimace assured Penelope that Claudia was well aware of the familial secrets Penelope was about to reveal. Claudia inclined her head. "I understand."

Penelope drew breath and commenced, "First, I have yet to meet or hear of anyone who feels even an iota of grief over Sedbury's death, which is remarkable in and of itself. I've been told that the reason I never met him socially is that despite being the heir to a marquessate, by the time I made my come-out, he'd already been struck off the hostesses' lists. It's also common knowledge, backed by first-hand evidence, that Sedbury was set on disowning the rest of the Hale family the instant he inherited the title. Consequently, every single member of the family, from the marquess himself to Claudia's youngest brother, Conrad, can be said to have had a powerful motive to do away with Sedbury. Against that, however, as one of my ladies observed, the question arises as to why any of them waited until now to act, as Sedbury's stance regarding the family has been known for years." She glanced at Claudia. "Have I got all that right?"

Somewhat stiffly, Claudia nodded. "All of what you've said so far is unarguable."

"In addition, there's a general view that Sedbury's shadow, as it were, has stymied the marriage prospects of his half siblings—specifically Jonathon and Claudia, but that would also apply to Bryan and Margot, who will shortly make her come-out. So I believe it's fair to state that all of the family and all those who are their active supporters had strong reasons for wishing Sedbury dead."

Penelope paused, reviewing her list of revelations yet to be made. "All of that speaks to a major motive that applies to every member of the family. However, we have at least two members with additional motives specific to them." She raised a hand and ticked them off on her fingers. "Jonathon, who Sedbury specifically and consistently goaded, including whatever was behind that unfinished letter. And Bryan, whose future wife Sedbury was doing his damnedest to steal.

"So that's the family." She blew out a breath and went on, "To that list, we apparently need to add a very large number of ton figures known to have had their lives adversely impacted by Sedbury." She looked at Stokes, who had been scribbling in his notebook. "And yes, it seems all those occurrences are of the ilk to give rise to sufficient motive for Sedbury's murder."

Frowning, Stokes glanced at her. "*All* of them?"

"All. There are at least twenty-three members of the ton known to be in that category." Her expression severe, she shook her head. "I have never come across any man so reviled by so many. In short, there is a very long list of people who would have wanted Sedbury dead. And that's just within the ton. As was stated to me, Sedbury was a man who delighted in gathering enemies, and given that behavior, we can be absolutely certain that there are many more who wished him ill among the lower classes."

Stokes appeared utterly confounded, and even Barnaby looked taken aback.

After a moment, as if feeling his way, Barnaby ventured, "In speaking of the family, why include the marchioness and Claudia and the younger children?"

Penelope evenly replied, "While no one imagines they would have— or indeed, could have—strangled Sedbury themselves..." She looked at Claudia. "Are there any trusted family retainers here in London?"

Claudia met her eyes, then sighed and tipped her head toward the street. "Fosdyke. Currently, he's acting as my coachman-cum-guard."

"His background?" Penelope inquired.

Claudia glanced at Charlie. "As I explained to Charlie, Fosdyke came to Rattenby with Mama on her marriage. He was her groom, and he's first and foremost devoted to her, but his vigilance extends to all her children."

Stokes fixed Claudia with a steady gaze. "Would he kill to protect any of you?"

Her gaze locked with Stokes's, Claudia hesitated, then sighed and said, "I really couldn't say."

And that, Penelope thought, was answer enough.

Charlie cleared his throat, and when they all looked his way, with an apologetic glance at Claudia, he offered, "Fosdyke has a nasty gash above his left eyebrow. Also, Jonathon Hale has a livid scrape down one cheek."

Stokes, who had been busily writing, looked at Charlie and frowned. "You met Jonathon Hale?"

Charlie explained how Jonathon, knowing Charlie to be a whip collector, had asked him for advice on what to do with Sedbury's whips. "But of particular note, when I looked over Sedbury's collection, I found a whip that, up until a week ago, belonged to Lord Napier."

Claudia sat straighter. "We—Charlie and I—called on Lord Napier, and he was kind enough to trust us with the story of how his son, who has recently come on the town, fell into debt, and how Sedbury had acquired those debts and insisted not only that the money be paid but that Napier throw in his whip for good measure." She looked at Penelope. "I imagine Napier's story is much like those you heard today concerning other members of the ton."

Penelope nodded. "Sedbury didn't exactly blackmail people, but extortion for immediate gain? Yes, indeed, that was his game."

Charlie said, "While I can't see Napier as the murderer, he certainly had as much motive as anyone. As did his son, although Napier sent the lad north to his sister nearly a week prior to Sedbury's murder, so the son, at least, seems to be off the list."

"Convenient." Stokes was still writing. "We'll need to check on the boy's movements, regardless." He looked at Penelope. "Do you have a list of those twenty-three names?"

She pulled a sheet of paper from her pocket. "I wrote down all the names, but as it happens, with this being the off-season, several are known to be in the country. Assuming they didn't hire someone to do the deed while they are far distant—always a possibility—then we have fourteen who were in town themselves when Sedbury was killed."

Stokes took the sheet, scanned the names, and sighed. "As matters stand, as well as the Hales and their people, and the Ellises and theirs, and now also Napier and his household, we need to investigate everyone on this list." He looked at Penelope.

She stared back unenthusiastically.

Barnaby stirred. "We should be able to at least make a cursory examination using my network"—he focused on Penelope—"as well as yours."

Stokes arched a brow at her. "You have a network as well?"

She lifted one shoulder. "The maids and the cooks' helpers the Foundling House has placed in service. Those girls are now distributed throughout the ton. I've taken on two of the older girls for training here, and with my encouragement, they keep in contact with all the others. In reality, the staff of all the houses in Mayfair have their own network—as we've all known for decades, given they are the speediest and most reliable source of ton gossip—and through my two girls as well as the staff here, we can tap into that wider network as well."

Stokes sat back. "That's…quite brilliant. I'm impressed."

Resigned, Penelope tipped her head at the list in Stokes's hand. "I have a copy of that, of course, and despite the number, accepting that everyone had motive enough, if we concentrate instead on who had opportunity, I would hope to reduce the list to possibles within a few days."

Stokes slowly nodded, then looked at Claudia. "How many days do you think we'll have before your father arrives in town?"

She plainly calculated, then grimaced and said, "Probably only another day, two at most. I know Aunt Patricia—Lady Selborough—is expecting Papa and Mama to arrive by the day after tomorrow."

Stokes grimaced, then briefly filled the others in on the progress—or lack thereof—in the search along the riverbank. "We're working on the theory that, assuming Sedbury was killed by the river or close to it, either there will be some physical sign of a struggle somewhere along the embankment or someone will have noticed an altercation. We know there was a fight, and given Sedbury's size and strength, the encounter had to have been notable. Alternatively, if he was killed somewhere else and his body brought there and dumped into the river, there should be someone who saw something. Despite the hour, in that area, there are taverns that would have still been open, and night watchmen and boatmen about as well." He concluded with, "Although it's been slow going, we've cleared the stretch from Limehouse Dock to the entrance to Regent's Canal. Tomorrow, we'll continue searching westward from there."

The sentiment *and hope we find something soon* didn't need to be articulated.

Barnaby looked around the faces, then said, "On a positive note, we've found witnesses enough to definitively strike Charlie from the suspects' list."

Charlie grinned and audibly exhaled in mock-relief.

Barnaby noted that Claudia also appeared quietly relieved. Smiling, he continued, "In addition, we now know that after leaving White's, Sedbury walked to Pall Mall and caught a hackney that he directed eastward. Whether he went directly to the docks or somewhere else, we've yet to learn, but my lads are presently searching for the hackney driver. Tomorrow, I'll send a group to ask at pawnshops, looking for any sign of Sedbury's whip. If it was left on the riverbank or anywhere else by his murderer, it's almost certainly no longer there. Someone will have picked it up and sold it on, and if we can locate it and, through that, contact who first found it, we might be able to deduce something useful from where it was discarded."

"Well," Stokes said, shutting his notebook, "it seems we have our work cut out for us."

Charlie glanced at Claudia, then looked at Penelope and rather carefully suggested, "If you like, we—Claudia and I—could question her brothers' and aunt's staff and see if we can establish alibis for Jonathon, Bryan, and Fosdyke."

"Please do," Penelope promptly replied. "I'll have my hands full with the rest of my list."

Stokes nodded his agreement. "Just make sure that you make it abundantly clear that you're only interested in hearing the truth. It won't help if the staff make up some story exonerating someone because they think that's what you want them to say."

Penelope studied Claudia and Charlie. "Do you think you can do that?"

Charlie and Claudia exchanged a glance, then Claudia looked at Penelope. "I'll make sure they understand we only want the truth."

"Onward, then." Stokes got to his feet.

Everyone else rose as well, and the company went into the front hall, where coats and hats were donned and farewells exchanged.

Penelope directed, "We'll meet back here and share what we've learned late tomorrow afternoon."

No one argued.

Charlie and Claudia were the first to leave, and Mostyn closed the door against the chilly breeze.

Settling his coat, Stokes caught Penelope's eye. "Do you think we'll be able to trust what Charlie and Claudia report?"

"I think so," Penelope replied. "Claudia may be protective of her brothers, but Charlie has good instincts about people, and he won't allow her to gloss over or invent anything, no matter how tempting." She smiled. "Besides, in case it's escaped your notice, Claudia is determined to prove her brothers innocent of the crime, and it's better that she employs her talents in a way that's useful to us rather than going off on her own and trying to discover, for instance, just where on the docks Sedbury died."

Stokes looked suitably horrified. "Heaven preserve us."

Barnaby laughed and clapped him on the shoulder, then he and Penelope saw their friend out.

With the front door closed, they turned and walked deeper into the house.

Barnaby glanced at Penelope's face and smiled at her focused expression. "You'll have a full day ahead of you, crammed with investigating."

She grinned and met his eyes. "I've decided that the only way to approach tomorrow's task is to view it as a challenge to see how fast and how far I can trim that list." She gestured as if giving the order to charge. "As Stokes said, onward!"

CHAPTER 6

$\mathscr{A}$s Barnaby had predicted, for all those investigating Viscount Sedbury's murder, Wednesday proved to be a day crammed with activity. By the time he stepped out of the house, Penelope was already closeted with her young assistants-cum-protégées, organizing their campaign to investigate the alibis of the potential ton suspects.

After drawing the front door closed behind him, Barnaby settled his hat on his head and left them to their endeavors. He had multiple lads to meet.

At that moment, Penelope was in the garden parlor, seated on one of the sofas with the two maids—Chrissie and Polly—perched on the sofa opposite.

Although faintly daunted by the task of investigating so many members of the ton all at once, Penelope believed she'd devised an approach that would at least give them enough information to eliminate some of their candidates. She'd just finished explaining her idea to her protégées and was pleased but not surprised to find them brimming with enthusiasm; she'd chosen them to train in investigative techniques for a reason. Both possessed an abundance of native curiosity as well as excellent memories, and neither was overly intimidated by the barriers of class.

"So," Polly said, eyes alight with eagerness, "in speaking with the staff, we focus on getting them to tell us where their people were on Saturday night and early Sunday morning—if they attended some ball or dinner or whatnot and when they got home."

Penelope nodded. "That's your first task. Coachmen and grooms will likely be the most useful sources, but butlers also will know when their master or mistress returned home and retired for the night. Or if they went out again later. As I've taught you, the best approach is to get your targets talking about whatever they want to talk about, then subtly lead them in the direction of the information you wish to know."

"But regardless of whatever answer we get on that point," Chrissie, equally eager, put in, "we should try to learn if their people had contact with anyone who might be a hired killer."

Penelope elaborated, "Either by having such a person call or by going out to meet someone unknown at an odd hour or specifically using an unmarked carriage. If they've had any mysterious meetings either under their roof or somewhere else in the past two weeks." She regarded the girls. "While the first part of your task should be easily enough accomplished simply by encouraging the usual household gossip, you'll need to be more tactful and careful probing for answers on our second point."

Chrissie frowned. "Which is more important? Where their people were on Saturday or if they met with some mysterious stranger?"

Penelope considered, then sighed. "Actually, both could potentially be our clue, so I suggest you try for the easier part first."

"What if," Polly said, "we make some comment about the viscount who was killed? A dresser or a gentleman's gentleman might know if their mistress or master knew the man or was particularly relieved on learning of his death."

"That's an excellent notion," Penelope replied, "as long as you can introduce the subject naturally. Just don't make it obvious that you have any real interest in Sedbury's murder."

Both girls nodded in understanding.

"Very well." Penelope consulted the list. "Now, who do we know at each of these houses?"

They progressed through the list of ton residences, cross-referencing each against the list of Foundling House alumni placements, and established that in every household, the girls had at least one Foundling House acquaintance on whom they could believably call.

"Can we say we've been asked to see how they're going in their job?" Chrissie asked.

"You can, indeed," Penelope replied. She was, after all, a patroness of the Foundling House and chair of the committee that oversaw placements. "And if there are any difficulties, do let me know. Now, the last thing we need to do to be as efficient as we possibly can is to order these houses in terms of location."

That didn't take long.

"Right, then." Penelope sat back. "We're ready. Chrissie, ring for the carriage, then both of you fetch your bonnets and cloaks. I'll meet you in the front hall."

Penelope smiled as the girls rushed from the room, then she gathered up her lists and followed.

She chatted with Mostyn as he helped her don her coat. She shook her head when he held out her bonnet. "I'll be remaining in the carriage throughout."

The girls came clattering down the stairs, breathless but ready to embark on their venture.

Mostyn smiled and opened the door. Penelope waved the girls ahead of her, then followed them down the steps.

Connor, her groom-cum-guard, stood holding the carriage door. Penelope shooed the girls inside, then took Connor's hand and climbed up.

The girls had claimed the rear-facing seat, leaving the forward-facing seat for Penelope. She settled, and when her coachman, Phelps, called down from above, asking for their direction, she raised her voice and informed him, "Hanover Square."

The coach rattled off, and she spent the short distance to their destination rehearsing the girls' initial sallies.

When the carriage drew up to the curb in the square, the girls eagerly descended, and each headed for a different house.

Penelope sat back and waited, something she'd never been good at. She would much rather be out, asking questions herself, but the truth was that ton staff were always tight-lipped in her presence, especially when it came to inquiries about their employers. The girls would fare much better than she; there was little restraint in gossiping among staff from different ton houses. "And, indeed," she muttered to herself, "this is precisely why I took them on as my assistants."

She sighed and tried to think of other things. Distracting herself with thoughts of Pip and Oliver playing together proved the most successful.

Uncounted minutes later, Polly appeared at the carriage door, her face alight with triumph. Penelope straightened and swung the door open, and as Polly climbed up, Chrissie appeared behind her and followed her into the carriage.

The instant the door clicked shut, Penelope looked hopefully at the girls. "Well?"

Polly spoke first. "Both the lady's dresser and their coachman chatted about how their master and mistress had been to some grand dinner in Grosvenor Square on Saturday night, and both said they'd come home about midnight and hadn't gone out again. And no one seemed to know anything about any unexpected meeting with unknown people. They were puzzled when I steered the conversation that way."

Chrissie was nodding. "I learned much the same at the Ferrises'. His lordship went out on Saturday, but was home by eleven o'clock, and her ladyship was at some ball, but came home just after midnight. And everyone was eager to learn whether I'd heard anything about the viscount's murder." Chrissie glanced at Polly. "Once I mentioned that, it was easy to slide in a question as to mysterious meetings with shady characters." Chrissie returned her gaze to Penelope. "But everyone in the household was sure their people hadn't met with any such person. No unexpected outings of any sort."

Penelope nodded thoughtfully. "It seems mentioning the viscount's murder might be a good tack to take with the rest of our inquiries." She glanced at her list and wielded a pencil, striking out the Ferrises and the Moretons. "That was an excellent start. Right, then." To Chrissie, she said, "Tell Phelps we're off to Brook Street."

Chrissie sprang up, tapped on the panel in the ceiling, and when Phelps opened it, gave him the new direction.

The instant Chrissie sat, the coach lumbered into motion.

As they rolled on along Mayfair's streets, Penelope wondered if the answers they extracted at Lord Napier's house would be similarly definitive.

After reporting on their progress to the commissioner, Stokes paused on the steps of Scotland Yard. The commissioner's parting words, "You need to find some concrete clue!" still rang in his ears.

The man was right. In this rather peculiar case, other than a dead body, clues of substance had been thin on the ground.

Belting his greatcoat more tightly about him, Stokes descended to the pavement. He hailed a passing hackney and, while waiting for it to come around, grumbled, "Napier's whip being found in Sedbury's collection surely qualifies."

Stokes hoped Penelope and her girls would find sufficient evidence during their inquiries at Napier House to rule his lordship either in or out. They needed definitive evidence, not equivocal findings.

The hackney drew up, and Stokes instructed the jarvey to drive to the docks west of the entrance to Regent's Canal.

While rattling through London's crowded streets, Stokes mulled over what they thought they currently knew. Ultimately, he concluded, "Lots of possible suspects, but precious few verifiable links putting any of them together with Sedbury on Saturday night."

Eventually, the hackney slowed, then halted. Stokes looked out and saw the rippling gray-brown waters of the river. He opened the door and stepped out into the brisk breeze that carried more than a hint of fish and rotting vegetation. After paying the jarvey, Stokes turned away from the canal and walked west along the narrow path that ran beside the embankment wall to where Sergeant O'Donnell stood, his gaze tracking several constables who were knocking on doors or walking into warehouses.

That morning, together with Morgan, O'Donnell was overseeing a group of six junior constables. As Stokes joined his sergeant, he could see three of the six talking with stevedores and workmen who were lounging outside two warehouses and a shipping office. Two other constables were stopping passersby and those visiting the various establishments and inquiring if they'd been in the area on Saturday night.

Stokes doubted any of the visitors would know anything; most didn't live in the area and only ventured into it during business hours. The stevedores, workmen, and navvies, however, might prove better prospects.

As if reading his mind, when Stokes halted beside O'Donnell, the experienced sergeant nodded at the constables chatting with the local workers. "I told them to ask that lot if they'd set eyes on a lordly cove like Sedbury anywhere near."

Stokes nodded. "Good thinking. If Sedbury came to the river under his own steam, he might have visited before."

"What I thought," O'Donnell returned, "but so far, no luck." He cut a glance at Stokes. "Can't say I'm surprised. The viscount might have been here all right, but finding anyone in this area who saw him on Saturday night well enough to register him as a gentleman and remember it, and we don't even know where exactly along this stretch he was, well, none of that seems all that likely."

"Normally, I'd agree," Stokes replied, "but you never saw Sedbury. Trust me, if he'd been here, someone would have noticed him. He wasn't just large and massive, but I'm reliably informed that he was so belligerently arrogant, he carried himself as if he owned the world. *That* sort of gentleman the locals hereabouts will always note, if for no other reason than to avoid him."

"Hmm." O'Donnell didn't sound entirely convinced. "Anyways, I sent Morgan and one of the bobbies to ask at all the possible watering holes—taverns, inns, whatever. Seemed best Morgan go in during the day and work his magic on the barmaids. If any of them know anything, he's sure to get it out of them."

Stokes grunted in agreement. It was well known throughout the Yard that the baby-faced Morgan could charm information from the crustiest old crone. For him, extracting information from barmaids would be as easy as falling off a stool.

The slap of the waves against the stone wall gave Stokes an idea. He tipped his head toward the river. "I'm going to take a wander along the waterline and see if there are any mud larks willing to talk to me."

"Mud larks" was the common term for the children of the poor who scavenged for bits and pieces—flotsam and jetsam—that washed up on the tide.

O'Donnell arched his brows. "Could be worth it. They see our uniforms and scarper, but they might be curious enough about you to hang around long enough to listen."

Stokes hoped so. In his experience, the children who haunted the river —indeed, street children anywhere—were highly observant.

With a nod to O'Donnell, Stokes set off along the embankment, looking for the nearest access to the shore. As he walked, he pretended to be unaware of the suspicious eyes that tracked his movements. In that area, the appearance of the police, especially in any numbers, made people uneasy and wary regardless of whether their consciences were clear or not.

As instructed by Claudia the day before, at precisely ten o'clock, Charlie knocked on the door of Selborough House in Farm Street. After informing the starchy butler who opened the door that he was there to see Claudia, he was immediately admitted and, after handing over his hat and relinquishing his coat, he was shown into the drawing room.

Within minutes, Claudia walked in, smiled, and gave him her hand. "Excellent! You're on time. Aunt Patricia has given us permission to interview the staff." When he released her hand, she swung around and gestured to the doorway. "I thought it would be best to use the back parlor. Rather less intimidating."

"A sound notion." Charlie fell in beside her, and they walked through the front hall and down a long corridor to a smaller, more comfortably furnished room at the rear of the house. The parlor was well lit via large windows that gave onto a leafy courtyard garden.

Claudia led the way to a sofa set before the main window, sat, and with a gracious wave, invited Charlie to sit beside her.

He did, rather nervously, truth be told, but Claudia's gaze promptly fixed on the butler, who had followed them into the room.

"Trestlewaite, I believe my aunt explained the need to verify Fosdyke's movements on Saturday evening through to Sunday morning." She glanced at Charlie. "Mr. Hastings is here by way of bearing witness to the information I gather. We all thought it best if I asked the relevant questions for the police, rather than have them here."

"Indeed, Lady Claudia." A hint of relief showed in Trestlewaite's expression. "On behalf of the staff, I quite agree. We do not need the police barging into this household."

"Quite." Claudia waved him nearer. "If you would step a little closer, we can begin."

Almost tentatively, the butler came to stand on the opposite side of the low table stationed before the sofa. In that position, the light from the window at Charlie's and Claudia's backs fell full on Trestlewaite's face.

"Now," Claudia began, "if you would tell us what you know of Fosdyke's movements from the evening of Saturday to first thing Sunday morning." Before the butler could speak, she held up a hand. "I ask for what you know, not what you think, believe, or assume."

The butler frowned slightly. "Well, I know Fosdyke was expected to act as groom when the coachman ferried her ladyship and you, my lady, to the dinner in Audley Street. You left the front hall at seven o'clock, and I recall seeing Fosdyke holding the carriage door for you and your aunt. The coach returned at just after midnight, and the footman opened the door, and as it was raining, James ran down with the large umbrella and escorted you and her ladyship in, and I met you in the front hall." Trestlewaite frowned. "As I didn't open the door, I didn't notice if Fosdyke was with the carriage."

Claudia frowned, clearly recalling the moment. "I have to admit, I could not say—not of my own knowledge—that he was. I assume he was, but that's not sufficient evidence."

"Perhaps Johns can shed some light on the matter," Trestlewaite suggested.

Claudia glanced at Charlie. "Johns is my aunt's coachman." She looked at Trestlewaite. "Perhaps we might have Johns in next."

Trestlewaite bowed. "I will summon him, my lady."

Her expression perplexed, Claudia stared at the door as it closed behind Trestlewaite. "You know, try as I might, I can't recall if Fosdyke was on the carriage when we returned to the house on Saturday night."

Charlie thought, then offered, "Good staff are like that. They know how to pass unremarked."

She tipped her head his way. "Good point. And Fosdyke is nothing if not 'good staff.'"

The door opened, and a large man with large hands and a faintly worried expression came in. "You wanted to see me, my lady?"

She smiled and waved him nearer. "Yes, Johns. I don't know if Trestlewaite mentioned it, but we're trying to establish where certain staff members were during the hours of last Saturday night. Now," she went on in bracing fashion, "when you ferried my aunt and me home after that dinner on Saturday, was Fosdyke still with you on the coach?"

"He was, my lady. The rain had started by then, and a right drenching it was for both of us. Luckily, James, the footman, came rushing down with the umbrella to shield you and the mistress up the steps and into the house. Fosdyke was beside me, and we saw the front door open before the carriage had even stopped—James must have been keeping an eye out, knowing he'd be needed—so Fosdyke didn't get down. No need, with James already on his way to open the carriage door."

"I see." Claudia was clearly reliving the moment in her mind.

"So," Charlie put in, "once their ladyships were inside, what did you and Fosdyke do next?"

"Well, we drove around into the mews and into the stable," Johns replied. "Tom, the groom, came hurrying down from our quarters above, and the three of us unhitched the team and saw to them. Then we went upstairs. We all share a room above the stable, see?"

"About what time was that?" Claudia asked.

Johns frowned, then ventured, "It was after midnight when we reached the house. I'd heard the bells as we drove through the streets. It'd've taken us a good half hour, likely more, to see to the horses, so we went up about one o'clock Sunday morn."

"And neither you, Fosdyke, or Tom left your room again that night?" Charlie asked.

"No, sir. We wanted our sleep. We rolled out of bed at five-thirty sharp to start on our chores and have his lordship's gelding ready when he called for it for his morning ride."

Claudia smiled at Johns. "Thank you. That's very clear."

"One last thing," Charlie said. "Fosdyke has a nasty gash above his left eye. Do you know how he got that?"

"Was it in a fight?" Claudia asked.

Johns grinned. "You could say it was a fight, but not with any man. It was that fractious gelding of your uncle's, my lady. Got a stone wedged deep in his hoof and wasn't of a mind to let any of us near. It took all three of us—me, Fosdyke, and Tom—to hold the beggar, and when Fosdyke got that stone out, well, the ungrateful beast lashed out and caught Fosdyke with his hoof. Opened up that gash, and you're right. Nasty, it was, but truth be told, Fosdyke was lucky it wasn't worse."

Charlie winced, then asked, "And that was when?"

"Sunday midmorning. After the master came back from his ride."

Looking pleased, Claudia nodded to the coachman. "Thank you, Johns." She glanced inquiringly at Charlie. "I believe that will be all?"

Charlie nodded. "Yes. Thank you. You've been most helpful."

"Happy to help." Johns bowed and retreated.

Once the door had closed behind the coachman, Charlie met Claudia's eyes. "Well, that was straightforward enough. So we can strike Fosdyke off our list, and that also eliminates all those who might have used him as their agent."

"Me, for instance," Claudia said.

"And your aunt and uncle, too." Charlie smiled confidently. "I doubt there's anyone else on the staff here who might have been a match for Sedbury."

"No," Claudia agreed. "Speaking more generally, not many could have bested him. He truly was a massive brute."

After a moment during which Charlie realized he'd been smiling vacuously while drinking in Claudia's more relaxed expression, he cleared his throat and asked, "So, where to next? Your brothers' lodgings?"

A faint frown puckered Claudia's brows as she considered the matter. "I was going to say yes," she eventually replied, "but it occurs to me that first, perhaps, we should return to Sedbury's rooms."

When, mildly surprised, Charlie arched his brows at her, she supplied, "Someone should question Duggan, and that might as well be us. As far as I know, no one's spoken to him or planned to do so, yet he might know or have seen or heard something pertinent."

Charlie's brows rose even higher. "That's true. Rather remiss of us all." He uncrossed his legs, rose, and offered Claudia his hand. "We should definitely catch up with Duggan."

After deciding not to avail themselves of Fosdyke's services given they were investigating, they quit the house, and Charlie hailed a hackney. On reaching Duke Street, they climbed to Sedbury's rooms and walked into the apartment.

They paused in the small front foyer, and Charlie closed the door behind them.

A man appeared in the open bedroom doorway, and from the way Claudia nodded at the fellow, Charlie assumed him to be Duggan.

"Lady Claudia." Duggan bowed, and Charlie seized the moment to take his measure.

Duggan was younger than Charlie had expected, somewhere in his late twenties. He was of average height and build, and garbed as he was in the neat and somber attire of a gentleman's gentleman, he was entirely forgettable. His face was round, his features unremarkable, and his straight dark-brown hair lay flat against his skull. He was the sort of man who would pass unnoticed on a deserted street.

Straightening, Duggan waved behind him, into the bedroom, and glancing past him, Charlie saw a half-filled portmanteau on the bed.

Duggan explained, "Lord Jonathon and Lord Bryan said they'd come around later and tell me what they want done with everything else. But they've already been through the clothes, and they said I could sell them on for whatever I can get for them."

Allowing staff to sell their employers' discarded clothes was a common practice, and Claudia nodded. "Good. However, we're here to ask what you know of Sedbury's movements over his last days." She beckoned Duggan to follow as she headed for the sofa. "Come and sit, and let's see what you can remember."

Charlie followed her to the sofa, and somewhat uncertainly, Duggan trailed behind them.

Claudia sat, and after Charlie subsided beside her, she imperiously pointed to the armchair facing them.

Duggan hesitated, then obeyed the unspoken command and moved to perch upright on the edge of the chair's seat, clasping his hands in his lap.

He was so patently uncomfortable, to put him out of his misery the sooner, Charlie said, "Let's start with the days leading to last Saturday. Did your master do anything different? Anything that seemed odd or unusual or not in the customary way of things?"

Succinctly, Claudia asked, "Did he alter his habits in any way?"

Duggan's brow furrowed as he dredged his memory.

Impatient, Claudia prompted, "Did Sedbury do anything he hadn't done before? Did he have any unexpected visitor or go out to some unanticipated meeting?"

Slowly, still frowning, Duggan shook his head. "I can't say as I remember anything unusual happening. Seemed like any other week, with him going out most evenings and getting back sometime in the wee hours." He glanced at Charlie. "He wasn't any gentle master, but he was easy enough to do for just as long as he got everything he wanted when he wanted it."

Claudia grimaced. "That sounds very like him."

"All right," Charlie said. "Now, think about Saturday. When did he rise for the day?"

"His usual time," Duggan replied, "a little before noon. He had me lay out the clothes he preferred for going around town during the day, dressed, and had his breakfast—his usual kippers, eggs, sausages, toast, and coffee—then he went out." Duggan looked from Charlie to Claudia. "Nothing different from any other day."

"So," Charlie said, drawing Duggan's gaze back to him, "when did he return?"

"Not until a bit after seven o'clock, and that was just to change for the evening. Then he went out again." Memory plainly struck, and Duggan's eyes lit. "He said he was eating at his club and then going on to some meeting."

Duggan looked pleased to have remembered that.

Claudia straightened. "He definitely mentioned going to a meeting?"

Duggan nodded.

"Was that normal—him going to a meeting after dinner?" Charlie asked.

Duggan thought, then frowned. "Now you mention it, no. Can't recall him going to any other nighttime meeting before." He paused, then clarified, "He was often out at night, but he'd never said it was to go to a meeting before."

Charlie thought to clarify, "And he took his whip with him?"

"Always did," Duggan said. "Even when he went to parties and dinners and such."

Charlie glanced at Claudia. "I'm not sure whether it was at White's that Sedbury dined, but we can check." He returned his gaze to Duggan. "After he left to go to dinner, did Sedbury return here at any time on Saturday night?"

"Or in the early hours of Sunday morning," Claudia put in. "And would you have known if he had?"

"I sleep in the nook off the kitchen," Duggan said, "and with him as a master, it paid to sleep light, so yes, I'd've heard him even if he didn't call me." He looked at Charlie. "But after he left just before eight o'clock on Saturday evening, he didn't come home again." He paused, then added, "I'd take my oath on that."

Charlie nodded in acceptance.

Claudia stated, "You didn't worry when he didn't show up the following day. When I called on Monday afternoon, you didn't seem bothered that he hadn't returned."

"Sometimes, he stayed out all night and late into the next day." Duggan grimaced. "When Monday dawned and he was still not back, I did start to wonder, but, well, he was the sort of master that raising any dust only to have him turn up wasn't worth my hide." He met Claudia's gaze levelly. "I was just his servant. He didn't tell me much about his life, just what he wanted me to know."

Charlie reflected that most gentlemen treated their gentleman's gentleman with a higher degree of trust, his relationship with Garvey being a case in point. Garvey knew a great deal more about Charlie, his hopes, fears, and dreams, than possibly anyone else alive, and that wasn't in any way unusual. However, accepting that Sedbury hadn't been the trusting sort, Charlie said, "Going back to the last time you saw him, when he left to dine at some club and then go on to some meeting, did he make any comment at all about when he expected to be back?"

"No. Not a word," Duggan replied. "But that wasn't unusual. He came and went as he pleased, of course, and just expected me to be here, to do whatever he needed at the time."

Claudia stirred. "This meeting he mentioned—did he give you any indication about where it was to be?"

"Or," Charlie put in, "when or with whom he was meeting?"

Duggan screwed up his features in thought. Plainly reliving the moment in his mind, he offered, "Not as such, but the way he said it— dinner, then a meeting—meant the meeting was after dinner, and he made it sound separate, a different event altogether. Other than that, he said nothing about where or who the meeting was with." Duggan paused, still lost in memory, then added, "But he was looking forward to it, the meeting. You could tell by the expression on his face. He was in a good mood, expectant like. He looked just like he did whenever he was going to squash someone under his heel."

Claudia winced.

Noticing it, Duggan said, "Beggin' your pardon, my lady, but he was like that. He took real pleasure in slamming people down, then grinding them down even more."

Charlie glanced at Claudia, at her pained expression, then looked at Duggan. "Thank you for speaking with us."

Duggan shrugged. "He's gone now, so there doesn't seem any reason to keep his secrets. But"—he looked at Claudia—"I'm not sure what I should do. Should I go off and look for another place?"

When Claudia looked uncertain herself, Charlie said, "I'd advise you to remain here for the time being and speak with Lord Jonathon and Lord Bryan when they return."

"Yes." Claudia regarded Duggan. "Sedbury might be dead, but you were in his employ for quite some years, and it's likely my brothers or the marquess will have some suggestion of further employment for you. At the very least, they can write you a reference."

Duggan's expression lightened, and he nodded. "I'll wait here for the nonce, then, and see what their lordships say."

Claudia rose, bringing Duggan and Charlie to their feet. "We'll be off, then. Thank you for answering our questions, Duggan."

Duggan bowed, and after bestowing a gracious nod, Claudia led the way to the door.

Charlie followed her down the stairs and out of the house.

On the pavement, he offered his arm, and she took it, then glanced at his face. "Do you think the family should let Duggan go?"

Charlie had been pondering that. "I think," he replied, "that it would be wise of your father if not your brothers to keep the man on in some capacity, at least until this business is settled." He met Claudia's eyes. "And even after that. Who knows what secrets of Sedbury's Duggan might have been privy to that he might remember later and think to put to good use?"

Her chin firming, Claudia nodded. "So it's a case of keeping a potential enemy close."

Charlie tipped his head. "For the moment, at least, but I have to say, he seemed a decent sort."

Claudia murmured, "Which was arguably more than Sedbury deserved."

They walked to where the hackney waited. Charlie opened the door, handed Claudia in, and followed.

Once they'd settled on the seat, Claudia directed the driver to take them to Bury Street, which wasn't far. As the hackney drew away from the curb, Claudia asked, "How much weight do you think we can place on Duggan's reading of Sedbury's mood?"

"Actually," Charlie replied, "I would say quite a lot. Staff like Duggan, living constantly with the one they serve in relatively close proximity, are usually very good at gauging their master's mood. And with a man like Sedbury, Duggan's health and continued employment very likely depended on his ability to accurately divine Sedbury's feelings. More, Duggan volunteered the information rather than constructed it in response to a prompt from us. It was him thinking back and remembering the moment when he last saw Sedbury that brought the point to his mind." Charlie met Claudia's eyes. "All in all, I would say Duggan's observation of Sedbury's anticipation of the meeting is very likely accurate."

Claudia faced forward. "If that's so, then we can take it as fact that Sedbury was intending to meet with someone later that night, and he was relishing the prospect of bullying and intimidating that person."

Charlie nodded. After a moment, he said, "If we put that together with Sedbury having his favorite whip with him, it might well be that he was expecting to use it."

Claudia glanced at him, but other than her lips grimly tightening, made no response.

～

As he'd arranged, Barnaby met with a large group of his lads in the churchyard of St. Paul's. It was an easy place for the lads to get to and, in this case, reasonably central to their area of operations.

He leaned against the stone wall marking the northern edge of the churchyard, and the lads who were free to attend, all aged between eight and fifteen, gathered around, perching on the stone slabs of graves or leaning against tombstones. Some were street sweepers, some stable lads, and others were errand boys. Some had graduated to being formal messengers or couriers for legal chambers or businesses in the City.

Barnaby had steadily recruited the group over the past few years, although he had only formally founded "the network," as they all called it, over the past six months. Working out the logistics and putting all the procedures in place had taken some thought and care, but now the group knew each other and could rapidly spread the word whenever he needed their talents.

The agreement was that only those lads who had the time free came to meetings, but others would be kept apprised of what was going on through a web of contacts within the group.

The lads had arrived in twos and threes, but there were no new arrivals in sight. Barnaby counted fifteen gazes fixed expectantly on him. He smiled faintly and pushed away from the wall. "Right, then. So far, we've found witnesses enough to verify Mr. Hastings's movements on Saturday night, when he left White's and returned to his house."

The boys nodded.

"That was good, solid work, and so we don't need any further information on Mr. Hastings." Barnaby had to call them off, or they would continue to keep an eye on Charlie. "Now, we need to concentrate on Viscount Sedbury. We already have sightings of him walking out of White's and down to Pall Mall, where he hailed and climbed into a hackney. That was at a little after eleven-thirty, and we know the hackney headed east."

One of the street sweepers, Tommy, raised his hand. "We—Murray, Joe, and me—think we know who the driver is. Least ways, we know what he looks like, but we haven't been able to find him again. Not yet. We'll keep looking."

"Excellent." Barnaby nodded his approval. He glanced around the group. "Let's leave you three—Tommy, Murray, and Joe—looking for the driver. Perhaps the lads who are about Trafalgar Square and the Strand could keep their eyes peeled as well."

Three other boys nodded and murmured, "We'll spread the word."

Tommy leaned forward to look at those boys. "I'll tell you what he looks like after, but his horse is a chestnut with a white blaze and a white nearside foot."

"Just so we're clear," Barnaby said, "the driver, when you find him, isn't in any kind of trouble. We only want to know where he took the viscount and what time he left him there. No need to spook the man. Just ask him to report to Inspector Stokes and his team at Scotland Yard."

The lads grinned, and Phil, one of the older lads, ventured, "Don't know as telling him that won't spook him anyways."

That brought a round of chuckles and even wider grins.

Barnaby chuckled himself, then went on, "There's also a whip we're now searching for. It's a particular type of horse whip with a short handle. As whips go, it's a special type and valuable because of that. We now believe that the viscount had it with him when he got into the hackney, and he took it with him to wherever he went. Our information is that the viscount was strangled with a whip, so we're assuming it was his whip that was used."

"Cor! So the whip's the murder weapon?" Marty, another of the older lads, exclaimed.

Barnaby looked around the circle of wide eyes. "That's what the police surgeon thinks, and no, it's not a common choice of murder weapon. But we think the viscount had his whip with him, so we think it's the one that was used to strangle him. It might have been dropped where he was killed or tossed into the river. Some of the mud larks are searching the riverbanks in case the latter is the case. However, it's equally likely the whip is still somewhere in town."

"If it's valuable, why wouldn't the killer take it and sell it?" Phil asked.

Barnaby nodded. "He might have, or he might not have realized it was valuable and simply thrown it away. Regardless, he wouldn't have kept the whip—the murder weapon—with him."

"No. 'Course not," Humphrey, another of the older brigade, said. "Someone would notice, and that would mark him as the murderer."

"Exactly." Barnaby looked around the faces. "That's why I suspect that if it's not in the river, then it'll be in a pawnshop somewhere."

"Oh, aye," Marty said, and the others all nodded sagely.

Hiding his amusement, Barnaby asked, "So, what are your thoughts on where the whip might be and how we should go about finding it?"

The discussion that ensued was lively and productive. In the end, they agreed that at least to begin with, they would canvass the pawnshops in two areas—around the docks between Limehouse Dock and the Tower and around Long Acre. As Phil, seconded by Humphrey, had pointed out, if whoever took the whip from the murder site had any brains at all, they would take it to the area in which gentlemen looked for whips, not the area where low-at-heel hackney drivers lurked.

Marty observed, "Even if the whip was sold into one of the pawnshops around the docks, likely the owner would be smart enough to sell it on to a shop in Long Acre."

Barnaby agreed. He and the lads, not counting those delegated to search for the hackney driver, worked out who would search in which area and which other lads they might call on to join each group.

With that decided, Barnaby declared the meeting concluded, and the boys dispersed, chattering happily with each other as they headed out of the churchyard.

Rather affectionately, Barnaby watched them go, then headed for the street to find a hackney to take him home. While he walked between the graves, a notion he'd been toying with resurfaced in his mind. He really should speak with Curtis, who owned and ran the Curtis Inquiry Agency, as to whether he might take on some of the older lads and train them up as inquiry agents. It would be useful to have a properly trained group on whom to call, and the boys could certainly make use of more steady employment leading to a potential career.

Barnaby made a mental note to speak with Curtis once this case was closed, then stepped out of the churchyard onto the pavement and, raising a hand, hailed a hackney.

CHAPTER 7

*C*laudia sat beside Charlie in the hackney, which was drawn in to the curb along Bury Street, opposite and two houses down from Bryan's lodgings.

She glanced at Charlie. "I'm sorry it's taking this long. I thought they would all have left by now."

Her brother shared a house with three other young gentlemen, all sons of the nobility.

Charlie smiled complacently. "Young gentlemen of their age frequently lie abed until noon. Understandable given they often don't hit the sheets until the small hours."

Claudia huffed. "Yes, well, they could be more accommodating."

Charlie chuckled, then, in an obvious effort to distract her, asked where she'd grown up, and she responded by telling him of the Rattenby estate. It passed the time, and he seemed to be genuinely interested in her answer.

Seizing the chance to satisfy her own curiosity, she asked about his childhood and learned that his family hailed from Surrey, and although he didn't precisely say so, she got the impression that the family line and principal estate were ancient.

"However, we were never ennobled." He didn't seem at all put out by that. "We Hastings have always opted for a quiet life."

Considering him, she found no difficulty believing that. The realization brought a smile to her lips. There was something intrinsically comforting about being with someone who preferred calm and peace to the hectic round that was the normal state of life in the ton.

Glancing at the buildings, she saw two well-dressed young gentlemen come out of the front door of Bryan's lodgings. She sat up straighter. "At last!"

The pair conferred, then set their hats on their heads, descended to the pavement, and set off with insouciant strides, heading south on the opposite side of the street. Claudia watched them walk away, then turned to Charlie. "Let's go."

Obligingly, he opened the carriage door, stepped down to the pavement, paused to confirm the pair hadn't turned back, then helped her down.

Without waiting for him to offer his arm, she looped her arm in his, and they crossed the street and went up the steps. Charlie plied the brass knocker on the front door.

The door was opened by a neatly attired man of average height and build, with wiry brown hair lightly touched with gray. The man looked at Charlie questioningly, but then recognized Claudia and bowed. "Lady Claudia."

"Good morning, Hughes." Claudia was relieved to be recognized; she and her mother had only visited once before. She waved at Charlie. "This is Mr. Hastings, a friend of the family. If we might have a word?"

"Yes, of course." Hughes pulled the door wider and bowed them in. He shut the door, then looked a trifle uncertain. "Ah...the drawing room?"

"Yes." Claudia turned to the left. "It's this room, isn't it?"

Hughes murmured an assent and quickly moved to open the door.

Claudia noticed that he peered around the door and swiftly scanned the room before standing back and waving her and Charlie inside.

On crossing the threshold, she understood Hughes's hesitation. The cushions were rumpled, and there were sporting magazines scattered over every surface. Ignoring all, she drew in her skirts and sat on the sofa. As Charlie came to sit beside her, she looked at Hughes. "Is Mrs. Hughes available? If we could speak with both of you at once, it will save time."

"Of course." Hughes bowed. "I'll fetch her."

He departed, leaving the door slightly ajar.

Claudia leaned closer to Charlie and whispered, "Mr. and Mrs. Hughes act as staff for all four lodgers. I believe there are no other staff here."

"That's probably wise," Charlie murmured. "Young men, wild oats, and all that."

Claudia hadn't previously thought of that, but it made sound sense.

Mr. Hughes returned, ushering in his wife, who was shorter than he but at least twice as wide.

Mrs. Hughes's soft features were worn and rather faded, with lines that declared her a kindly soul, yet her brown gaze was shrewd. She curtsied to Claudia and Charlie, then clasped her hands before her. "How can we help you, my lady?"

Rather than refer to a murder, of a family member no less, Claudia serenely stated, "My parents will soon be visiting town, and they've asked me to learn what I can about how Bryan is faring." She smiled with just a touch of fond exasperation. "Living in the country as they do, they are prone to worry. Not over anything specific—more in general, if you take my meaning."

Mrs. Hughes nodded readily. "The parents of our other lads have occasionally inquired as well. Parents do fret sometimes."

Straightening, Hughes stated, "In the case of the four we have here now, all such concerns have proved unfounded, I'm pleased to say."

Relieved, too, Claudia thought, but she nodded encouragingly. "Just so. From that, I take it that you know of no problems—quarrels, arguments, anything like that—involving Bryan?"

Mrs. Hughes shook her head, and Hughes replied, "Nothing of any significance. Indeed, the four here get along very well. Lord Bryan has been no trouble at all. Well," he amended, "no more trouble than other lads of similar age and station."

Claudia stared back, momentarily flummoxed as to how to progress to the question she needed answered.

Beside her, Charlie stirred, and when she glanced his way, he suggested, "In order to allay your parents' concerns, why not simply ask about Bryan's doings on a particular evening? Say last Saturday evening. You can then relay that to your parents as evidence there's no reason for them to worry."

"An excellent idea!" Claudia turned to the Hugheses and smiled. "So, what were Bryan's movements last Saturday?"

The Hugheses exchanged a meaningful look, but what meaning the look carried, Claudia couldn't tell. Then Hughes cleared his throat and returned his attention to Claudia and Charlie. "As is often the case, all four went out at about eight o'clock on Saturday night."

Mrs. Hughes nodded. "Together, the four of them."

"They tend to stick together," Hughes put in, "which, to my way of thinking, is reassuring."

Claudia nodded, and Mrs. Hughes went on, "They mentioned they were going to some ball in Mount Street, and after that, they planned to go on to some other entertainment, but they didn't say what that was."

"No, they didn't," Hughes corroborated, "but they came home together at around three in the morning."

Mrs. Hughes huffed fondly. "Heard them come staggering up the stairs just after three o'clock."

"All four?" Charlie asked.

Hughes nodded. "Aye. We can hear them each go into their rooms, and I take special note, as once they're all in, I go down and lock the front door, which I did."

"So," Claudia summarized, "the four spent their evening together, and they were here, in their beds, from three o'clock onward."

Charlie caught Claudia's gaze. "If your parents want to know more, we can always ask the other three if they were with Bryan the entire night." He smiled at the Hugheses. "It sounds as if the four look out for one another."

Hughes was starting to eye them with suspicion, but he nodded. "Aye, they do that, the four of them." He looked at Claudia. "However, if you're wanting to know definitely where any one of the four was between whenever they left the ball and three last Sunday morning, I don't think asking them will help."

Frowning in puzzlement, Claudia asked, "Why? If they were all together...?"

Mrs. Hughes sighed. "Drunk as only lords can be, they were. You should've heard them stumbling around getting up the stairs. Legless, they were. So no matter what they say happened or didn't happen, you wouldn't want to be putting any faith in anything any of them say."

Claudia's expression blanked. "Ah. I see."

Charlie rose and thanked the Hugheses for their time and their help, then grasped her hand and drew her to her feet. She was still digesting what they'd learned—and what they hadn't—when they reached the pavement.

She heard the door close behind them and, still frowning, halted. "That's really not all that helpful."

"Sadly," Charlie said, "I have to agree." He studied her face. "We'll just have to hope that, inebriated or not, Bryan can remember where he went and that it's the sort of place we can prove he was at."

Claudia sighed and started for the hackney. "Hopefully, we'll get more useful information from Jonathon's man. Jonathon's rooms are in Jermyn Street."

Jermyn Street was just half a block away, but the time was now long past noon, and when Charlie inquired, she admitted that she was, indeed, famished.

At her suggestion, Charlie paid off the jarvey and, arm in arm, she and Charlie strolled the short distance to Piccadilly and a nice little eatery she knew of there.

By mutual if unvoiced agreement, while they enjoyed a light luncheon, they once again spoke of other things.

To Claudia, more interesting things—certainly much less worrying things.

But soon enough, they were back on the street, and with somewhat renewed and refreshed determination, they made for Jonathon's door.

As they walked along Jermyn Street, Charlie glanced at her, then nodded to a door opposite. "I live there—number twelve—if you ever need to send for me."

Immensely curious, she studied the building. It was of similar vintage to others in the street, neat and well-kept with a bow window on the first floor. "You lodge there." It wasn't a question, more her fixing the building in her mind.

"No," Charlie said, surprising her. When she glanced his way, he explained, "Well, I did lodge there at first, but a few years back, I bought the whole house, and the couple who had owned it stayed on to do for me. I have the first-floor apartment and rent to two other gentlemen, who have the ground- and second-floor rooms."

Claudia could only approve and had to own to being rather impressed. Not all gentlemen were so forward thinking as to seize opportunity when it beckoned.

They reached Jonathon's lodgings, which were farther down the street. Charlie knocked, and when the door was opened by Jonathon's man, Hobbs, Claudia smiled and asked, "Is my brother in, Hobbs?"

"No, my lady." Hobbs looked rather surprised she'd asked. "Not at this hour." A fact of which he knew she was well aware; gentlemen of Jonathon's age did not languish through the afternoon in their rooms.

Claudia's smile deepened. "In that case, Hobbs, do let us in."

Knowing her quite well, Hobbs stood back and held the door wide.

As she breezed past, Claudia informed him, "This is Mr. Hastings. He's assisting the family with this bother over Sedbury's death."

"Yes, my lady." Hobbs ushered them into the drawing room, which, contrary to their earlier experience at Bryan's lodgings, was reasonably neat.

Claudia sat, and Charlie claimed the armchair beside hers. She fixed Hobbs with a direct gaze. "Now, Hobbs, we are endeavoring to simplify matters for the police by learning of and verifying my brothers' movements on the night Sedbury was killed." She saw no sense in beating about the bush with Hobbs; he'd been with the family for decades.

Hobbs straightened to attention. "Yes, my lady."

"So," she inquired, "do you have any information as to where Jonathon went on Saturday, from evening to night to the time he returned here?"

"Also," Charlie put in, "who he was with during those hours."

Hobbs frowned slightly. "Well, Lord Jonathon was out the whole evening. As I understood it, he had a dinner with one group of friends, and after that, he was intending to attend some gathering, also with friends, although I can't say if the dinner friends were also at the later event."

Claudia wasn't actually expecting an answer when she asked, "Do you have any idea who hosted either event?" but Hobbs surprised her.

"Actually, my lady, I suspect I can tell you that. If you and Mr. Hastings will wait a moment, I'll retrieve the invitations. I cleared both from Lord Jonathon's pocket, but I haven't thrown them away as yet."

Claudia beamed. "Bless you, Hobbs. Of course we'll wait."

Hobbs vanished, and they could hear him rustling around in the rear of the apartment, then he returned holding two ivory invitation cards. "These are the two events he attended on Saturday." Hobbs handed Claudia the cards.

She took them, and Charlie leaned across to read over her shoulder. Claudia stated, "The dinner host was Peregrine Fitzwilliam, and the party later was thrown by Lord Satchwell."

Charlie sat back. "I'm acquainted with both sufficiently well to ask what they recall of Jonathon that night. If they or others at the event can swear he was present and sufficiently in sight throughout the night, that will alibi him completely." He glanced at the mantelpiece. The clock there showed it was just after three. "If we leave now"—he pushed to his feet—"with any luck, I should be able to catch both Fitzwilliam and Satchwell at Boodle's."

Claudia eagerly gave him her hand and allowed him to help her up. "Thank you. That will be such a relief." She smiled at Hobbs and started for the door. "And thank you, too, Hobbs. Your help with the invitations will likely see your master cleared of all suspicion over Sedbury's death."

"Indeed, my lady. I'll be most happy if that's so." Hobbs followed Claudia and Charlie from the room, then stepped ahead to open the front door for them.

Claudia swept out, and Charlie was about to follow when he paused, then turned to Hobbs and asked, "Hobbs, when was it that you noticed the scrape on Lord Jonathon's face?"

Hobbs blinked in surprise, but answered readily. "Lord Jonathon often goes riding of a Sunday morning—he says it's quiet then, with few others about. He enjoys a good gallop. Last Sunday morning, he came back with that wound. He said he'd run into a branch. Truth be told, I wasn't all that surprised. He'd got to his bed only a few hours before and was barely compos mentis."

"You're sure he didn't have the wound before he went riding?"

"Quite sure, sir. I would have noticed it while I was helping him dress."

Charlie smiled in satisfaction and, with a nod to Hobbs, joined Claudia on the pavement. He met her relieved gaze. "So we have confirmation of Jonathon's story of how he got that scrape, which is another point in his favor."

"Excellent." She took his arm. "Thank you for remembering to ask."

"Not at all. Now"—Charlie met her gaze—"as you won't be able to accompany me into Boodle's, I think we'd better hail another hackney so you can wait inside it while I go into the club and see what I can learn from Fitzwilliam and Satchwell."

Claudia would much rather have gone with him and listened to the interrogation, but... She nodded. "Very well. I'll wait outside with what patience I can muster."

∾

One glance at Claudia's face had been enough to warn Charlie that she wouldn't consent to return home and wait for him to see Fitzwilliam and Satchwell and then report. The concern in her eyes was evident. She was so determined to clear at least one of her brothers that he was grateful she'd consented to wait in the hackney.

Picking his battles was a knack he'd learned long ago.

The hackney rattled onto St. James Street and drew up outside Boodle's. Having recollected that eyebrows would be raised at the sight of a lady on that street, even one waiting inside a hackney, Charlie climbed down and directed the jarvey to turn down nearby Ryder Street. To Claudia, Charlie said, "Better you wait there."

Although her lips tightened, to his relief, she merely nodded. He shut the door, and the carriage rumbled on and turned left at the next corner.

Charlie didn't want to think of what her brothers—let alone her father—might say if any gossip touched Claudia's name over something she did while with him. In his care, so to speak. Deeming himself to have dodged a bullet, he climbed the single step to Boodle's door, and the doorman, recognizing him, bowed him in.

Luck was with him, and he found Fitzwilliam in one of the front rooms, chatting with a group of friends. Fitzwilliam was a few years younger than Charlie, but was friends with two of the Cavanaughs, and he and Charlie had met at several of that family's events. Consequently, it wasn't difficult for Charlie to hail Fitzwilliam and, while exchanging the usual trivialities, mention hearing of the dinner Fitzwilliam had hosted the previous Saturday.

Nothing more was needed to induce Fitzwilliam, who was a naturally garrulous sort, to launch into a happy recollection of the event—who had attended, the venue, the menu, and the good time had by all. Without specifically asking, Charlie confirmed that Jonathon Hale had been one of Fitzwilliam's guests and that the gathering had dispersed just before midnight, with everyone going their separate ways.

Accepting, therefore, that Fitzwilliam's event would not furnish Jonathon with an alibi for a murder that was committed sometime after midnight, Charlie congratulated Fitzwilliam on his acumen in organizing such a successful dinner and asked after the venue as if that had been the aim of his inquiry. After appearing to take due note of the place—a room above one of Fleet Street's public houses—Charlie parted from Fitzwilliam and his cronies and went in search of Satchwell.

He found that gentleman—also a few years Charlie's junior—in the smoking room, reading a news sheet. Charlie knew Satchwell as a decent sort, and as Satchwell's family estate was also in Surrey, not far from the

Hastingses' property, despite the disparity in age, he and Satchwell had been acquainted for years.

Satchwell hadn't yet married, and although Charlie knew Satchwell had a shrewd brain, he also had a penchant for hosting parties for his bachelor friends that might best be described as quietly wild.

Even elegantly wild.

Charlie claimed the armchair to Satchwell's right and waited until the other man—well aware of his approach—lowered the news sheet.

Satchwell fixed him with a faintly curious eye and nodded. "Hastings."

Charlie nodded back. "Satchwell."

"To what do I owe this pleasure?"

"I understand you held a card party last Saturday night—or more correctly, through the early hours of Sunday morning."

Almost warily, Satchwell nodded.

Charlie went on, "I need you to tell me who was there, where it was, and when it broke up."

Satchwell regarded Charlie for several silent seconds, then said, "If I ask the obvious question—why—you're not going to tell me, are you?"

Charlie smiled. "No. It's not my place to divulge the reason. Suffice it to say that I'm asking on behalf of others who have an interest in your answers."

Satchwell knew enough of Charlie's association with Barnaby and Penelope and, through them, Stokes to interpret that reply as meaning that the police might well have questions about his event. The calculation that Satchwell would prefer to speak to Charlie rather than to some policeman wasn't a difficult one, and Satchwell reached the expected conclusion in a blink.

"Oh, that makes it so much better!" Satchwell shook his head resignedly and folded the news sheet. "I don't know why I should humor you, but as we've nothing to hide, the party was held in a room above the Racy Lady in Haymarket."

The Racy Lady was one of the premier brothels in London. "I see," Charlie said.

Satchwell nodded. "I'm sure you do. A part of the arrangement was that guests could—at their own expense—avail themselves of the offerings provided below and, of course, many did."

Charlie frowned. "How many guests were there?"

"Somewhere north of fifty. At least, that was the number of invitations I sent out, and everyone accepted, but many brought friends as well." Satchwell arched his brows at Charlie. "It was a very convivial night."

Charlie could imagine the scene all too well. He sighed and said, "This stays between you and me, but the person whose whereabouts we're trying to confirm is Jonathon Hale. Do you recall seeing him at the party?"

Satchwell clearly thought back, then nodded decisively. "Yes. He came up to me and congratulated me on the event."

"Any idea when that was?"

Satchwell frowned. "Later. I know that much. We kicked off at midnight, so it must have been about two-thirty or three?" He grimaced. "Some time about then."

Charlie thought, then asked, "What would be my chances of finding any of your guests who might remember seeing Hale during the party?"

Satchwell gave a choked laugh. "I'd be truly surprised if anyone could say where anyone else was at any given time. The brandy was flowing freely, and the room was so crowded that people were constantly going in and out, not just to enjoy the delights downstairs but into the corridors so they could chat without shouting." Satchwell met Charlie's eyes. "You know how such events go. Everyone was free to come and go and return as they pleased."

Charlie sighed, but nodded. "Thank you. At least I know what the situation was with your party."

He rose, and Satchwell caught his eye. "I assume this is something to do with that devil, Sedbury, turning up dead. If you want my opinion, if Jonathon or any of the Hales had wanted to bump the man off, they would have done so years ago. He's been a bane on their existence for the last decade at least."

Soberly, Charlie replied, "I agree, but sadly, the law wants facts."

"Well, good luck with finding them." Satchwell sat back and shook out the news sheet. "Jonathon's all right. It won't be him."

Charlie inclined his head and, wrestling with a fresh problem— namely how to break this latest set of facts, such as they were, to Claudia —made his way out of the club.

He emerged from Boodle's and walked along St. James Street, then turned onto Ryder Street. The hackney was waiting by the curb, with Claudia even more impatient for news. Charlie instructed the jarvey to wait and climbed into the carriage.

Claudia all but pounced on him. "What did you learn?"

Stifling a sigh, Charlie duly reported that Fitzwilliam's dinner had ended before midnight, and all had gone their separate ways. "So there's no one there who can say where Jonathon went next. And the party he attended later started at midnight, but the rooms were so crowded, with people constantly going in and out, that it's difficult to see how anyone could give Jonathon any meaningful alibi."

Claudia's expression had grown increasingly grim. "So," she concluded, "as matters stand, neither Bryan nor Jonathon have alibis for the period during which Sedbury was killed."

Charlie met her eyes. "To be perfectly frank, given their activities on that night, I can't see how we could secure alibis strong enough to convince the police, let alone solid enough to stand up in court."

Claudia's expressive lips turned down, and the light in her eyes dimmed.

Charlie shifted on the seat and faced forward. "At least we've crossed Fosdyke and all associated with him off the suspects list."

Frowning, she said, "This investigating business is more difficult than I'd thought."

Glancing at her face, Charlie said, "We should head back to Albemarle Street and report our findings. Perhaps the others have had better luck."

After two seconds of glumness, Claudia raised her head and nodded. "Yes. Let's go and see."

Charlie pushed up the hatch and directed the jarvey to take them to the Adairs'.

CHAPTER 8

$\mathcal{C}$harlie ushered Claudia into the drawing room in Albemarle
Street and was surprised and not a little dismayed to find Penelope seated on the sofa with a dejected expression on her face.

She rose and greeted them with "I hope you've had some luck."

Her delivery implied that she hadn't.

"We made some progress," Charlie informed her.

"But not," Claudia added, "as much as we would have liked."

Penelope sighed. "The others should be here shortly." She waved
them to armchairs, and they'd just taken their seats when they heard the
front door open, and the next instant, Barnaby and Stokes walked in.

Both men looked at them in hopeful inquiry, but were met with no
encouraging sign.

After exchanging greetings, Stokes claimed the armchair farthest from
the hearth, and Barnaby elegantly subsided onto the sofa next to
Penelope.

"Right," Stokes said. "To business." He looked at Claudia and Charlie. "What did you two manage to learn?"

"First," Charlie said, "I believe we can retire Fosdyke as a suspect,
along with anyone who might have used him as an agent. He was with at
least two others from Saturday evening to at least one o'clock on Sunday
morning, and he shares quarters above the stable with Selborough's
coachman and groom."

"That gash on his forehead?" Penelope asked.

"Fosdyke got that on Sunday midmorning from the hoof of my uncle's horse." Claudia looked at the others. "I don't think Fosdyke could have left Farm Street before two o'clock in the morning. He would have had to wait until the others fell deeply asleep to sneak out undetected, and he would have had to have returned, also undetected, before first light."

"By five-thirty, when the coachman and groom awoke for the day." Charlie looked at Barnaby and Penelope. "I really can't see how Fosdyke could have got to the docks, met with Sedbury and strangled the man, then got back to his bed. The timing would have been excruciatingly tight."

"And that's assuming he didn't wake either of the other two while sneaking in and out," Claudia said.

Stokes had been taking notes. He looked at Claudia. "At present, all we know is that Sedbury was killed sometime between midnight and three o'clock on Sunday morning. Until we get a better idea of when, exactly, he was killed and even more importantly where, Fosdyke remains an outside chance." Stokes faintly grimaced. "That said, it sounds as if we'll have many more likely suspects."

Claudia grimaced as well.

Charlie cleared his throat and, when the others looked his way, went on, "We also spoke with Duggan, Sedbury's man. We realized none of us had spoken with him, so as we were in the area, we dropped by Sedbury's rooms. Duggan was quite forthcoming, and what he had to say was rather illuminating."

"Apparently," Claudia took up the tale, "Sedbury mentioned that after having dinner at his club—"

"Not sure if he dined at White's or somewhere else," Charlie put in.

Claudia dipped her head his way. "According to Duggan, Sedbury said he was going to some meeting later, after dinner, and Duggan says that wasn't something he normally did."

"Or had ever done before," Charlie said, "at least to Duggan's knowledge."

"A meeting?" Penelope, along with Barnaby and Stokes, had come alert. "Did Sedbury say with whom?"

Charlie shook his head. "He didn't mention where, either. However, Duggan got the distinct impression that Sedbury was looking forward to the meeting, meaning that he was anticipating bullying and intimidating whoever he was meeting with."

"What Duggan actually said," Claudia clarified, "was that in mentioning the meeting, Sedbury looked 'just like he did whenever he was going to squash someone under his heel.'"

They all sat back and digested that. "So," Stokes concluded, "Sedbury knowingly, willingly, and with intent went to a meeting with someone he expected to—indeed, anticipated—cowing."

After a moment, Stokes huffed and said, "Let's put that to one side for the moment." He refocused on Claudia. "Did you manage to catalogue your brothers' movements over the relevant hours?"

Claudia sighed feelingly. "We know where they were for some of the time, but..."

Charlie filled in, "There seems little chance of finding witnesses able to alibi either of them." Briefly, he outlined Bryan's outing with his three co-lodgers, then described the events that Jonathon had attended. "Satchwell is a sensible sort, and he made it clear that he seriously doubted any of his guests—or any group of his guests—could vouch for Jonathon's whereabouts during the hours from midnight to three or so in the morning."

Stokes grimaced. "Regardless, I'll need to interview both Hales. Who knows? They might recall something of their evening that opens the way to establishing alibis of sorts."

"Speaking of alibis of sorts," Penelope said, "I regret to report that each and every one of the fifteen potential suspects on my list—including Napier—was either at home or known to be at some major ton event in the company of many others throughout the hours of midnight to three o'clock on Sunday morning. In this season, most were at home, with that attested to by at least two staff members. More, as far as their staff are aware, over the past weeks, not one has been involved in any unexpected or mysterious meeting with anyone at all, much less the sort of person who might be a killer for hire."

Rather glumly, she looked at Stokes, then glanced at the others. "It's still possible that one of the fifteen had some long-standing agreement with a hired killer to murder Sedbury, but in light of what we now know, were that so, I simply can't see why Sedbury would have so readily gone to meet with said hired killer."

Frowning slightly, Stokes slowly nodded. "Given what Charlie and Claudia learned from Duggan, assuming that what he said about Sedbury going to a meeting and Sedbury's attitude toward that meeting is accurate, and I can't see why Duggan would lie on such points, then the problem with our killer being Fosdyke or any other person who inhabits Mayfair or even a killer such a person had hired is that—assuming Sedbury was killed by the river or nearby—I have difficulty believing that Sedbury would have agreed to meet in such a location." Stokes looked at Barnaby. "Yet we know that at about midnight, Sedbury climbed into a hackney in Pall Mall and directed the driver eastward. Toward the docks."

Penelope turned to Barnaby. "We need to learn where that jarvey took Sedbury. Was it to the docks or somewhere closer?"

Barnaby nodded. "The lads believe they know who the jarvey is and are currently tracking him down."

Stokes sat up and slid his notebook into his coat pocket. "On the Yard's part, we're pushing ahead with the search along the riverbank. By its very nature, such a comprehensive canvassing is necessarily slow. Exceedingly slow. That said, I feel confident we haven't overlooked the spot in which Sedbury was put into the river. In that area, even dead, his body wouldn't have passed unnoticed. We just have to find the people who saw him—dead or alive—and learn what they can tell us."

Barnaby grimaced. "Sadly, until you find evidence to say yea or nay, we have to allow for Sedbury being killed elsewhere and his body carted to the river. Because of that, I've directed my lads to search for the whip over a wide area. As well as the pawnshops around the docks, they're looking at those closer to Mayfair, for instance, the shops along Long Acre."

"A good thought, that," Charlie said. "If anyone recognizes the quality of that whip, they'll likely think to pawn it around there."

Penelope pulled a face. "Unless it's in the river."

"As to that," Stokes said, "I've asked the mud larks along that stretch to keep their eyes peeled for it. I only spoke to five of them, but they'll pass the word up and down the river and among the rivermen as well." He smiled faintly. "Useful beggars, they are, over anything to do with the river."

Barnaby nodded. "If the whip was tossed into the river when Sedbury's body was dumped in, there's a decent chance it'll wash ashore somewhere."

The doorbell pealed, and the sounds of male voices and boots in the front hall had everyone looking toward the door. Seconds later, it opened, and Mostyn walked in and announced, "Lord Jonathon Hale and Lord Bryan Hale."

Claudia's brothers. Penelope rose and went forward to greet the two very large gentlemen who followed Mostyn into the room. A quick glance at the window told her it was already dark outside. She smiled and held out her hand. "Good evening, gentlemen. I'm Penelope Adair."

They duly mumbled greetings and bowed over her hand. "And this gentleman"—she gestured to Barnaby, who had risen and come to stand at her shoulder—"is my husband, Barnaby." As soon as the three men had shaken hands, Penelope waved at Claudia. "Your sister, of course, and I believe you're already acquainted with Mr. Hastings."

Jonathon and Bryan exchanged nods with Charlie; it was plain to all that they were bottling up a degree of irritation, but were forced by Penelope's actions to behave with decorum.

"And this," she concluded, smiling at Stokes, who had risen and turned to face the pair, "is Inspector Stokes of Scotland Yard, who is leading the investigation into Sedbury's murder."

The brothers were taken aback at finding Stokes there, and they were not adept at hiding their sudden surprise or the wariness that followed.

Penelope urged the pair to armchairs. "Please, do sit down."

The pair shuffled, yet had no option other than to follow her direction.

But the restraint that had held them back didn't last long. Once they sat and everyone else had returned to their places, the brothers fixed quite ferocious scowls on their sister.

Jonathon opened fire with "You've been questioning our staff about where we were on Saturday evening."

If she was in any way intimidated by those scowls, Claudia gave no sign of it. "Of course I have." She spread her hands. "We need to establish alibis for both of you. You must see that."

"You can't possibly believe we killed the blighter," Jonathon retorted.

"It's not what I believe, but what can be proved," Claudia countered.

Bryan eyed his elders, then grouched, "You could have just asked."

Stokes drew out his notebook. "We're asking now. Officially." He fixed his gaze on Jonathon. "Where were you, Lord Jonathon, and who can confirm that?"

A full minute of silence ensued as Jonathon debated his wisest move, but after slanting glances at Barnaby, Penelope, Claudia, and even Charlie, patently hoping for some intervention, he cleared his throat and reluctantly replied, "I attended a dinner." As Stokes led him to relate his subsequent movements, even Jonathon realized how difficult it would be to prove that he hadn't slipped away and met and murdered his half brother. By the time his recitation ended, he was looking decidedly uneasy and shooting imploring glances at Claudia, as if hoping she would suggest something that would help him.

But Claudia simply looked glum, and Stokes turned to Bryan. Again, as the younger Hale described his activities on Saturday night, it became increasingly clear that there simply was no hope of reliable witnesses to attest to his whereabouts during the crucial hours.

After jotting down the brothers' replies, Stokes arched a questioning brow at Barnaby and Penelope.

Barnaby grimaced. Addressing the Hales, he summarized, "The hours the pair of you were with others can—in theory—be verified, but in Jonathon's case, it seems likely there will be periods during which you could have left the house, met with Sedbury, and murdered him, then returned, and securing viable testimony that you didn't will be difficult." He transferred his gaze to Bryan. "And as we already have testimony that you and your three friends were all three sheets to the wind, their word as to your presence with them will not hold up in court."

He studied the two downcast faces and felt moved to observe, "Sadly, proving you didn't do something is often more difficult than proving you did."

Frowning, Jonathon darted a glance at his brother. "So you're saying that we—Bryan and I—are in a sort of suspended state of possibly being suspects in Sedbury's murder."

Penelope inclined her head his way. "That's a reasonably accurate assessment."

Jonathon and Bryan looked around the circle, and when no one disagreed, their faces fell even further.

Reality, Barnaby thought, had finally bitten.

The doorbell pealed, not once, but twice, the sound somehow conveying impatience.

They all heard Mostyn cross the front hall, then a gruff voice, speaking in a rather demanding tone, reached them.

Instantly, all three Hales stiffened. They were already starting to rise from their seats when Mostyn opened the drawing-room door.

"I believe," Barnaby uncrossed his legs and murmured to Stokes, "that the marquess has arrived."

Barnaby rose with Penelope as Mostyn halted and announced, "The Marquess of Rattenby."

The marquess was as tall as his sons, but although still physically imposing with a rigidly upright posture, he no longer carried the heft and muscle they possessed. He was older than might be supposed, well into his sixties, and expensively if conservatively dressed with neatly coiffed steel-gray hair. While his features carried the same handsome stamp as his younger sons' did, his expression was all ageing aristocrat accustomed to wealth and privilege and to getting his own way.

Smoothly, with her most graciously confident smile in place, Penelope moved past Barnaby to welcome the senior Hale. "My lord, do come in and join us. Despite the circumstances, it's a pleasure to welcome you to our home."

The marquess clearly hadn't thought of what he would encounter at their house. His suddenly blank expression suggested that, certainly, he hadn't expected to be taken in hand by a socially adept hostess, and for a moment, he was knocked a trifle off-kilter. As Penelope rolled on, following the established social script for receiving a senior noble and ensuring he was properly introduced to those of the company he did not know—namely, Barnaby, Charlie, and Stokes—the marquess had no real alternative but to fall in with her direction.

The marquess duly shook hands with Barnaby and Charlie, but when it came to Stokes, Rattenby fixed a glowering look on Scotland Yard's finest.

But before Rattenby could challenge Stokes in any way, Penelope took his arm and solicitously guided him to the armchair by the fireplace. As that was a prime spot from which to observe everyone else, Rattenby gruffly thanked her and sat.

Everyone else resumed their seats, allowing the marquess to catch his breath. He fixed his steely gray gaze on Stokes and stated, "Inspector. Mr. and Mrs. Adair. I'm told the three of you work together on such cases as this, those that involve members of the haut ton." Penelope and Barnaby inclined their heads in acknowledgment, and Rattenby rolled on, "I'm keen to learn what you've discovered in the matter of Sedbury's death."

Death, Barnaby noted, not murder. He also noticed that Rattenby hadn't labeled Sedbury his son. Or even his heir.

Stoically, Stokes listed the facts they'd already ascertained and, without missing a beat, moved on to describing their current avenues of investigation. "Through her sources, Mrs. Adair identified fourteen members of the ton presently in London who might have had reason to wish Sedbury dead. Via diligent investigating, she's established that none of those fourteen or Lord Napier, who more recently had an encounter with the viscount, were directly involved in his murder."

Barnaby noted that Stokes did not address the issue of any of the fifteen having hired a killer to do the deed. Instead, Stokes continued, "My sergeant is currently overseeing a squad of constables who are searching the north bank of the Thames and questioning all those who live and work in the area in a push to locate the spot where the body went into the river. If the viscount was murdered in the vicinity, it's possible we'll also identify the site of the murder."

Rattenby was frowning with the air of a man trying to imagine a scenario that, to him, was entirely foreign.

"In addition," Stokes went on, "we're endeavoring to locate Sedbury's whip, which, as I mentioned, we believe to be the murder weapon. Accepting that, if discarded by the murderer, such an item is unlikely to still be where he left it, Mr. Adair has agents scouring the pawnshops of London, and I've alerted those who make their living trawling through the debris washed up on the riverbank to our interest in that item. Unless it's been destroyed, which is possible but overall unlikely, we stand a reasonable chance of finding it, and where it was initially discovered will likely give us some clue as to where the viscount was murdered." Stokes added, "The site of the murder will help define who might be the murderer. And further to that, Mr. Adair's agents are also seeking the jarvey who ferried Sedbury east from Pall Mall on the night in question. Learning where he let the viscount off will significantly advance the investigation."

Amused to hear his lads referred to as "agents," Barnaby made a mental note to share that fact with the lads themselves when next he saw them.

Meanwhile, Stokes had paused, and Barnaby sensed he was weighing his next words very carefully. Then, tucking his notebook away, Stokes said, "We're also working to, if at all possible, establish sound alibis for Lord Jonathon and Lord Bryan, both of whom have arguably the most powerful motives for doing away with Sedbury."

Rattenby's reaction was reminiscent of a rigidly contained explosion. Instantly, he rapped out, "Jonathon and Bryan had absolutely nothing to do with Sedbury's death."

Stokes inclined his head and said nothing more.

Rattenby glowered, first at Stokes, then at Barnaby. "I expect," he barked, "that the culprit will be identified in short order, the required evidence assembled forthwith, and the matter dealt with expeditiously."

Returning his glower to Stokes, his tone forceful, he went on, "I do not wish to hear any suggestion that any of my surviving children were in any way involved." Belligerently, he stated, "They weren't, and that's all there is to it."

Barnaby was starting to see from where Sedbury had inherited his arrogance. Mildly, Barnaby stated, "That Sedbury's body was put into the river along a stretch of embankment in a decidedly rough and seedy area rather than being left in some alley in Mayfair suggests his murderer had some reason for choosing such a site."

Rattenby huffed, and the heightened color in his lined cheeks receded somewhat. "Just so. There's no reason to suppose the murderer is anyone in the ton."

That wasn't what Barnaby had meant, but he was glad to have calmed the marquess.

Rattenby looked from Barnaby to Stokes and back again, plainly calculating, then he fixed Stokes with a level gaze and stated, "I'm happy to answer any questions you have regarding Sedbury, although I freely admit that since he came into his majority, I have seen little of him and am not well informed as to his habits."

Barnaby seized the offer. "Do you have any idea why Sedbury might have ventured along the riverbank between the Duke Stairs and the Tower? Do you know of any association that might have taken him to that area?"

Rattenby shook his head. "I'm not aware of any interest he had that might account for him going there. Certainly, the family has no business or holdings in the vicinity."

Barnaby saw Stokes glance his way and minutely shook his head. While he could think of countless questions about Sedbury they would be glad to have answered, he judged that despite Rattenby's declaration, there was little chance the marquess would make any useful revelations.

Stokes shifted and, from his pocket, drew out Sedbury's unfinished letter. "Perhaps, my lord, you or Lord Jonathon might know something about this." He passed the letter to Jonathon, who was closer. "We found it on Sedbury's desk the day after he was murdered. It appears he broke off writing it and left it as if he intended to return later to complete it."

Barnaby watched Jonathon scan the single sheet. A frown formed on Jonathon's face and progressively deepened. When Jonathon reached the end of the piece, Barnaby asked, "Do you know to whom Sedbury was referring?"

Jonathon's expression matched his reply. "I have no idea." He glanced at the ladies, then at Barnaby and Stokes, and colored. "I mean..." He swallowed and went on, "It could refer to any number of ladies. Women. Girls." Helplessly, he looked at the letter. "Without more to go on, I really can't say." He shook his head. "I couldn't even begin to guess."

Given Jonathon was twenty-six years old and decidedly handsome, Barnaby could understand that.

Stokes tipped his head toward Rattenby, who was barely restraining himself from grabbing the sheet. "Perhaps your father might have some insight."

Jonathon drew his gaze from Sedbury's writing, rose, and carried the letter to his father.

Rattenby seized the sheet and studied the brief message. His features hardened, and he continued to stare at the written words.

After a moment, Stokes inquired, "My lord, do you have any idea to whom Sedbury was referring?"

"No." There was enough puzzlement in Rattenby's tone to suggest that was the truth. "I've not the faintest notion." As if speaking to himself, he went on, "It could be someone in town or in the country. In fact, whoever he means could be anywhere at all." Rattenby frowned at the letter, hesitated, then said, "I assume this"—he raised the note—"is evidence?"

"It is, my lord." Stokes held out his hand. "I'll need to keep it, at least for the moment."

With obvious reluctance, Rattenby handed the letter to Jonathon, who returned it to Stokes, then resumed his seat.

Barnaby could almost feel Stokes's relief as he tucked the letter back into his pocket.

The marquess was, once again, scowling, although this time, his ire wasn't directed at anyone there. "I would suggest," Rattenby stated, "that letter is simply another example of Sedbury's maliciousness." He focused on Stokes. "I will tell you now, Inspector, that I view Sedbury's removal from this world as a benevolent act of fate. His death will not be mourned by anyone. I would much prefer that you ceased your investigation, and I propose to tell the commissioner as much tomorrow morning."

Claudia stirred. She shot a worried glance at her brothers, then turned to their father. "You might want to reconsider that notion, Papa."

The marquess's scowl deepened as it swung Claudia's way. "Why? For goodness' sake, girl, this investigation is going to focus far too much attention on the family." Voice strengthening, he declared, "I won't have it!"

Claudia didn't waver. "With respect, Papa, how much interest becomes focused on the family isn't something you can control. The news of Sedbury's death was reported in the news sheets this morning—thankfully in highly restrained fashion, for which I believe we have Scotland Yard to thank—so the murder is now common knowledge. Inevitably, the ton has started to speculate, and the gossip will only grow more extreme as the days pass. Until someone is taken up for the crime, the most obvious suspects"—she waved at her brothers—"namely, Jonathon and Bryan, will remain just that. Suspected of murder. Do you really want their futures tainted and tarnished by the suspicion that one or other of them killed Sedbury?"

From under beetling brows, Rattenby stared hard at his daughter, who held her nerve and regarded him levelly, then he looked at his sons. "But…" He seemed to deflate and looked a trifle lost.

"We didn't do it," Jonathon said, "but Claude's right. We are the prime suspects—especially me. With Sedbury gone, I'm your heir, and that alone is motive enough. But the gossipmongers will pick and poke and hunt for more as long as the question of who killed Sedbury remains unresolved, and who knows what they'll turn up?"

"We didn't kill him," Bryan averred. "*We* know that, but the ton will make a great mystery of it. You know they will, and they'll relish the scandal, and that will hang over our heads forever if Sedbury's murderer isn't caught."

Penelope sensed it was his younger son's summation that decisively cracked the wall of the marquess's stubbornness. Despite his retreat to the country and his consequent eschewing of ton society, she doubted he would be so out of touch with ton habits that he couldn't appreciate what his children were very sensibly telling him. Nevertheless, she drew breath and stated, "Sadly, my lord, your children are entirely correct. If left unsolved, Sedbury's murder will have no good outcome for them or, indeed, any of your family. In order to stop the gossip, the real murderer must be identified."

The marquess studied her for several long moments, then he looked at his children. Ultimately, he transferred his gaze to Stokes. "I accept that you need to find Sedbury's murderer. However, I would ask that you investigate this affair with minimum public fuss. I will also reiterate that I am not inclined to view Sedbury's murder as an evil. Knowing Sedbury, the act was almost certainly some form of well-deserved retribution or revenge. It gives me no joy to state that, but I cannot pretend I didn't know Sedbury well enough to be sure that will be so." Rattenby paused, then said, "Do what you need to do, Inspector. Mr. and Mrs. Adair." His gaze shifted to Penelope and Barnaby. "However, know that I reserve the right to sit in judgment as to what happens once you have your answers."

Stokes briefly met Barnaby's and Penelope's gazes, then formally inclined his head to the marquess. "We'll bear your stipulations in mind, my lord, and proceed on that basis."

"In that case"—Rattenby rose, bringing everyone else to their feet— "I will leave you to your deliberations. Kindly keep me informed of any progress."

Stokes nodded. "We will."

Rattenby half bowed to Penelope and Barnaby, nodded curtly to his children and Charlie, then, stiffly upright, made for the door. Barnaby accompanied him into the hall.

Everyone else remained standing until the sound of the front door closing reached them, after which everyone breathed more easily.

Barnaby returned as the others resumed their seats.

Penelope was curious that the junior Hales hadn't left with their sire. Instead, seated once more, the three exchanged glances, then Jonathon sighed. "He means well. He just wants to protect us, but…"

Determinedly, Claudia completed the sentence. "The only way to do that is to find Sedbury's killer."

"We might feel like giving whoever it is a bouquet," Bryan said, "but sadly, that's the sum of it."

Bracingly, Penelope said, "I believe we're all in agreement on that point. So"—she glanced at Charlie, Stokes, and Barnaby—"what are our next steps?"

Stokes and Barnaby reiterated their intention to continue their respective searches for the riverbank site and the whip.

Claudia eyed her brothers. "Can either of you remember more about where you were that night?"

Bryan came up with several places he recalled looking in at, while Jonathon believed he'd spent much of his time at Satchwell's event in the company of three like-minded gentlemen. "I suppose," Jonathon said, "I could ask what they remembered of me during those hours."

"Before you do that," Penelope said, "it would help if each of you constructed a timeline of where you were and who you were with. Then, depending on where the murder site proves to be and how far that is from where you were and how long it would have taken you to get to the place, strangle Sedbury, and return, you might be able to assemble enough verified sightings through the critical hours to prove you couldn't be his killer."

Charlie nodded encouragingly. "And we shouldn't forget that there are doormen, barmen, and footmen as well as street sweepers and the like who might have noticed you going to, during, or leaving the events."

When the Hale brothers looked somewhat at a loss, Charlie offered, "I'll help. Just write everything down, then we'll see what we can learn."

Claudia glanced at the clock. "Look at the time! I must get back to Selborough House." She looked at her brothers. "I'm sure Mama will have come down with Papa, so we all need to present ourselves there. Writing your lists will have to wait until tomorrow."

Everyone roused themselves and rose.

After seeing the Hales and Charlie out, Penelope turned to Stokes and confessed, "I feel utterly at a loss. In inquiring into the movements of my fifteen possible suspects, while I didn't imagine I would find confirmation that any of them had gone to meet Sedbury that night, I fully expected to stumble over *something*. Some indication of possible involvement. But"—she raised her hands palms up—"nothing! Not a shred of suggestion of even the vaguest connection."

Stokes looked like he was struggling to hide a smile. "Sometimes, investigations go like that."

She almost growled, "But that leaves me with nothing to do."

Stokes glanced at Barnaby, then looked back at her. "Sleep on it," he advised. "Something will occur to you. Some factor we've missed that you can pursue."

She huffed and waved him off, adding a directive to bear her best wishes to Griselda, who was heading toward the end of a rather trying confinement.

After Barnaby closed the door, Penelope looped her arm with his. "We'd better go up to the nursery and see how our two are faring."

Barnaby smiled in acquiescence, and they headed up the stairs.

As they climbed, Penelope mused, "One point my usual sources raised that we haven't pursued at all is that Sedbury was as horrible—possibly even more horrible—to those of lesser station. So there may well be many others not of the ton—people or families who Sedbury wronged

—who might have wished him ill. People we, the investigators, have no inkling of."

Barnaby inclined his head. "Sadly, with our victim being Sedbury, that's very likely true. Equally true is that his unfinished letter to Jonathon might have no connection to Sedbury's murder."

"Hmm." Penelope's gaze turned speculative. "I wonder if there's any way I can learn more on that front."

CHAPTER 9

$\mathcal{T}$he next morning, after Barnaby had left for a meeting with his lads to check on their progress, Penelope played with their sons for another hour, then, after relinquishing the boisterous pair to their nursemaids for a walk in the park, she sat in the garden parlor and pondered her investigative options.

After dwelling on the outcome of the previous day, she'd concluded that her disaffection with her own contribution stemmed largely from her failure to advance their understanding of any aspect of the crime. While necessary to collect, the information she and her assistants had gathered had been entirely negative, and she wasn't accustomed to having no investigative thread to tug and follow. *That* was what had left her so dejected—the waiting around with nothing to do and no idea of how to advance their cause.

Determined to put an end to her frustration, she decided that there was one member of the Hale family she had yet to interview. It was the matter of a moment to call for the carriage and don her coat and bonnet, then she directed Phelps to drive to Farm Street and Selborough House.

When the butler opened the door, she smiled and extended one of her cards. "Please convey my compliments to the marchioness and that I would very much appreciate a few minutes of her time. I believe she will know which subject I wish to discuss."

The butler took the card, read the name, and bowed. "If you will wait in the drawing room, Mrs. Adair, I will inform her ladyship that you have called and wish to speak with her."

"Thank you." Penelope walked into the hall and allowed the butler to usher her into a sizeable drawing room decorated in peach-and-cream-striped silk. She sat on the long sofa and looked around. She was acquainted with the Selboroughs, but had only met them socially, as was the case with Rattenby and his marchioness.

She didn't doubt that the marchioness would see her. Even if Rattenby or Claudia hadn't mentioned Penelope's involvement in the investigation, over the years, together with Barnaby, she'd developed something of a reputation for assisting Scotland Yard with their inquiries into crimes involving the ton.

Sure enough, less than five minutes later, the marchioness swept into the room. Georgina Hale, Marchioness of Rattenby, was a tallish lady, elegant and svelte, with her dark hair upswept into a simple knot on the top of her head. She was nearing fifty, Penelope supposed, and was dressed in a fashionable day gown of mulberry cambric.

The marchioness paused only to hear the door shut behind her, then her blue eyes fixed on Penelope, and she continued gracefully across the room, extending her hand as she neared. "Mrs. Adair. I'm pleased you've called. If you hadn't, I likely would have called on you."

Penelope lightly touched the marchioness's fingers, and when the marchioness waved her back to her seat, she sank down and watched as Georgina Hale claimed the armchair opposite.

Before Penelope could venture any question, the marchioness said, "I understand from my daughter Claudia that you and your husband are assisting the police in this matter of Sedbury's death, and I must say that it's something of a relief to know that the investigating team is aware of…shall we say, the peculiar ramifications that can and usually do surround criminal actions within the haut ton."

Penelope interpreted that as an opening salvo designed to inform her of what was expected of her. She smiled serenely and told herself she would be unwise to underestimate the marchioness. Her blue gaze was sharp and direct, and if she was included in Helena Cynster's extended circle, Georgina Hale was very likely to have a shrewd and quick-witted mind to match. Especially when it came to matters affecting her family's social standing.

As if confirming that, the marchioness sat back and said, "I take it you are here because you believe I can help."

"Hoping, rather." Choosing her words with some care, Penelope explained, "While we've established that those of the ton known to bear enmity toward Sedbury are not directly involved in his death, and we are aware that indirect involvement remains a possibility, there is no question but that the pair of suspects currently at the top of the list are your sons, Jonathon and Bryan." She met the marchioness's very blue gaze. "On the face of the evidence in our possession, both had excellent reasons—powerful motives—to wish Sedbury dead."

Her estimation of the marchioness's acumen rose by several degrees when, instead of leaping to heatedly defend her offspring, she took several silent moments to consider her response, then, finally, nodded. "I can't say your conclusion surprises me. However, I believe it will assist you in understanding the full gamut of Sedbury's many enemies if you understand how the man came to be as he was."

Penelope's investigative heart leapt. Trying to veil her eagerness, she inclined her head. "Please do enlighten me."

The marchioness faintly smiled and said, "The first thing you need to know was that Sedbury was an infant when his mother died. Throughout his early years, as an only child and his father's heir, he was dreadfully spoilt and grew accustomed to invariably being the cynosure of attention for everyone in his orbit." She paused, then went on, "I married Gerrard —Rattenby—when Sedbury was seven years old, and from the first instant he laid eyes on me, he hated me. Not because of anything I did— of course, I tried to be kind and understanding and motherly toward him —and certainly not in the sense of me replacing the mother of whom he had no memory but because I took his place as the center of attention, not just for his father but for everyone in the household. That was the driving source of Sedbury's abiding anger and his never-far-from-the-surface resentment toward me and my children. In his eyes, we supplanted him."

Penelope contemplated the image the marchioness's words conjured.

Her gaze fixed in the distance, the marchioness continued, "He hated us, and I do not use that word lightly. His wasn't any sort of mild emotion, not even a childish one. It was a passionate fire that burned in him—he had to be the king of the castle, and everyone had to bow down before him. Because of that, because of his overweening sense of supreme entitlement, he quickly grew apart from his father. Rattenby is definitely not like that. He's arrogant, sometimes bullishly so, but underneath, he's a reasonable and even conscientious man, one protective of those he considers in his care. Rattenby didn't know how to handle

Sedbury, much less how to bridge the widening chasm between Sedbury and the rest of the family."

The marchioness met Penelope's eyes. "Sedbury was never one to share, not with anything, and when he was given no choice in the matter of his father's attention and the attention of all others associated with the marquessate and, indeed, that extended to society as a whole, he grew ever more rancorous."

The marchioness paused, then said, "I am aware that Sedbury diligently sought any lever he could wield to cause Jonathon and Bryan not just difficulty but pain. That was Sedbury's way. As you might imagine, that's not an attitude that endeared him to the rest of the family, all of whom have suffered at some time to one degree or another from his machinations, but Jonathon and Bryan were his favorite targets. They were the ones who stood highest in his mind as having taken or detracted from his own importance, the two who most challenged what he saw as his rightful dominance within the family." The marchioness smiled faintly. "My sons may be more gentle souls, but they never cowered or bowed before Sedbury's aggression. Sadly, that only entrenched his hatred."

Recapturing Penelope's gaze, the marchioness said, "Now that I've explained Sedbury's unbending and unwavering attitude, you won't be surprised to learn than none of us have shed so much as a single tear over his demise." She tipped her head, indicating the rest of the house. "Not even Patricia, who was his godmother."

Patricia was Lady Selborough. Penelope thought to clarify, "Lady Selborough is Rattenby's sister, I believe?"

The marchioness nodded. "My sister-in-law. We've always been close."

"I see." Penelope took a moment to reorder her thoughts. Now she was there and had the marchioness's undivided attention, she wanted to make the most of the opportunity. "There is one possible clue on which I hope you might be able to shed some light." She met the marchioness's gaze. "Sedbury started writing a letter to Jonathon earlier on Saturday. He broke off mid-letter and left it as if he intended to return and complete and send it later, but then he was killed. The letter itself is in the hands of the police, but the few sentences Sedbury had penned went..." She closed her eyes and called up a mental picture of the unfinished letter. "Dear Jonno," she recited. "I thought you'd like to know that a few months ago, I ran into that little maid you used to be so fond of. You know the one—

pretty as a picture with rosy cheeks and blonde pigtails. I could see what caught your eye. I have to confess that I had my wicked way with her."

She opened her eyes. "That was the extent of it." The marchioness was now frowning. Penelope asked, "Do you have any idea to which 'little maid' Sedbury was referring?"

Slowly, still frowning, the marchioness shook her head. "No. I can't imagine who that might be."

Penelope hesitated, debating whether to air a notion that had been brewing in the back of her mind. She hadn't spoken of it to Barnaby or Stokes yet, but she was there with Sedbury's stepmother... She refocused on the marchioness. "According to Duggan, Sedbury's man, Sedbury left the letter uncompleted and went out to dine and subsequently attend some meeting. Sedbury took his favorite whip with him, and in Duggan's opinion, Sedbury was looking forward to that meeting with considerable anticipation. As if he was expecting to, in Duggan's words, 'squash someone under his heel.'"

The marchioness looked faintly disgusted. "Sadly, I can imagine that all too clearly. Sedbury was a bully through and through and not just with the family."

"Quite." Penelope fixed the marchioness with a direct gaze. "However, it occurred to me that the unfinished letter and the meeting might be connected." She couldn't quite imagine how, but... "I wondered, you see, if the reason Sedbury left the letter unfinished was because, after his meeting, he expected to have more to add on the subject. Namely, about the 'little maid' he had presumably seduced."

The marchioness considered that, then inclined her head. "Clearly, that's one potential interpretation of his actions."

"Yes," Penelope went on more eagerly, "and that makes the identity of the 'little maid' even more important. If we knew who she was, that might give us some clue as to whom Sedbury met with, who we currently believe was his killer."

The marchioness was slowly nodding. "You think Sedbury might have met with a member of the little maid's family?"

"I think that's at least a possibility," Penelope replied. "That's why I asked if you knew or can even hazard a guess as to who the 'little maid' might be."

Several seconds ticked past as, judging from the concentration apparent in her face, the marchioness trawled through her memories, but in the end, she grimaced and met Penelope's gaze. "The truth is that

Jonathon has been dallying with maids—in the country, at friends' estates, and in town—for more than a decade. I couldn't begin to guess which one amid that legion of candidates is the one to whom Sedbury referred. And as at various times, Sedbury would have visited the same family estates, many of the same country houses, and certainly had access to the same haunts in town as Jonathon, then Sedbury might have stumbled across one of Jonathon's ex-paramours in any number of locations." The marchioness raised her hands in a helpless gesture. "I can't even begin to guess who she might be."

Penelope grimaced. "The description…"

"Could apply to any number of girls." The marchioness shook her head. "It might mean something to Jonathon—clearly, Sedbury believed it would—yet to be deliberately obtuse and teasing was quite Sedbury's way."

Penelope sighed a touch glumly. "Well, it was a theory and, I suppose, worth asking."

The marchioness studied her, then, her blue gaze shrewd, said, "Actually, something you mentioned earlier, about those in the ton known to wish Sedbury ill not being directly involved in his murder."

"Yes?"

"You referred to 'indirect involvement' remaining a possibility, by which I assume you mean hiring some thugs to kill Sedbury."

When Penelope nodded, the marchioness went on, "The truth is that anyone—anyone at all—who had interacted with Sedbury would have known better than to attempt to murder him themselves. A member of the ton, a shopkeeper, a tradesman, a navvy, or anyone who decided to kill him would have hired a pair of brawlers, at the very least, to get the job done."

Penelope held the marchioness's gaze. "You're saying that we can't strike anyone off our list of suspects on the grounds that they, themselves, didn't kill Sedbury."

The marchioness smiled faintly. "I believe that means that your suspects list will, sadly, remain a very long one."

Penelope screwed up her nose as the reality of the situation crystallized in her brain. "Unless we can directly identify the man who strangled Sedbury—for instance, via a witness—there is no way of solving this case." She extrapolated further, then disgustedly shook her head. "We have a detested victim and far too many viable suspects, yet precisely because of that very large number, we absolutely must identify Sedbury's killer in order to lift the taint of suspicion from the legion of those innocent of the crime."

"Indeed." The marchioness was trying not to look pleased. Her sons might be at the top of the suspects list, but she'd just ensured that the investigators understood that the list remained impossibly long. With a faint smile curving her lips, the marchioness said, "I'm glad you came to speak with me, Mrs. Adair. If there's anything more I can do to help, please do ask."

Penelope eyed the marchioness and shut her lips on the observation that, given the outcome of this interview, which had only increased her frustration, she would think again before repeating the exercise. Instead, she inclined her head politely, thanked the marchioness for her time, then rose and quit the house.

~

Stokes stood at an intersection on the lane that followed the riverbank a short block back from the embankment and impatiently waited for news of what he hoped would, at last, be a definitive sighting.

Typically, it had been Morgan who had first heard the whisper—a mere thread of a rumor—of a fight by the Cole Stairs. More specific and insistent questioning had elicited the information that this fight was thought to have occurred not long after midnight on Saturday night.

Subsequently, O'Donnell, Morgan, and the junior constables had concentrated their efforts along the narrow lanes and alleyways surrounding the Cole Stairs. Unlike most of the river "stairs," the Cole Stairs were partly natural—an outcrop of gray rock that swept along the river's curve for more than fifty yards, and along most of that length, the rock shelf was several yards wide. For centuries uncounted, the rivermen had used the shelf as a loading dock, and several sets of steps had been carved into the river-facing edges, giving easy access to the water.

Stokes had taken station directly north of the center of the shelf, where the junction of Gold Street and Dean Street formed a small square. All around, lanes and alleys barely wide enough for a man to walk along snaked between warehouses and other buildings. The area was among the older sections along the north bank of the Thames, and the stone along the river's edge was dark with age and dank with weed, and the scent of the river was pervasive.

Although the autumn sky far above was reasonably clear, between the buildings, shaded from the sun, the day felt gloomy.

Finally, Stokes saw a fresh-faced constable chivvying a weakly protesting boatman up the cobbled lane toward the square.

The constable fetched up before Stokes and, with an eager smile, presented the boatman with "Says he saw two men wrestling by the bank here on Saturday night, guv."

Stokes eyed the boatman, a slight, wiry fellow. But he was clear-eyed and, Stokes judged, had his wits firmly about him. Stokes acknowledged the constable's information with a brief nod and asked the boatman, "Where were you when you saw these men?"

Transparently disgruntled but knowing better than to think he could slide away with a mumble, the boatman replied, "I was just about where you're standing now. I'd been in the Drunken Duck." He tipped his head to the east, toward a large, dark-timbered building a little way along Dean Street. The sign of a staggering duck holding a frothing mug of ale jutted out from above the door. "I don't normally drink 'round 'ere—usually, I stay closer to 'ome in Bermondsey—but that night, one of me mates 'auled me down 'ere. Said the porter were right good. And it was. But I was heading off 'ome, must've been before one judging by the bells, and I came along 'ere. I'd left me boat tied up at Shadwell Dock, and that's where I was 'eading."

"Your mate?" Stokes's fingers itched to draw out his notebook, but doing so would only make the boatman more nervous and less likely to be forthcoming.

"He stayed on. It was just me, walking back to me boat." He paused, then added, "Mind you, there were others about, 'eading to their 'omes and such, but I don't know who they be."

Stokes nodded. "Right. So you were standing here when you saw these men." Stokes stepped forward to stand at the boatman's right, and obligingly, the boatman turned and joined Stokes in looking toward the river. Stokes said, "Point to where you saw them."

Without hesitation, the boatman raised a hand and pointed straight toward the river, to the Cole Stairs. "There. They was right there. Other side of the embankment wall, on the main part of the Cole Stairs. Two big men—large, heavy bruisers—wrestling hard as can be."

Stokes observed, "That's a fair way to see in the dark."

The boatman scoffed. "I'm a boatman—we need sharp eyes. 'Sides, the rain had blown over, and the moon was out, and with moonlight playing on the water, I could see the pair's outlines well enough."

Stokes accepted the assurance. "So what, exactly, did you see? Was it just the pair of them, or were there others hanging about who might have been a part of it?"

"Nah. It was just the pair of 'em, I'm sure of that. Watched 'em as I walked across this square, but I didn't stop to gawp. Not the sort of thing you do 'round 'ere—it's not 'ealthy, if you get me drift."

Stokes nodded, imagining the scene in his mind. "So just the two of them. Think back. How were they standing? Face to face or...?"

Frowning, the boatman took his time, then offered, "Well, to begin with they were, one lashing out at the other, but now you mention it, that changed, and one of 'em was facing the river and 'ad 'is back to the other. And that other man—I'd say 'e was the taller and heavier—had his arms up, elbows high." The boatman raised his hands to his collarbone and stuck his elbows out level with his shoulders. "Like this. And 'e was rocking a little, side to side. Like pretending to be a waddling duck."

Stokes caught the eager constable's eye in time to shake his head. He was not about to ask the boatman if the larger man could possibly have been strangling the other; he'd leave that to the coroner. Instead, Stokes asked, "Did you see anything else?"

"Nah. I didn't 'ang 'round, just put me 'ead down and kept walking. None of me business what they were up to, was it?" The boatman hesitated, then asked, "Given you lot are running 'round all 'bout and asking 'bout this fight, what 'appened?"

Stokes hesitated, then replied, "A large, heavy bruiser of a man was pulled out of the river on Sunday. We're trying to learn where he went into the water, and it's likely what you saw gives us our answer." Stokes turned to the constable. "Deliver this man to Morgan. He'll take a formal statement."

The boatman looked hopeful. "And then I can go?"

Stokes suppressed a cynical smile. "Just be sure to give Morgan your real name and address, and the chances are you won't hear from us again."

Stokes watched the boatman and constable head toward the main body of police canvassing the lanes. Normally, the boatman would be called to give evidence at the inquest into Sedbury's death, but Stokes had a strong premonition that there would be no public inquest held into the death of Viscount Sedbury, the Marquess of Rattenby's late, much-detested, and entirely unlamented heir.

Stokes was standing staring, unseeing, at the Cole Stairs and mentally reviewing the customary outcomes when the nobility and the justice system collided when Barnaby hove into view.

Barnaby trudged up from the riverbank and, when he saw Stokes had noticed him, briefly waved and smiled. As soon as he was close enough, he called, "O'Donnell said you might have found a witness."

Stokes allowed a satisfied smile to bloom. "It appears we have. At last."

When Barnaby stopped beside Stokes, Stokes nodded toward the Cole Stairs. "A boatman heading home from the local public house saw two large, heavy bruisers wrestling on the stairs."

Stokes started down the cobbled street, and Barnaby fell in beside him. As they walked, Stokes described what the boatman had seen.

"So," Barnaby concluded, "it seems highly likely that your witness saw Sedbury being strangled."

Stokes nodded. "The boatman's recollection was clear, and he seemed quite certain of what he saw." They reached the embankment wall and stepped over the low stone parapet onto the rock shelf that formed the main part of the stairs. "Therefore," Stokes continued, looking about the uneven surface, "it appears that Sedbury came down here for his meeting, and it was here that he died."

Barnaby joined Stokes in a thorough visual examination of the stone platform, but there was no hint of a struggle or fight to be found.

"Also no sign of the whip," Stokes said, "but even if it was here, it wouldn't have remained here for long."

It was Barnaby's turn to smile with satisfaction. "As it happens, I, too, have a breakthrough to share."

"Ah-ha!" With an expectant grin, Stokes returned, "As ever with investigations, it never rains but it pours."

"Indeed. And I'm here to report that it seems my lads have found what we believe to be Sedbury's whip."

Stokes's expression lit. "Where?"

"A pawnshop in Aldgate High Street."

"So not far away?"

"No. I came here first to see if you wanted to come with me on the off chance it is Sedbury's whip and therefore the murder weapon. If it is and we can get the pawnbroker to say from whom he received it, then…"

"Indeed." Stokes nodded. "And if we can tie it to somewhere around here, that will further help our cause." He turned to the buildings. "Come on."

They walked back up Gold Street, cast around through the nearby lanes, and found O'Donnell conferring with Morgan, who had informed the sergeant of the boatman's revelations. Stokes brought the pair up to date with the news about the whip and directed them to see who else they could find who'd seen the fight in the small hours of Sunday morning.

O'Donnell's expression turned even more dogged than it usually was. "Now we know it was on the stairs, we can press the locals harder. There'll be others who saw what the boatman saw, and hopefully, someone saw more."

Morgan offered, "I'll check with the other boatmen who ply their trade in the small hours. Plenty of them on the river of a Saturday night, even along this stretch."

Barnaby nodded approvingly. "It sounds as if the fight would have been readily seen by anyone on the river."

O'Donnell and Morgan saluted. "Right you are, sir," O'Donnell said. "We'll get on with it."

Stokes nodded a dismissal, and he and Barnaby walked briskly to where Barnaby had left his curricle in the care of Jeremy, one of his lads. "He's from the local area," Barnaby explained as he and Stokes neared the curricle, "and it was he who tracked down the whip."

On reaching the carriage, Stokes smiled at Jeremy. "Good work on finding the whip."

Jeremy colored and bobbed his curly head. "Wasn't hard. Just had to ask."

Stokes smiled. "Nevertheless."

Barnaby grinned and took the reins and, with Stokes, climbed to the box. At Barnaby's tip of the head and his "Come on!" Jeremy eagerly scrambled up behind. Barnaby flicked the reins and set his chestnut trotting. Following directions from Jeremy, Barnaby navigated the narrow streets, eschewing the crowded byways around the docks and striking north to turn onto Commercial Road. From there, they made their way to Whitechapel and followed the road west until they reached Aldgate High Street.

Jeremy pointed out Sullivan's Pawnshop, and Barnaby drew the curricle up to the curb.

"It's old Mr. Sullivan in there," Jeremy said. He accepted the reins and Barnaby's instruction to wait for them there, then Barnaby led the way inside, with Stokes hanging back in his shadow.

Mr. Sullivan was a round man, dressed in browns, whose hair and whiskers gave him the appearance of a badger. With the briefest of glances, he assessed Barnaby's station in life and smiled toothily. "Good day, sir. Are you looking for anything in particular?"

Barnaby smiled easily back. "I am, indeed. A whip. I'm told you have one that arrived recently?"

"Indeed, indeed!" Mr. Sullivan reached below the counter and brought out a short-handled horsewhip, coiled and tied with a leather thong. "You're in luck. This came in a few days ago. Lovely specimen, it is."

Almost reverentially, Sullivan laid the whip on the glass counter.

Barnaby had never seen Sedbury's whip, but from what little he recalled of Charlie's description, this whip could definitely be it. Even without touching it, he could see the quality of the workmanship and the soft, subtle sheen of highest-grade leather, and the embossing on the handle was first rate. Barnaby picked up the whip, hefted it in his hand, then half turned to Stokes and arched a brow. "How likely is it that two whips of this quality would be found around here?"

Stokes grunted and pulled out his warrant card, and Mr. Sullivan's face fell. "This whip," Stokes said as he took the coil of leather from Barnaby, "is wanted in relation to a murder investigation. I'm therefore claiming it as evidence. We will get an expert to confirm it is the whip we seek. If it proves not to be, I'll make sure this whip is returned to you."

Mr. Sullivan didn't look the least bit mollified.

Barnaby leaned on the counter and, in conspiratorial fashion, asked, "So, do you know anything of where the whip was found?"

A golden guinea appeared between Barnaby's long fingers, and Sullivan's eyes fixed on the gleam.

After a moment, his gaze still on the coin, he said, "There's an old codger, name of Cedric. We all call him Cedric the Long. He prowls for bits and pieces along the riverbank and brings me anything he thinks I might be interested in." Before Stokes could ask, his expression turning sour, Sullivan went on, "At this time of day, you'll find Cedric in the Sun Tavern, just down the street"—Sullivan tipped his head to the east—"no doubt drinking the shillings I gave him for that blessed whip."

Barnaby smiled, straightened from the counter, and flicked the guinea toward Sullivan.

The pawnbroker snatched the coin out of the air, and his toothy smile returned. He dipped his head to Barnaby. "Thank ye, sir. You're surely a gentleman."

Barnaby laughed and followed Stokes out of the door.

Barnaby asked Jeremy if he knew the location of the Sun Tavern, and the lad pointed east along the street. "That's it just there. You can see the sign above the door."

They could just make out the faded sign and, after some debate, left the whip safely tucked beneath the curricle's seat, under Jeremy's watchful eye, and walked on and into the tavern.

Barnaby paused just inside the smoky taproom to allow his eyes to adjust to the gloom. There were several groups of old men gathered about tables with mugs in front of them and—having taken in Barnaby and Stokes—shuttered expressions on their faces, but Barnaby's attention was drawn to the very tall, very thin, aging man in an ancient frieze coat who was sitting at the bar and who had yet to notice Barnaby and Stokes's arrival.

Barnaby went forward and claimed the stool on the man's left. As Stokes slid onto the stool on the man's right, Barnaby saw that the man— assuredly Cedric the Long—was nursing a pint of lager.

Abruptly, Cedric stiffened. He slid his gaze in Stokes's direction, then glanced warily at Barnaby. Then he returned his watery blue gaze to Stokes. "Police?"

Stokes smiled amiably. "You've sound instincts, Cedric."

Cedric licked his lips, but didn't seem all that nervous. "So, what can I do for you gents?"

Stokes replied, "We'd like to know where you found the whip you sold to Sullivan up the street."

"Hmm." Cedric screwed up his face. "Me memory's not what it used to be, you know?"

Barnaby clinked two florins on the bar, seizing Cedric's attention. "Perhaps the sight of these might help clear the fog away?"

Cedric's gaze had locked on the coins. "Oh, aye. They've done that, right enough." Briefly dragging his gaze from the silver, he glanced Stokes's way. "You know the Cole Stairs?"

Stokes nodded. "We do."

"That whip was just lying there, in the lane this side of the wall." His gaze distant, Cedric tipped his head, as if studying the picture in his memory. "'Twasn't coiled up, but just lying there like someone had dropped it. Wasn't anyone around—I checked—so I took it." He glanced at Stokes. "Finders keepers and all that."

"When was this?" Stokes asked.

"Sunday morning," Cedric promptly replied. "The bells were all ringing loud as can be. That's when I found that whip and picked it up."

Barnaby met Stokes's eyes and saw his friend had no more questions to ask. Barnaby tossed the florins on the bar and pushed up from his stool. "Just don't drink them all tonight."

His gaze once more locked on the coins, shining against the dark wood of the bar, Cedric only hummed and made no promises.

Barnaby met Stokes's gaze, and feeling much more satisfied than they had that morning, they headed for the curricle.

CHAPTER 10

*P*enelope was seated on the sofa in her drawing room, with Charlie and Claudia sitting on the sofa opposite and Jonathon and Bryan in armchairs, when Barnaby and Stokes walked into the room, their smiles and their attitudes exuding success.

"You obviously have news." Impatiently, Penelope waved the pair to chairs. "What have you learned?"

Barnaby sank elegantly onto the sofa beside her, while Stokes claimed the armchair next to Jonathon's and declared, "*Finally*, we know where Sedbury was murdered, and that it seems he was killed by a single man."

"Where?" Penelope asked.

"On the Cole Stairs in Upper Shadwell," Stokes replied. "It's more a wide landing place than the usual narrow jetty and steps. A boatman on his way home from a local pub saw two men wrestling on the platform."

"Right time—before one o'clock on Sunday—and expected descriptions," Barnaby said. "However, his account of a large, heavy bruiser, taller and larger than Sedbury, is still too general to point a finger at the murderer, especially in that area."

Stokes grunted. "At least not without some other clues to go with it."

The door opened, and Mostyn appeared, carrying a whip. "I had to cut the leather thong to remove it, Inspector."

Stokes shrugged as Mostyn handed the unfurling whip to Barnaby, who grasped the handle and explained, "Courtesy of the lads' network, we located what we believe to be Sedbury's whip."

Charlie leaned forward, peering at the whip. He held out a hand. "Here, let me see."

Barnaby handed the whip over, and Charlie took it and examined the handle, then the thongs. Then he looked at Stokes. "This is definitely Sedbury's whip. The braiding here"—he pointed to where the thongs left the handle—"is quite unique. I noticed it when I took the whip off him on Saturday morning, and I've only ever seen that working on his whip."

"Perfect." Stokes's smile was smugly satisfied. "That's exactly the confirmation we need."

Claudia had been studying the whip and looked inquiringly at Barnaby. "Where did you find it?"

He described the pawnshop and their visit to the Sun Tavern. "Cedric the Long told us that he picked up the whip from beside the Cole Stairs, where it was lying discarded when he came past on Sunday morning."

Penelope sighed. "Well, I'm glad you two have significant advances to report, because as I was explaining to the others before you arrived, I fear that, on mine and their parts, there's little to no chance that we'll get anywhere pursuing the question of who might have had motive as well as opportunity to kill Sedbury." She couldn't help but look as dejected as she felt. "I interviewed the marchioness today, and as she most sapiently pointed out, the simple truth is that legions of people in all walks of life likely had a motive to kill Sedbury, and as for opportunity, as every one of those motivated souls ipso facto had to have met him, then if moved to kill him, every single tortured soul would have hired a brawler to do it." She pulled a face at Stokes. "Indeed, just such a brawler as the man who, according to the boatman, did away with the wretch."

Barnaby caught her eye and smiled sympathetically. "You never met Sedbury, so that wouldn't have been obvious to you."

"Yes, well." She huffed in frustration. "With my usual mode of investigation utterly stymied, I'm not sure what more I can contribute."

"Actually…" Stokes's expression of dawning comprehension suggested he'd seen a light. His gaze distant, clearly speaking as he followed his developing thought, he continued, "I think it very likely that even if we could wave a magic wand and learn if any of Sedbury's many victims had, indeed, hired a brawler to kill him, given what we learned today, the information will prove irrelevant, at least in terms of identifying our murderer."

Barnaby frowned and asked the question forming on all the others' tongues. "Why do you think that?"

Clasping his hands between his knees, Stokes leaned forward. "Because the location raises one critical question." He looked around the circle. "Why was Sedbury there?"

Stokes studied their faces, then reiterated, "What was Sedbury doing —expecting to accomplish—on the Cole Stairs at between twelve-thirty and one o'clock on Sunday morning? We haven't yet found the hackney driver, but it seems Sedbury went to the spot willingly, apparently to meet with someone who was at least his equal in size and strength."

Digesting the implications of their latest clues, Barnaby slowly nodded. "More, was Duggan's sense that Sedbury was looking forward to quashing someone under his heel a reflection of Sedbury's expectations of that meeting?"

"Only," Penelope put in, "the meeting went horribly wrong for Sedbury, and he was the one who got quashed by his intended victim." She thought about that. "Huh! How ironic."

Claudia said, "Everything seems to hinge on why Sedbury went to that spot."

Jonathon and Bryan exchanged glances, then Jonathon offered, "I— well, we—have heard rumors that, and I quote, 'he frequents rougher circles far removed from the ton.' I never paid much attention to the whispers." Jonathon grimaced. "The truth was, I didn't want to know."

"I can't say I did, either," Bryan put in. "But perhaps that was why he was in that area. Because he had some sort of interest there."

Stokes nodded. "That's possible, and it's an angle we can pursue on the ground." He looked at Penelope and Barnaby. "As I see things now, our most pressing question is how did he get to the Cole Stairs? We assume he took the hackney the whole way, but did he?"

Barnaby stated, "We need to find that hackney driver and learn where he set Sedbury down."

"And when," Penelope added.

"That," Stokes said, "will tell us whether Sedbury went directly to the stairs and his putative meeting was, indeed, with the bruiser who killed him, or whether the meeting Duggan knew of occurred earlier and the encounter on the stairs was something else entirely."

Barnaby nodded. "We won't be able to tell until we find that driver." He met Stokes's gaze. "I'll speak with my lads. Now we've found the whip, we can concentrate on locating the driver."

Frowning, Penelope shook her head. "Regardless, what was Sedbury doing in such an area?" She looked at the other Hales and Charlie. "A liking for rougher circles or not, it's hardly an area that gentlemen frequent."

"There has to be a reason," Stokes stated. "I'll put my men onto scouring the area for witnesses. Now we know where he was, we can be much more thorough."

Again, Jonathon and Bryan exchanged a glance, then Jonathon looked at Stokes. "We'll help. It might be useful to have someone to point to instead of just a vague description, and as much as it pains me—and Bryan—to admit it, Sedbury and the pair of us are similar enough to be mistaken at a glance."

Barnaby nodded. "That would help, possibly a great deal. Having you along might jog someone's memory." He glanced at Stokes. "Enough for them to react and, thus, label themselves as a person with information."

Stokes's wolfish grin said he approved of that tack. He looked at Jonathon and Bryan. "We'll be happy to have you two along. Anything we can do to better our chances of learning all we need has my vote."

"Meanwhile…" Penelope had been thinking and, now, looked at Claudia. "When I spoke to your mother, I received the distinct impression that while she didn't have any specific information, she suspected that there was more to Sedbury's nefarious activities in London than she and the family knew. For instance, she alluded to many of Sedbury's victims in town—those with motive to kill him—coming from outside the ton." Her gaze on Claudia's face, Penelope tipped her head. "Your mother mentioned that your aunt, Lady Selborough, was Sedbury's godmother. I would describe her ladyship as the meddling sort. Do you think she might know more about Sedbury's London activities?"

Claudia looked much struck and eagerly replied, "I would be very surprised if she didn't. Aunt Patricia is one to poke her nose into her relatives' lives without quarter." She glanced at her brothers, both of whom plainly agreed with that statement. "So yes!" Claudia straightened and returned her gaze to Penelope. "We should definitely ask Aunt Patricia what she knows and wheedle whatever she does from her."

Penelope nodded decisively. "We—you and I—will interview her tomorrow." She looked inquiringly at Charlie. "It might help if you came along as well. You might be able to make more of what her ladyship tells us than Claudia or I."

Charlie readily nodded. "Happy to help." He paused, then, frowning slightly, added, "Just as long as I don't have to interrogate her ladyship."

By the looks on all the other men's faces, they agreed with that stipulation, but Claudia just smiled, and Penelope laughed. "I believe," she told Charlie, "that you can leave that to me and Claudia."

Claudia beamed, and in much better moods, each with their task for the following day settled and before them, the company made arrangements where to meet and when, then broke up.

～

As arranged with Claudia, at precisely eleven o'clock the following morning, Penelope stood beside Charlie on the porch of Selborough House and watched him pull the bell chain.

The butler recognized them both and bowed them in, then took their hats and coats.

Claudia peeked out of the drawing room, then came quickly to join them. "Aunt Patricia has agreed to speak with us." She lowered her voice to add, "It took quite a bit of convincing to make her see the need, but Mama helped." Claudia pulled a face. "While none of us want to air Sedbury's linen in public, Mama pointed out that the alternative was potentially much worse. We can't simply ignore his murder and hope the situation goes away. Unless the murderer is caught, the speculation over who killed him is only going to grow worse."

"To the detriment of all the Hales," Penelope added.

"Exactly!" Claudia led them toward the open drawing-room door. "I just wanted to warn you that Aunt Patricia remains reluctant over speaking of Sedbury and his habits." Just outside the door, Claudia paused and, in the tone of one struck, concluded, "That likely means she knows something she believes will be detrimental to his and the family's reputations."

"Indeed." Penelope's eagerness to question her ladyship escalated. "Let's see if we can induce her to tell us what that is."

With Charlie beside her, Penelope followed Claudia into the drawing room. Lady Selborough sat in one of the chairs before the fireplace, while the marchioness sat on the sofa, in the corner closest to her sister-in-law.

Lady Selborough was of average height and build, with faded curly blonde hair and pale-blue eyes. Being Rattenby's sister, she was several years older than the marchioness and was a typical matron of her vintage, with her rather fussy taste in dress a reflection of her fussy nature. She was fidgety, too, and as Claudia made the introductions, incessantly fiddled with her rings, turning them around and around.

After acknowledging Penelope's greeting, her ladyship gushed, "I do hope, Mrs. Adair, that we can rely on your discretion."

Penelope blinked, then countered, "I can assure you that the only information we will carry from here will be facts relevant to establishing who murdered your nephew."

Lady Selborough looked faintly peeved. "Well, I suppose..."

The marchioness patted Lady Selborough's arm bracingly. "Stop worrying, Patricia. As Claudia and I explained, we all need to know anything pertinent you can tell us." The marchioness waited until Penelope and Charlie sank onto the seats Claudia steered them to, then commanded, "Now, my dear, please enlighten us as to what you know of Sedbury's doings."

Lady Selborough continued to look uncertain. She glanced at Penelope, and Penelope schooled her expression to one of mild inquiry.

Finally, her ladyship cleared her throat and said, "When Sedbury came on the town, as his godmother, I made an effort to keep in touch. He used to call occasionally, albeit only when I sent around a note to summon him to tea. Some years ago—three or four years after he started living in London—I became aware, largely from comments he made, that he had developed a liking for...I believe the term is 'roughing it.'" Faint color appeared in her ladyship's cheeks. "Apparently, some quirk of his nature led him to seek entertainment in circles far removed from the ton. After noting my reaction to his occasional revelations, he took positively evil delight in slipping tidbits about his low life into our conversation purely to disconcert and worry me."

Plainly captured by her memories of such exchanges, Lady Selborough raised her hands to her lined cheeks. "I was so thankful that Selborough was never around to hear some of the things Sedbury claimed to have done. It was...*mortifying* to think of a Hale behaving in such a way."

Lowering her hands, her ladyship hauled in a fortifying breath. "In the end, I grew so *angry* with him—at the way he was thumbing his nose at the family and, indeed, at the very values that are the hallmark of a gentleman—that I pretended not to listen anymore, and gradually, I invited him less and less frequently, until over the past year or two, he hasn't been to this house."

Carefully, Penelope probed, "What, exactly, was he doing that so bothered you?"

Her ladyship's lips firmed, and her eyes flashed. "He was using his position to satisfy his darker cravings. I firmly believe that the power of being heir to the marquessate had quite gone to his head. While within the ton, his position would let him go only so far, in lower circles, he was able to lord it over anyone and everyone." Her voice lowered, and she went on, "Even as a child, he'd shown a tendency toward being viciously cruel. As a man, by exploiting his position, he was able to feed his liking for cruelty and unspeakable pleasures—he literally enjoyed causing others pain."

The marchioness had paled. Now, she said, "Perhaps it's fortunate for the ton that Sedbury preferred the lower orders on whom to visit his tastes. That said, I wouldn't wish the fate of being Sedbury's victim on anyone."

Penelope regarded Lady Selborough. "I accept that you will not know details, but from what you did gather, how low had Sedbury sunk?"

For a moment, Lady Selborough pale's gaze remained fixed on Penelope's face, then in a low tone, she replied, "The last time I encountered him in private—the last time he indulged me with any comments about what he did with his life—he was well beyond the pale and striding down the road to depravity and damnation." She shuddered, then with her voice gaining strength, went on, "He was a *fiend*, plain and simple. And it's my *firm* opinion that the family should reward whoever removed him from this earth, thus sparing us from what would undoubtedly, at some point, have been untold ignominy and wretched grief."

Slowly nodding, Penelope digested that, then refocused on Lady Selborough. "One last question. Did Sedbury ever mention any particular part of town in relation to his deplorable activities?"

Lady Selborough frowned, clearly trawling through her memories. "Dockside." She nodded and met Penelope's gaze. "He mentioned the docks and being near the river several times."

"Thank you for your help." Penelope included the marchioness in her nod. "Your candor has given us much to think about."

She rose, as did Charlie and Claudia. Charlie took his leave of the marchioness and Lady Selborough and, with Penelope and Claudia, walked into the front hall, leaving the older ladies sharing reassuring whispers.

Penelope sighed, halted, and glanced at Claudia and Charlie. "Quite obviously, Sedbury was a massive scandal in the making, a volcano that could have erupted at any time."

Claudia looked faintly shocked. "I had no idea he'd become that bad."

"Hmm." Penelope frowned. "We came here hoping to learn whether Sedbury had any interest in the area around the Cole Stairs—the sort of interest that might have led to him going to a midnight meeting there." She looked at Claudia. "It seems your aunt has given us the answer."

His expression grave, Charlie said, "Because that area was the one to which he went to satisfy his darker urges. He went to meet someone with his whip in hand and in an expectant mood. Odds are that meeting was connected to his usual activities in the area."

Penelope nodded. "Precisely."

Claudia was frowning. "If Sedbury regularly went to that area to indulge his warped tastes, doesn't that mean that the locals will very likely know him?"

Penelope blinked. "An excellent point." She looked at Charlie and Claudia with renewed enthusiasm. "We'll send a messenger at once to Stokes, Barnaby, and your brothers. In canvassing the locals, they need to know what to ask."

By the time Penelope's groom-cum-guard, Connor, caught up with Barnaby down by the river and conveyed her latest information with the implication that Sedbury would be known to the locals in a more definite way than the investigators had supposed, Barnaby and Jonathon, who had been doing their damnedest to reassure the locals and glean what they knew of Sedbury, had already come to the same conclusion.

"This"—Barnaby flicked Penelope's note with one finger—"confirms that Sedbury was regularly and quite deeply involved with those living in this area."

Jonathon looked utterly mystified. "Why, for heaven's sake?" He turned, arms extended, indicating the drab reality of the narrow lane in which they stood. "What on earth brought him here?"

"According to Penelope, your aunt believes it was his warped tastes that drove him, in that he could indulge his habits to the hilt around here, and no one could say him nay." Barnaby looked disgusted. He refolded the note and returned it to Connor. "Find Stokes and give him that. Lord Bryan Hale is with him." Barnaby pointed eastward. "They were questioning locals over that way."

Connor saluted and left.

Jonathon frowned. "So what now?"

Barnaby looked at the next house along the cramped lane. "Now we go on as we were, but dig a bit deeper. We need to frame our questions in a way that conveys we already know that Sedbury was often around and see what confidences we can entice."

The area was a hodgepodge of tiny houses and cramped shops interspersed with stores and warehouses crammed with goods. They continued along the lane, knocking on doors and venturing into businesses and warehouses. About them, four constables did the same, and several of Barnaby's lads were working along the nearby lanes in their own way. It was easier for the lads to get chatting with the locals, and Barnaby had encouraged them to range ahead of where he and Jonathon were plodding along.

Barnaby and Jonathon came out of a shipwright's store to find one of the lads, Jordan, waiting.

Barnaby arched a brow in question, and Jordan tipped his head down an alley. "Reckon you need to hear what this old lady has to say, guv."

Barnaby nodded. "Lead the way."

Jordan turned and trotted down the alley, then veered into a connecting lane.

They were halfway down the lane when an old woman—probably not more than fifty but worn down by life—leaned out of an open doorway a few paces ahead. Her stained apron fluttered in the breeze, and her iron-gray hair was caught up in a net.

Her gaze landed on Jonathon, and for a second, she froze. Then her eyes flared wide, and she tensed to pull back.

Jonathon halted and called out, "I'm not Sedbury." Barnaby and Jordan halted as well.

The woman blinked. After a pregnant pause, she shuffled into the doorway proper and stared hard at Jonathon, scrutinizing his face, then running her gaze down his long length. Eventually, she nodded and looked into his face. "Aye, you ain't that devil. But who's to say you're not cut from the same cloth?"

Jonathon waved at the pair of uniformed constables who were coming up behind him and Barnaby. "Do you think I would be helping the police if I was?"

The woman looked at the constables, then sniffed. "Not sure talking to you or the rozzers is like to do any of us around here any good."

Barnaby stepped forward and, with an easy smile, said, "Still, it can't hurt, can it? You see, the man you called 'that devil'—Sedbury—wasn't well liked in our circles, and from talking to those who live around here, we're realizing he wasn't anyone's favorite in this area, either."

"Favorite? Hah!" The woman crossed her arms over her chest. "He was a monster! Why, he near broke my Donnie's arm just because the boy accidentally jostled him in the pub, and he used that evil whip of his on Jonas Henry and nearly cut off his foot! Then there's the maids who live in fear of catching his eye, all scurrying around like mice these days. And I shouldn't forget Old Man Higgins, who that brute pushed into a wall so hard it broke the poor old codger's ribs. And that's just the happenings I know of. No telling what you'll learn if you ask a few blocks down."

She paused to draw breath, then looked at Barnaby before transferring her gaze to Jonathon. "We all heard someone offed him last Saturday night. I don't have a clue who did it, which is good because I'd not be inclined to tell on whoever did the world a favor and killed the blighter." She regarded Jonathon severely. "Even if he was kin of yours, he was a bad 'un to the bone."

Jonathon held her gaze and quietly said, "I know. Trust me, I know."

She must have read something in his expression, because after a second, she nodded. "Aye. Seems you do."

Satisfied, Barnaby thanked the woman, and Jonathon added his own thanks, along with a few shillings for her time. Barnaby commended Jordan and left him to continue along that lane, and he and Jonathon returned to the lane they'd previously been investigating.

They'd drawn a blank at another warehouse and had just come back outside when Barnaby saw one of the older lads, Finch, striding along with a man in a driving cape in tow.

Barnaby halted, and Jonathon stopped beside him.

Finch spotted Barnaby, and his face lit. He reached back and tweaked the man's cape. "This way. This is the gen'leman I told you about."

Barnaby smiled as Finch halted before him.

Finch beckoned the jarvey, who approached uncertainly. "This is the jarvey who took up the viscount in Pall Mall."

Barnaby nodded to Finch. "Good work." Barnaby waved the jarvey closer, then glanced at Jonathon and, to the jarvey, said, "You picked up a gentleman who looked like this man in Pall Mall on Saturday at close to midnight?"

The jarvey regarded Jonathon warily. "Aye." After a second, looking puzzled, he added, "But it wasn't this cove."

"No. But can you describe the man you took up?" Barnaby asked.

The jarvey eyed Jonathon. "Very like this one, but maybe older. Meaner looking, anyways. And the man I took up carried a whip, coiled in his hand. Short-handled sort."

Barnaby nodded. "That's the man we're interested in. So, from Pall Mall, where did you take him?"

"Here—well, close by." The jarvey pointed northeastward. "He had me drop him off at the corner of Gold Street and Upper Shadwell."

Gold Street ran for two short blocks from Upper Shadwell to the Cole Stairs. "Did he have you stop anywhere along the way?" Barnaby asked.

The jarvey shook his head. "Straight here from Pall Mall." He paused, then added, "He first told me to go to Upper Shadwell, then when I turned onto the street, he told me to go on and stop at Gold Street."

Barnaby nodded. "What time did you drop him off at Gold Street? Any idea?"

The jarvey screwed up his face in thought, then offered, "Best I can say is it was heading to one o'clock. The bells tolled for one as I was passing London Dock on my way back to Mayfair."

"About a quarter before the hour, then." Barnaby couldn't think of anything more they needed from the jarvey. He thanked the man and paid him generously for his time and for driving all the way to the docks.

"Happy to be of service." With a tip of his hat, the jarvey strode off, his cape swishing.

Barnaby turned to Finch, who was looking pleased as punch. Barnaby smiled. "Well done! Now, head back to Albemarle Street and tell Mostyn that you found the jarvey and that the man's spoken with me, and we have all the information we need on that score. And, of course, Mostyn will have something for you."

Barnaby had recruited Mostyn as his major-general in charge of the lads. Mostyn would know how best to reward Finch and would also get the word out to the other lads to stand down from their search.

"Yes, sir!" Beaming fit to burst, Finch saluted, then took off at a run.

Barnaby laughed. "Ah, to have the enthusiasm of youth."

"And its energy," Jonathon added.

"That, too." Barnaby considered how the latest information fitted with what they already knew. "If Sedbury was brought straight here and dropped off at the top of Gold Street at a quarter to one, then the encounter on the Cole Stairs must have been the meeting he'd been looking forward to."

Jonathon nodded. "No time to go anywhere else. Not before he was seen wrestling with some man on the stairs."

"The only possibility—and it's barely even that—is if Sedbury stopped off at one of the buildings along the way." Barnaby looked in the direction the jarvey had indicated. "Let's go to Gold Street and concentrate our efforts around there and see if we can find anyone else who can shed light on Sedbury's movements that night."

$\sim$

Half an hour later, Barnaby and Jonathon came out of a shop and found Stokes and Bryan waiting in the street.

Earlier, Barnaby had dispatched one of the constables who had been supporting him and Jonathon to convey the jarvey's information to Stokes.

"So," Stokes said, as Barnaby and Jonathon joined him and Bryan, "any further sightings?"

Barnaby glanced around at the sad-looking houses. "No. We couldn't turn up anyone who saw him or anyone else after Saturday midnight."

"However," Jonathon said, looking rather grim, "as to what brought him here and the likely reason for his meeting, it seems he'd taken to playing his games of intimidation and coercion on a larger scale and to a much deeper, darker degree in this neighborhood."

Bryan, whose complexion had turned a trifle pasty, nodded. "That sounds the same as the stories we've heard, and you can tell that no one's making them up—the passions are too raw." He, too, glanced around. "I wouldn't have thought it possible, but Sedbury was even more loathed and detested around here than he was in the ton."

"With reason," Stokes growled. "If even half the tales we've been told are true, Sedbury had taken to treating this area as his personal fiefdom. In more genteel society, he risked running afoul of all manner of social and similar strictures, but here?"

"Here," Barnaby responded, "he could do whatever he wished, and no one was in any position to even bring pressure to bear against him, much less say him nay."

"In other words," Jonathon said, "assuming he was killed by a local— someone he pushed too far—then the suspect list will run into the hundreds."

"If not thousands," Bryan put in. After a moment, he admitted, "And having heard all we have, I don't even know that I want whoever did for him caught."

Stokes grunted. "On a more positive note, we now have three more witnesses who noticed the fight. The one with the clearest view of the action and who, therefore, gave the best description of the man who killed Sedbury was another boatman. He was out on the river, but closer to the opposite shore than this one. Sadly, he was too far away to be able to identify our murderer, but he said the man was a trifle taller and broader than Sedbury—overall, definitely larger."

Barnaby whistled. "There can't be that many men of such stature around here."

Stokes dipped his head in agreement. "The boatman also said the murderer had dark hair, and he thinks it was curly. Our unknown man wore a long, heavy-looking dark coat, but no hat. The boatman saw both men arrive and step onto the platform. Sedbury first—although, of course, the boatman didn't know who he was—then the other man lumbered out from the shadows at the east end of the stairs. The boatman says the other man nodded to Sedbury, but they didn't shake hands."

"Well, Sedbury wouldn't, would he?" Bryan said. "He barely acknowledged anyone in the ton as an equal."

Stokes continued, "The boatman said the pair faced off about a yard apart, and they talked. The boatman thought the exchange lasted for several back-and-forths, then Sedbury stepped back and flicked out his whip. He paused, then raised the whip and struck at the other man. But the man raised his left arm—the boatman thinks he was wearing leather gauntlets—and the whip wrapped around his forearm, and he wrenched hard, but Sedbury didn't let go. The murderer jerked Sedbury closer and smashed his other fist into Sedbury's face."

Barnaby nodded. "That accounts for the damage to Sedbury's face."

"Yes. And it tells us that the boatman's information is reliable," Stokes said. "Sedbury staggered, but didn't go down. The murderer used the moment to unwind the whip from his arm, then Sedbury flung himself at the man, lashing out with his fists, although the boatman didn't think he managed to land many blows. That said, he didn't stop until the murderer thrust him off, and when he came in again, the murderer looped the whip about Sedbury's throat, stepped behind him, and pulled."

"The boatman saw Sedbury strangled?" Jonathon swallowed.

Stokes waggled his head. "Not quite, and he didn't truly realize what he was seeing until it was all over, because a laden barge passed down the river and cut off his view of the platform for the critical moments. When he could finally see the stairs again, only the other man—our murderer—was still there. He was standing on the edge of the platform and looking into the river downstream, then he turned and walked away into the shadows."

"In which direction did he walk?" Barnaby asked.

Stokes shook his head. "All the boatman could see was him leaving the platform, and he thinks it was more or less in the middle, near the end of Gold Street."

All four of them turned and stared down Gold Street toward the Cole Stairs.

Jonathon huffed. "So the murderer could have gone in any direction—east, west, or north—into the lanes."

No one argued the obvious.

"Well, from all we've learned today," Barnaby observed, "it seems that any number of denizens of this area had excellent reasons for wishing Sedbury dead."

Stokes sighed. "No matter how much he deserved to die, we still need to find the man who actually did the deed."

"A hired killer or someone local?" Barnaby mused. "He could be either."

Jonathon stirred. "Regardless of who he is and how much gratitude I feel he's owed not just by the family but by so many others, I suppose we have to find him in order to clear our own names."

The Hale brothers exchanged glances; neither of them looked all that keen to expose their half brother's murderer.

With his gaze narrowed on the stairs, Barnaby said, "One point we have established is that far from this being a ton matter, the reason Sedbury was murdered almost certainly lies somewhere around here."

The other three looked at him. No one disagreed.

CHAPTER 11

$\mathcal{T}$he enlarged investigative team once again gathered in the drawing room in Barnaby and Penelope's house. Together with their host and hostess, Stokes, Claudia, Charlie, Jonathon, and Bryan had only just settled on the chairs and sofas when the doorbell pealed, and seconds later, the marquess walked in.

Everyone rose, and Penelope and Barnaby welcomed Rattenby and saw him to the armchair by the hearth hurriedly vacated by Jonathon, who moved to the chair between his brother and Stokes.

As everyone resumed their seats, from under heavy lids, Rattenby surveyed them all, then commanded, "Tell me what you've learned."

The question sounded more like a quiz, the marquess's tone hinting that he knew far more about his late heir's less-than-acceptable proclivities and was concerned about how much they'd uncovered.

Stokes responded by inviting Penelope, Claudia, and Charlie to share what they'd learned. "Even though you sent us word, it would be useful to have the critical points restated."

For the marquess's understanding were the words that Stokes didn't need to say.

Penelope shared a glance with Claudia, then opened with "It seems that Sedbury had a liking for what Lady Selborough termed 'roughing it.'"

Her expression severe, Claudia cut in, "By which Aunt Patricia meant indulging in all manner of cruelties and darker dissipations." Her tone rang with haughty disgust.

"Apparently," Penelope continued, "Sedbury had chosen an area by the docks—or at least, somewhere near the river—in which to practice his despicable activities." She looked at Stokes. "Given Duggan's sense that Sedbury was looking forward to his meeting that night, it seems likely that the subject of the meeting was something to do with Sedbury's contemptible deeds in that dockside area."

"So," Charlie concluded, "after he left Pall Mall, his destination might well have been somewhere near the Cole Stairs."

Stokes nodded. "We canvassed the locals in the area surrounding the Cole Stairs and, informed by your report"—he tipped his head to Penelope, Charlie, and Claudia—"we learned that Sedbury had, indeed, taken to treating those in the local area as if they were his serfs."

Barnaby confirmed, "Distinctly medieval behavior of the most cruel and vicious sort."

"It was as if he'd decided that area was his personal territory, and he could do whatever he pleased. Anything and everything." Jonathon looked almost accusingly at his father, and Barnaby saw the marquess faintly wince.

"Subsequently," Stokes continued imperturbably, "one of Barnaby's lads brought us the jarvey who took Sedbury up in Pall Mall, and the jarvey confirmed that he drove Sedbury directly to an intersection two short blocks north of the Cole Stairs, leaving him there at about a quarter to one o'clock."

Stokes made a show of consulting his notebook, although Barnaby was sure he didn't actually need to refresh his memory. "Subsequently," Stokes went on, "we found three further witnesses to the fight between two men on the Cole Stairs at close to one o'clock. One of those men was Sedbury, the other his murderer. We have a sketchy description of that man—taller and broader than Sedbury, with possibly curly dark hair." Stokes paused, then looked at the marquess. "In terms of motive and even opportunity, our suspects are legion, but courtesy of what we now know, it appears most likely that the reason Sedbury was killed relates to his activities in the area around the Cole Stairs."

The marquess's eyes narrowed. "So not anyone of the ton?"

Stokes calmly replied, "While not impossible, a killer hired by a member of the ton who happened to know enough to lure Sedbury to an area he considered his own to kill him seems considerably less likely." He glanced at his notebook, then raised his gaze and said, "Based on what we now know, our next step is to find Sedbury's killer. He will either be a local or someone known to the locals, and his size and strength will mark him."

Bryan said, "There simply can't be that many men of such a size in that one area."

Stokes nodded. "So at last, we're progressing. I'll have constables crawling all over the area tomorrow, searching for our man."

The marquess studied Stokes, then steepled his fingers before his chin. "I take it, Inspector, that you feel confident in your ability to lay hands on this man."

Stokes paused, then replied, "I would like to say yes, but with us having asked questions about Sedbury all around the area, it's possible he's heard of it, realized we're closing in, and fled. If he has, then catching up with him won't be easy."

Silence lengthened as the marquess and the rest of the company considered that prospect.

Eventually, the marquess lowered his hands and said, "I have thought long and hard about this situation—about the rights and wrongs of it—and subsequently, I consulted with several of my peers, as well as with my wife and sister and her husband." He focused his steely gaze on Stokes. "As much as I would infinitely prefer that you dropped this investigation and left the matter of Sedbury's murder unresolved, I've been counseled that I must, however reluctantly, accept that, in order for the innocent to be cleared of suspicion, we need Sedbury's murderer identified.

"Nevertheless"—the marquess's gaze swept the company—"I wish to make it plain that I am not in the least delighted by the prospect of having Sedbury's distasteful activities investigated and aired for all the world to goggle over. That would rank as a final evil act, one enacted from beyond the grave to adversely impact the futures of his relatives, most especially Jonathon, Bryan, Claudia, Margot, and Conrad."

The marquess paused, and his gaze grew weighty as it circled the faces of the company. "So I caution you all that, while I accept the need to pursue Sedbury's killer, I expect and will continue to insist that all information regarding Sedbury's activities remains closely held, shared only among those who need to know."

Stokes met the marquess's gaze and inclined his head. "I take your point, my lord, and accept your stipulation." He glanced at the others.

"We will do our best to catch the killer with the least possible dust raised." He returned his gaze to the marquess. "Once we have our man, what happens next will be in the hands of the commissioner and the courts."

The marquess held Stokes's gaze, then nodded. "Just so. Very well." He shifted his gaze to Penelope and Barnaby and inclined his head. "Mr. and Mrs. Adair. Inspector. And the rest of you. I will leave you to your deliberations."

He made to rise, but Jonathon held out a staying hand. "One moment, Papa." When the marquess eased back into the chair and looked questioningly Jonathon's way, Jonathon continued, "I wanted to ask..." He broke off and looked at Stokes. "Do you have that letter that Sedbury started to write to me?"

Stokes hunted in his pocket and drew out the folded note. He handed it to Jonathon.

Jonathon unfolded the sheet, read the words again, then huffed. "I thought so." He looked at his father. "Do you remember the Weatherspoons? The family that had the smithy in Rattenby village?"

The marquess frowned. "I remember them, yes."

Jonathon looked around at the others. "I've been racking my brain over who Sedbury might have meant with his reference to a 'little maid,' and finally, I remembered the bit about the pigtails." He looked at his father. "The only pretty little maid with pigtails that I ever had my eye on was Weatherspoon's daughter. But they left Rattenby years ago, while I was at Oxford. Do you know where they went?"

The marquess took his time before he replied, "No." He continued to stare at his son; it seemed obvious the marquess was debating how much to reveal. Eventually, he said, "I don't know where they went, but I know why they went."

When he didn't elaborate, Stokes gently prompted, "And why was that?"

The marquess sighed. "This was back...it must be eight years ago. I was surprised to hear that Weatherspoon was selling the forge and the business—his family had been blacksmiths in Rattenby since before my father was born. By the time I heard of it, he'd sold up, but he did come to see me before he and his daughter left, to tell me why he was going." The marquess's gaze returned to Jonathon. "Unbeknown to me, Jonathon had been...flirting with the girl. Weatherspoon's wife had died long ago, and the girl was all the family he had left. Unsurprisingly, he was protective of her, and he'd noticed Jonathon hanging around. And when Jonathon returned to his studies, Weatherspoon learned that the girl was harboring unrealistic dreams of becoming a lady... Well, the man was solid, respectable, and above all sensible. He was a working man, at his forge most of the day—he could never hope to keep an eye on his daughter all the time. So he decided to take her out of harm's way. That was why they left the village."

The marquess paused, then went on, "I thanked him most sincerely and bestowed a sizeable parting gift. Oh, he hadn't come hoping for anything of the sort—I had to insist he take it. He'd come to tell me because he'd felt the family quitting the village without any explanation to me was rude. As I said, he was a solid, decent man."

Jonathon looked faintly aghast. "I had no idea..."

"No," the marquess replied. "In my experience, young gentlemen rarely do. You don't think through the consequences of your actions."

"Oh, God." Jonathon paled and looked down at the note in his hand. His fist clenched. "So it's my fault if Sedbury..."

"No." Barnaby spoke decisively. "When it comes to Sedbury's actions, the only person at fault is Sedbury himself."

"Indeed." Penelope looked at Jonathon. "How old was the Weatherspoon daughter when they left the village?"

Jonathon swallowed and frowned. "Fifteen, I think." He raised tortured eyes to Penelope's face. "She was sweet and innocent and very pretty in that fresh-faced country way."

Thinking aloud, Barnaby said, "So on Saturday afternoon, we have Sedbury starting a letter to Jonathon about the Weatherspoon girl. What prompted him to commence writing that letter at that time?" He glanced at Penelope. "Was there a reason the Weatherspoon girl was on his mind?"

Rather grimly, Penelope returned, "What you mean is, was the meeting arranged for that night something to do with the Weatherspoon girl?" She looked around the circle of faces. "If so, that might explain why Sedbury left the letter unfinished—he expected to have more to add to it later." She looked at Stokes. "After he returned from the meeting."

Stokes stared back, then sat up. "He was meeting with Weatherspoon." Stokes looked at the marquess. "You said Weatherspoon is a blacksmith. How large is he? Taller than Sedbury?"

The marquess was nodding, but it seemed most unhappily. "He is a very large man."

Stokes got to his feet. "So it's likely to be Weatherspoon we're searching for. A very large man, possibly still a blacksmith. I'll get the word out to my men and, through them, to our informants on the docks." He nodded to the marquess. "No need to make it a hue and cry. If Weatherspoon's been living in that area, he'll be known, and even if he has run, we will, at least, know he's our man."

With the briefest of nods to the company, Stokes strode from the room.

The others exchanged glances, then rose and followed more slowly, all wondering and pondering about what would come next.

The following morning, having heard nothing from Stokes in the interim, Barnaby and Penelope were enjoying a quiet and peaceful breakfast and trying not to speculate over what the day would bring or whether they should head for the docks to be in on the end of the case when the doorbell pealed, and seconds later, Stokes—looking very much as if he hadn't slept at all, but was nonetheless relieved—walked into the room.

With the barest of nods in greeting, he drew out a chair and slumped into it. "One of our snitches finally told us what we wanted to know." He helped himself to a crumpet.

Along with Penelope, Barnaby remained silent and waited for more; never before had he felt more empathy for his wife's impatience.

Stokes took a large bite of the crumpet, chewed, swallowed, then went on, "The entire population of the docks was beyond reluctant to even tell us if Weatherspoon lived in the area, much less give us his address. When any of my men uttered the name Weatherspoon, everyone—even our most reliable chatterers—buttoned their lips. More, they grew stony and hard of hearing. We'd been asking for most of the night and got nowhere until we spoke with one of those who has more reason than most to keep us sweet. As he put it, and I quote, 'How's a man to make a living with all you rozzers clomping about?'"

Penelope leaned forward. "So, what did he tell you? Is Weatherspoon there?"

"It turns out"—Stokes blotted his lips with a napkin—"that Weatherspoon is the owner and publican of the Drunken Duck."

"The pub in the lane just up from the Cole Stairs?" Barnaby clarified.

Stokes nodded. "That's the one. And although Weatherspoon knows we've been searching all around—a constable questioned him and his helpers early on—it seems he's stayed put. Yesterday evening, before I'd got the word down there, Morgan had a pint in the Drunken Duck, and he said the man behind the bar matches the description we got from the boatman and had a slightly bruised face. But he's a publican and is constantly wading in to stop fights, so Morgan didn't get too excited over that."

Barnaby grinned. "I bet Morgan's excited now."

Stokes nodded. "He volunteered to keep an eye on the place for the rest of the night, although if Weatherspoon's made no move to leave yet, I doubt he'll bolt now. O'Donnell's rounding up some experienced men and will meet us near the stairs."

Barnaby raised his coffee cup. "So when are we leaving?"

Stokes eyed the half-filled platters before him. "How about as soon as I've soothed my hunger pangs."

Penelope huffed, drained her teacup, set it down with a *clink*, and rose. "Five minutes," she declared and bustled out.

Barnaby smiled and sipped while Stokes dutifully applied himself to the ham and eggs.

Six minutes later, the three of them walked down the front steps to where Penelope's carriage stood waiting by the curb. They gained the pavement only to be hailed by Charlie, who was heading their way with Claudia, Jonathon, and Bryan.

"Ho!" Charlie called. "Where are you off to?"

The four lengthened their strides, patently eager to join the investigators.

Claudia said, "We were just coming to see what you thought we should do next."

Stokes exchanged a resigned look with Barnaby, then explained that they'd located Weatherspoon.

Naturally, Jonathon, Bryan, Charlie, and Claudia insisted on being a part of the expedition to the Drunken Duck. With no way of deterring let alone denying the four, Stokes reluctantly agreed, and when Barnaby tipped his head toward their carriage, Penelope promptly climbed up. As Barnaby and Stokes prepared to follow, Jonathon hailed a passing hackney, and Charlie did the same.

Charlie called to Barnaby, "Lead on—we'll follow."

With a nod and an inward sigh, Barnaby climbed into the carriage and sat beside Penelope, and as soon as Stokes was aboard, the carriage rattled off.

~

The bells had just finished pealing for ten o'clock when their company joined a bevy of uniformed policemen gathered at the corner of the lane within sight of the Drunken Duck's front door.

Morgan had been waiting for them and promptly reported, "No sign of activity inside the place." He looked toward the pub. "But apparently, that's normal. According to other locals, he usually opens his door sometime after eleven."

Barnaby glanced at the buildings around them. Many were already alive with the hustle and bustle of a working day. "It's likely Weatherspoon's up and about, but keeping his door and shutters closed against any early drinkers."

"Is there a rear entrance?" Stokes asked.

Morgan nodded. "Into a yard, and from that, into a runnel at the rear of the buildings."

Stokes sent three beefy constables to wait in the runnel in case Weatherspoon tried to flee.

Given that Stokes kept both O'Donnell and Morgan with their group, Barnaby concluded that Stokes thought Weatherspoon fleeing wasn't at all likely and had to agree. The man had stayed put so far; he was clearly not disposed to run.

Stokes gave the constables five minutes to get into position—five minutes their group spent in impatient fidgeting—then, flanked by O'Donnell and Morgan, Stokes walked down the lane. With Penelope by his side, Barnaby followed, and the rest of their company trailed behind them.

Barnaby noticed that several others who had been in the lane stopped what they were doing and watched. He had to wonder how the locals would take the arrest of one of their own—one, moreover, who, if their reluctance to identify him was anything to judge by, seemed to be respected by many—but Stokes had brought a sizeable force. Ten more constables followed their group down the lane, taking up positions here and there, plainly on guard against any interference.

Stokes reached the Drunken Duck and halted before the door. Morgan stepped forward and thumped his fist on the panel, but refrained from announcing them as police.

They waited. Barnaby wasn't sure any of them were breathing and certainly not deeply.

Then the sound of bolts being drawn back reached them.

The door swung open, revealing a massive bear of a man filling the entryway. Taller than Jonathon definitely, and much more heavily built, that this man had been a blacksmith for most of his life wasn't hard to believe. Despite the shadows, Barnaby confirmed that Weatherspoon had curly dark hair, streaked here and there with gray.

Weatherspoon stared, his gaze swiftly taking them in. His eyes widened a fraction on seeing Jonathon and Bryan, then he looked at Stokes and grunted. "Wondered when you'd get here." He tipped his head into the pub. "Best come inside."

Weatherspoon turned and retreated into the dimness. Stokes threw a glance of mild surprise at Barnaby and followed.

Their host led them into a large taproom. The heavy black-painted beams running across the smoke-stained ceiling made Barnaby want to duck, but although the atmosphere still smelled faintly of hops and stale ale, enough air had seeped through the slatted shutters during the night to alleviate the worst of the fug.

Weatherspoon pulled upturned chairs off the round tables and set them on the floor, creating a large circle around one of the tables nearest the bar. Only once everyone who had ventured inside and wished to sit had claimed seats did Weatherspoon pull up a chair for himself and settle his bulk upon it. He didn't react when O'Donnell and Morgan drifted as unobtrusively as they could to stand behind him. Instead, Weatherspoon —like the rest of him, his head and features were large, but his face gave the impression of being comfortably worn, and his brown eyes held no hint of either shame or malice—focused his clear-eyed gaze on Stokes and said, "Right, then. What do you want to know?"

In the silence that followed the simple question, Penelope studied Weatherspoon. He was truly huge, with massively muscled arms straining the sleeves of his cloth jacket, and his hands, clasped in his lap, looked more than adequate to the task of strangling a brute bigger than Jonathon.

She was on Stokes's left, sitting a little way back from the table across which Weatherspoon faced them. The others were still settling in their seats when a faint creak reached her ears, and she glanced toward the alcove that screened the front door just in time to see a shadow slide inside—a very tall man moving slowly and carefully.

Penelope turned back to the table. The company had been focused on Weatherspoon; no one else seemed to have noticed the interloper. As she had a very good idea of his identity, she made no comment and gave her attention to the proceedings as Stokes commenced by asking, "Did you strangle Viscount Sedbury on the Cole Stairs just before one o'clock on Sunday morning?"

Weatherspoon thought, then slowly nodded. "I did. He set on me with his whip. He struck at me first. I took the whip off him, and then he came at me like a vicious animal. He wasn't going to stop until he had that whip and was beating me with it—according to him, like a misbegotten cur, until I was dead." Weatherspoon lifted his huge shoulders in a faint shrug. "So I ended it. I had the whip in my hands, and I looped it about his throat and hung on. Didn't have to do much more than that, and then he was dead, and I let his body slide into the water, threw that blasted whip away, and came home."

Weatherspoon paused, then, his gaze level, went on. "Can't say as I'm sorry. He was a blight on the lives of all hereabouts, and I'm glad he's gone."

Penelope glanced around, but no one protested. In fact, the comment elicited several small nods.

Barnaby, seated on Stokes's other side, said, "You came to meet him at the stairs. Did you arrange that or did he?"

"He sent me a note by errand boy telling me to meet him there at half past twelve that night. He was late, but with him, that was par for the course. Lesser mortals had to wait on his convenience."

"Do you have the note?" Stokes asked, his tone suggesting he held little hope of that.

But Weatherspoon nodded. "Aye. Happens I do." He reached into his pocket and drew out a crumpled sheet. He regarded it for a moment. "Meant to throw it away, but didn't get around to it." He held it out over the table to Stokes. "For what it's worth."

Penelope suspected that as matters were unfolding, the note might be worth Weatherspoon's life. If Sedbury had summoned him and come armed with a whip, which he'd used and, when denied, he'd refused to back away... That surely had to qualify as self-defense.

Stokes accepted the note, smoothed it out, read it, then handed it to Penelope, who was their writing expert. Swiftly, she scanned the bold strokes. "This is definitely in Sedbury's hand." For the others—including the one lurking in the shadows by the door—she read, "'Meet me at the Cole Stairs at twelve-thirty on Sunday morning. I'm prepared to discuss your proposition.'"

Penelope looked at Weatherspoon, and before Stokes could, asked, "What proposition was that?"

Weatherspoon's gaze shifted to Jonathon, seated a little way beyond Barnaby. Weatherspoon regarded Jonathon for a moment, then returned his attention to Barnaby, Stokes, and Penelope. It was to her he said, "I wrote to him last week. About my daughter, Millie." He glanced again at Jonathon, then refocused on Penelope and said, "My wife died long ago, and Millie was all I had left. Back when I was the blacksmith in Rattenby village, when Millie was just blooming, I saw the interest yon lordling took in her, and then I heard she was getting airs above her station, thinking he'd take her to wife. I knew that wouldn't happen—that nothing good would come of anything between the pair—so when I got a decent offer for the business, I took it, even though my folks had been black-smiths there for generations. It was the only way I could see to keep Millie safe and give her something new to think about." He paused, then added, "It worked, too. We traveled about a bit, then settled here. The money from the blacksmith's and the extra the marquess had given us allowed me to buy this place. I enjoy company, and although some might think this neighborhood scruffy and down-at-heel, the people here welcomed us and made us feel at home. We were comfortable here."

Then he grimaced. "Well, we were for the years before that devil came strutting around. He—Sedbury—started haunting the area, no idea why, but he's been lording it over people hereabouts for the past two years at least." Weatherspoon's lip curled. "He was an animal. Might have been well-born, nobility and all, but he was a godforsaken animal beneath the skin. Any woman he fancied—anyone at all—he'd simply take. No question, and no such thing as saying no. He didn't know the word. He behaved as if he was our feudal lord, and people seethed, but no one could work out what to do about him, marquess's son that he was. And well he knew that, too—our resentment and our helplessness—and he rejoiced in that as well."

Weatherspoon paused, and his face clouded with anger and grief. "Then he came in here about six months back and spotted Millie. She was just a girl, a good, sweet girl, and that set a match to Sedbury's lust. I—and others about, too—tried our best to keep her safe—" Weatherspoon choked, then determinedly cleared his throat and went on, "He found her alone one day, and he...hurt her. Bad. She had to keep to her bed for more'n a week, just to stop the bleeding. And when she finally got back on her feet, she was never the same. She never recovered. And it came to the point of her not being able to live with what he'd done to her. She took herself off early one morning, while it was still dark, and threw herself into the river."

He paused to wipe a hand beneath his nose. Not so much as a rustle of cloth sounded throughout the room.

"I raged, of course, and then I had so many around here consoling me and telling me their tales. Some were as bad as what he did to Millie. I'd known for a time that there were whispers about some of his doings, but I hadn't heard the whole. But after Millie was gone, I listened to it all." He looked squarely at all three Hales. "Your kin was a monster."

It was Jonathon who, sympathy in his eyes, simply said, "We know."

Weatherspoon studied him for a moment, then looked at Bryan and Claudia. He saw the empathy in their faces and nodded. "Aye. P'rhaps so."

He paused as if gathering his thoughts, then went on, "After a time, I calmed down. I thought long and hard, then I wrote to Sedbury. I listed his crimes against us and asked for restitution. Payment in coin, not just for Millie but for all the others, too. I wrote that if he didn't pay up promptly, I'd take all the stories to Fleet Street and see who might be interested in printing them. I told him he had a week to decide, and he knew where to find me, but if I didn't hear from him by Sunday night, I'd be on my way to Fleet Street the next day."

Barnaby stirred. "So you weren't surprised by his note asking you to meet him?"

Weatherspoon shook his head. "Not surprised, but I wasn't born yesterday, either. I didn't see the likes of him shaking in his boots—at least, not yet. I didn't think he'd just turn up and pay, although I'm sure he'd've had the blunt for what we asked. Still and all, I wasn't surprised he wanted to meet. I expected him to bluster and threaten, and I knew about his whip, so I wore the gauntlets I used in the smithy. I knew they'd stop a whip if he thought to take a crack at me. As he did." He paused, then went on, "I was early to the meeting place. I wasn't sure I trusted him to come alone, but he did. I was standing back in the shadows by the steps when he sauntered down and walked out on the stairs, cool as you please."

In a mild tone, Stokes said, "You and the others around here could have come to the police with your stories."

Weatherspoon snorted. "Not likely. What possible use would that have been? We're just the rats from the docks, and he's a fancy viscount. Even if you lot had believed us—and I'm not saying you wouldn't have, given the number of stories we had to tell—you wouldn't have even been allowed to talk to him. Or if you had, like as not, he'd have claimed it was all lies and turned you around and set you on us—"

Weatherspoon's gaze rose over Stokes's head, and he blinked.

The rest of them turned and watched with varying degrees of surprise as the marquess walked out of the shadows of the entryway. He nodded to Weatherspoon. "Good morning, Weatherspoon." Rattenby picked up a spare chair, lifted it to the table to Barnaby's right, and sat.

Unsurprisingly uncomfortable, Weatherspoon warily inclined his head. "M'lord."

With a glance at Barnaby, Stokes, and Penelope, in an even tone, the marquess said, "As to your expectation that complaints from locals would have fallen on deaf ears, I can't be certain, yet at least in this instance concerning Sedbury, I believe that procedures have changed sufficiently that something would have been done."

The marquess caught Stokes's eye. "Inspector. I arrived in time to hear the entirety of Weatherspoon's confession. As per my earlier reservations regarding this case, I have spoken with the Law Lords"—his gaze shifted to Barnaby, and he inclined his head—"and also with those peers charged with overseeing Scotland Yard, and all have agreed that whatever charges might be laid in relation to Sedbury's death should take into full account any and all mitigating circumstances."

Calmly, the marquess went on, "From what you told me of the evidence previously amassed and what we've heard explained and confirmed by Weatherspoon here, it seems that Sedbury was undoubtedly the aggressor and that in more ways than one. It was Sedbury who caused harm to others, not the reverse, and while that fact fills me with no joy whatsoever, it will come as no surprise to all who were even distantly acquainted with the man he had become. In considering the incident on the Cole Stairs, it was Sedbury who struck the first blow, with his whip no less. In my eyes, and I respectfully suggest in the eyes of any judge and jury of sensible men, Weatherspoon was present because he was driven to put right a manifest wrong—a wrong the authorities should have seen and acted on themselves, but for a multitude of reasons had not—

and in the face of Sedbury's attack, Weatherspoon was forced to defend himself."

The marquess paused, then, in the same even tone, said, "There are any number of people who will testify that Sedbury wasn't one to stand down. He it was who pushed Weatherspoon and prolonged the fight, until Weatherspoon had to act to save his own life." The marquess looked at Barnaby, Stokes, and Penelope. "That is my reading of the essentials of this case. Do you agree?"

Stokes studied the marquess, then allowed, "I see no reason not to agree, but I'm left unsure as to what, in such circumstances, my next actions should be."

The marquess smiled faintly and inclined his head. "In that respect, in light of the circumstances of this particular case, the Law Lords suggested, and the commissioner and the relevant peers agreed, that should matters fall out as in fact they have, then while Scotland Yard should, indeed, trumpet their success in having taken up Sedbury's murderer, possibly mentioning that said murderer was a denizen of the docks, as the victim, namely Sedbury, was the true villain in this case, the charge should be manslaughter in self-defense and that Weatherspoon be left free pending further legal action, which, of course, will never eventuate. The charges will evaporate due to the lack of any willingness to pursue them, and the entire matter will be allowed to fade away. Along with, as far as possible, all memory of Sedbury."

Penelope had to restrain herself from applauding, but, it transpired, the marquess hadn't finished.

He turned to Weatherspoon. "You spoke of seeking retribution for all the suffering Sedbury caused to those in this area. Can I ask you to please consult with those around about and gather the details of all the harms perpetrated by Sedbury that you judge to have truly occurred, then bring the list to me? In gratitude for what you had the courage to do, I will pay all appropriate restitution and gladly. I should have reined the devil in long ago, but I could never work out how to manage it." The marquess held Weatherspoon's gaze, then half bowed. "Thank you. From the bottom of our hearts, my family thanks you. In removing Sedbury from this world, you have acted as the Hand of Justice. By your action, you have freed countless people from the depredations of the monster Sedbury had become. You have removed a millstone from around the neck of my family, one that threatened to sink us all. Never doubt that you have my"—the marquess glanced at his sons and daughter—"and my family's genuine thanks. If beyond this time, you have need of help, know you have only to ask."

Weatherspoon blinked, then in a faintly bewildered tone, replied, "That's very nice of you to say, m'lord, but…" He looked at Stokes.

Stokes faintly smiled. "Those Law Lords the marquess mentioned are the lords who oversee the country's laws. They are the ultimate authority regarding the way the courts and the police operate. If they decree that we should not put you in jail, then we won't. Indeed, I suspect we can't."

Barnaby sensed Stokes had thought the case would end this way for a while and was inwardly pleased it had.

"Good Lord." Weatherspoon blinked, then blinked again as the realization that he would remain a free man sank in.

After a moment during which the others present shared Weatherspoon's relief, the marquess ran his gaze around the company, then stated, "Let us all be clear. Sedbury received nothing more than what he deserved. Weatherspoon and all like him who Sedbury exploited, including my family and many others throughout the ton, were Sedbury's victims. In this case, true justice—not blind but clear-eyed—has been served." He looked around again, then his gaze deflected to the front door, through which the murmurings of a gathering crowd could be heard. The marquess returned his attention to the company. "I suggest the right path for all of us is to accept that and feel vindicated. And now, we should head home to Mayfair and Scotland Yard and allow Weatherspoon here to open his business for the day."

Weatherspoon glanced toward the door, then returned his gaze to the marquess and bobbed his head. "Thank ye, m'lord." He looked around the circle. "I'm thinking them out there will be curious as all get-out. You sure you don't want to leave through the back?"

The prospect was discussed, but in the end, more than anything else to underscore Weatherspoon's continued good standing with the authorities, they elected to depart via the front door and rose to do so.

As they milled, trying to decide on an order of departure, Penelope was heartened to see Jonathon and Bryan shake Weatherspoon's hand and hear Jonathon swear with considerable feeling that if he'd known what would come from it years later, he would never have even looked at Millie.

To his credit, Weatherspoon gruffly conceded that Jonathon could not have known how black-hearted his brother would become.

"Half brother," Jonathon stressed. He glanced at Bryan, then looked at

Weatherspoon. "If you hear of any other woman Sedbury abused, will you please let us know? We'd like to make what amends we can, in Millie's memory as it were, but if we advertise…"

Weatherspoon was touched, but managed a chuckle. "Aye. You'd be paying 'til kingdom come and never knowing the rights of it. Leave it with me, and I'll send word of those I know of once I check with them."

Jonathon and Bryan readily agreed, and Jonathon gave Weatherspoon his address.

Penelope smiled and, happy and content with how matters had played out, took the arm Barnaby, also smiling, offered, and following Stokes, they walked out of the Drunken Duck.

In procession, their company, each smiling and genuinely and openly pleased, emerged through the inn's open doorway. Among the considerable crowd watching, their expressions and attitudes caused some consternation and puzzled whispers, but when Weatherspoon, also smiling, appeared in the doorway and waved them on their way, the brittle tension gripping the onlookers evaporated.

Their party reached the corner of the lane, and from behind them, they heard a barrage of eager questions hurled at Weatherspoon. His rumbling replies were greeted with exclamations of amazement tinged with incredulous disbelief.

As they walked on to where they'd left the carriage, Penelope mused, "Somewhat unexpectedly, I feel deeply content. Despite having a veritable army of suspects, we managed to find our way to the truth."

"And"—Barnaby tipped his head closer to hers—"despite there being no one charged, it was rather uplifting to see justice—as the marquess labeled it, true justice—delivered in such a comprehensive way."

"Exactly! And we were a part of it." Looking ahead, she smiled. "True justice is rare, and we should applaud and savor the experience."

Barnaby grinned. "Hear, hear!"

EPILOGUE

Quite by chance and somewhat unexpectedly, those who had accompanied Penelope and Barnaby from Mayfair to the Drunken Duck to witness the culmination of the search for Viscount Sedbury's murderer reconvened that evening in Lady Conningham's ballroom.

Stokes, of course, wasn't present, but her ladyship's ball was a select affair, and attendance by the likes of the Hales and the Adairs was virtually compulsory.

When, having reached the ballroom's foyer, Penelope and Barnaby approached their host and hostess, Lady Conningham welcomed them with near-rapturous delight. "My dears! We are all *so* relieved!"

The commissioner had been at pains to ensure that the news of Viscount Sedbury's murder had been reconfirmed in the evening news sheets together with the information that Sedbury had instigated a fight in a dockside area and had died as a result of injuries received, and his body tipped into the river. The public had been assured that due to the quick work of Inspector Basil Stokes, assisted by Mr. and Mrs. Adair, the viscount's murderer had been apprehended, and Scotland Yard considered the case successfully closed.

Lord Conningham echoed his wife's sentiments. "Huge weight off so many shoulders, y'know?" He shook Barnaby's hand. "Well done!"

Barnaby and Penelope shared a laughing glance and, after exchanging a few words about their respective families, parted from the Conninghams and descended the stairs to join the throng of other guests.

They had barely gained the ballroom floor when Jonathon materialized from the crowd and, his face lit by a smile that was more relaxed and genuine than anything Penelope had previously seen from him, planted himself before them.

After the briefest of greetings, he said, "We thought you should know —m'father and I went back to the Drunken Duck this afternoon and met with Weatherspoon and settled the matter of restitution over Millie's death." A cloud passed over Jonathon's open face, then he cleared his throat and, raising his chin a trifle, stated, "We also set up a way for Weatherspoon to contact our solicitor in London directly, regarding all the other claims, of which we expect there will be many." He met Penelope's and Barnaby's eyes. "Sedbury was an unmitigated villain, and the family can't just bury the results. We need to set all right, or at least as right as we can."

Penelope smiled encouragingly. "That's commendable and also very wise. The burden of Sedbury's actions should not be a weight you and the others carry forward." She pointed at the black armband Jonathon wore. "Should I take it the family is not going into full mourning?"

Jonathon glanced at the band. "We decided we couldn't be that hypocritical—that false. M'father, Bryan, and I opted for armbands—it's at least an acknowledgment of a death in the family. Mama and Claude have opted to wear muted colors for a month, but none of us felt it appropriate to retreat from society." He smiled. "Not even for one night."

Barnaby nodded. "Impossible to mourn when, in fact, everyone is rejoicing."

"Exactly." Jonathon raised his head; his smile hadn't dimmed. "And of course, it's not just us."

"Indeed," Penelope said. "I seriously doubt that even the most censorious hostess will comment adversely. Too many in the ton know what Sedbury was like, and as you say, in the wake of his passing, society as a whole feels buoyed." Nonetheless, she made a mental note to check with her usual sources.

Barnaby, too, was smiling. "Now that you are your father's heir, what are your thoughts about taking up Sedbury's title?"

Jonathon shuddered. "No, thank you. Luckily, Papa has another I can use, and we've agreed I should simply be Viscount Hale." He smiled.

"And without the bane of Sedbury hanging over my head, I might even be able to venture forth and find a bride."

Penelope beamed. "I predict you'll have no trouble finding a suitable young lady." In fact, she would make sure of it.

Faintly bashful, Jonathon shrugged, and with good wishes all around, they let him go.

Barnaby chuckled softly as they moved into the crowd. "So now you have another challenge before you."

"Pfft!" Penelope responded. "Finding a bride for him now will be more a matter of beating off the unsuitable hordes. Remind me that I must call on the marchioness before she and the marquess leave town."

As it transpired, Penelope didn't have to remember anything.

Ten minutes of wandering through the crowd, many of whom seized the chance to quiz them on the case, brought them face to face with the Rattenbys.

"My dears," the marchioness said as soon as the exchange of greetings was complete, "I want to most sincerely thank you for all your help in resolving this so-distasteful matter. Your assistance in dissipating the ominous cloud that has hung over the family and our children's futures for so long leaves us forever in your debt."

Rattenby nodded. "Quite so. I have to say I was deeply impressed by the dogged team effort that prevailed." His gray gaze was shrewd as it rested on Barnaby's and Penelope's faces. "You and Inspector Stokes have formed a formidable partnership, and for that, you are to be congratulated."

They would have politely demurred, but the marchioness leapt in to say, "As I told Gerrard"—she clasped her husband's arm—"paying restitution is all very well and should definitely be done, but that's in the nature of putting the past to rest, and we should, in all thanks, also do something, take some positive step, that will impact the future." The marchioness arched her brows inquiringly. "I've been told, Penelope, that you have interests in various charities, and I wondered if you could direct us toward one that might suit our purpose."

Penelope didn't have to think. "Actually"—she shot a glance at Barnaby—"Barnaby's lads' network was instrumental, critically so, in solving the Sedbury case, and I believe the time has come to discuss setting up a foundation, one that would encourage the brightest lads to further their development by underwriting their employment in, for instance, the police force or the inquiry agency business." She looked at the Rattenbys. "We have excellent contacts in both fields, and some of the lads have the potential to go far. They really are quite bright."

Rattenby was nodding, and the marchioness looked eager.

Regarding his wife with a faintly fascinated smile, Barnaby admitted, "Assistance with their living expenses for their first years of employment would go a long way to encouraging them to pursue further advancement."

Rattenby gave a more decisive nod. "By all means, let's pursue that tack. Perhaps we can call on you in the coming days, before we return to Gloucestershire."

They made arrangements to meet the next week, then parted, and Barnaby guided Penelope on.

"That was an excellent idea," Barnaby murmured, his eyes dancing. "Have you been incubating it for long?"

Smiling brightly, Penelope admitted, "Only since this case. The lads were such a help, it seems foolish not to advance your network onto a more formal footing."

Soon after, through the crowd, they spotted several of her usual sources gathered on long sofas at the end of the room. Knowing that a report would be expected, she and Barnaby dutifully presented themselves to the older ladies and meekly submitted to their inquisition.

When the exclamations and congratulations came to an end and Penelope inquired as to how the Hales' rejection of mourning was being received, Lady Osbaldestone was quick to reassure her, "No need to worry on that score. Everyone else is so relieved, we're all quite happy to see the family regaining their feet, as it were."

Horatia confided, "We're hoping to convince Georgina Hale that she should join us in London more often."

Relieved that, on the social front, all was well, Penelope and Barnaby moved on.

The strains of a waltz rose over the guests' heads, and after exchanging a glance, they made their way to the dance floor.

Once they were revolving, circling the cleared space, Barnaby surveyed the other dancers, then dipped his head to tell Penelope, "Look ahead. Three couples on."

He waited for her reaction and wasn't disappointed.

"Great heavens!" She leaned back in his arms to peer around the intervening pairs at the couple in question. "That really is Charlie! He's waltzing! I've never been sure he could, much less would."

"It seems," Barnaby said, equally amused by her comments and by seeing his friend circling rather carefully with Claudia, "that he merely needed the right encouragement."

"I did wonder." Penelope settled in Barnaby's arms and fixed her gaze on his face. "Do you think he's truly taken with Claudia? Because she's so…well, managing, I wasn't sure that she hadn't merely conscripted Charlie for the duration, as it were, so that via him, she could remain involved in the investigation, and that once we solved the case, she would calmly bid him goodbye, and that would be the end of it."

His gaze returning to Charlie and Claudia, Barnaby smiled. "That doesn't appear to be the case. If anything, they seem equally smitten. I believe we can reasonably expect an invitation in due course."

Penelope beamed. "Wonderful! And for once, I didn't have to prod anyone." She glanced at the crowd around them. "Lady Conningham will be ecstatic, and so will Mrs. Hastings! They're quite good friends, which is another nice touch."

"Indeed." Barnaby gathered his wife closer as they went through the turn and, knowing her as he did, wondered what she would do next regarding Charlie and Claudia.

Sure enough, when the music ended and the dancers halted, Penelope all but towed him across to where Charlie and Claudia stood.

They exchanged delighted greetings, then supper was announced, and with the bulk of the guests, the four of them moved into the supper room. By dint of superior strategy, they secured a table for four in one corner and settled to nibble on the delicacies provided, sip champagne, and catch up with the ramifications of the revelations gained at the Drunken Duck.

"I cannot adequately describe," Claudia said, "the depth of the relief that everyone in the family is feeling. Aunt Patricia was so affected, she actually cried. What with being constantly in town, I believe she'd sensed for longer than anyone that Sedbury had gone quite beyond the pale, and she'd been so worried he would do something that would bring the entire family down, but of course, she felt helpless to do anything about it."

Charlie put in, "Even your uncle described the event—Sedbury's death without any ensuing scandal—as having lifted a pall from not just your family but his household as well."

"I think," Claudia said, "that we'd all grown so accustomed to the pressure, to the weight of Sedbury's threat, that having that suddenly removed has left us all feeling light and airy and rather giddy." She smiled at Charlie. "You know what I mean."

Penelope watched Charlie readily nod and smiled to herself. Barnaby had been right in thinking wedding bells featured in Claudia and Charlie's future.

Charlie turned to Penelope and Barnaby. "Here, I say, as the original prime suspect, I want to thank you both for steering our ship through this case. I'm truly grateful you were there for me to appeal to. I don't know what I—or Stokes, for that matter—would have done without you."

Penelope smiled, and smiling, too, Barnaby replied, "You're very welcome, and we enjoyed the challenge."

Penelope quipped, "Do feel free to bring any future accusations and crimes to our door."

Claudia shuddered. "I sincerely hope to never be involved in a murder investigation again."

Penelope shared a smile with Barnaby and made no comment.

Charlie said, "I was talking with Napier earlier, and he, too, was hugely relieved to learn that the Sedbury case is closed. He pointed out that there's no saying how many Sedbury blackmailed over the years and knowing that the threat of his continued malevolence has been permanently removed will, in all likelihood, be a huge blessing to a large number of our peers."

With a proud smile for Charlie, Claudia said, "Lord Napier and Charlie have suggested that the family consider donating Sedbury's whip collection to a museum."

"Or perhaps the Jockey Club," Charlie said, faintly coloring under Claudia's regard. "Some place like that where the collection will be appreciated."

"Given the collection is of whips, the Jockey Club might be best." Penelope looked at Barnaby.

He nodded. "And if you do decide on approaching the Jockey Club or the British Museum, do remember we have connections at both, which might be of some help."

"Thank you." Claudia looked a touch relieved. "We'll likely take you up on that. I'll tell Jonathon—Papa put him in charge of the dispersal of Sedbury's possessions."

With supper consumed, they rose and strolled back into the ballroom. At Penelope's suggestion, she and Claudia parted from the men and went in search of the ladies' withdrawing room.

Once in the corridor and away from any interested ears, Penelope asked, "What are your plans? Will you remain in London or accompany your parents on their return to Rattenby?"

Claudia met Penelope's eyes, then drew breath and said, "I wanted to ask—you're in a position to advise me—would Charlie Hastings be considered a suitable match for me?"

Penelope could barely contain her delight. "He would, indeed. The Hastingses might not carry a title—or at least, his branch don't—but the family is ancient. Indeed, they're every bit as much a part of the fabric of English nobility as the Hales or the Adairs."

Claudia exhaled in relief. "Thank goodness. I suddenly wondered if I was...well, drawing him along a path that ultimately couldn't lead anywhere."

Penelope pressed Claudia's hand. "Speak to your mother. I'm sure she'll be encouraging."

"I'm hoping to be able to invite Charlie to visit Rattenby next month," Claudia confided. "We have quite good shooting, and a shooting party might be the right sort of event to introduce him to the wider family."

"An excellent notion," Penelope concurred. "I know he's quite a good shot."

They'd reached the withdrawing room and had to pause their confidences while there were other ladies around. But when they were on their way back to the ballroom and once again alone, Claudia said, "I've been waiting for years to find a suitable gentleman, but with Sedbury hovering, I never felt able to step forward. It seems quite ironic that it was Sedbury's murder that brought me and Charlie together."

Penelope smiled and nodded. "Ironic, indeed. In the best way."

Smiling in faintly bemused fashion, Claudia shook her head. "While I've been hoping to find a husband, until I met Charlie, I'd never met a man with whom I could imagine living a future life, but Charlie... I find him restful yet entertaining and, overall, rather absorbing."

"That's a very good recommendation," Penelope said as they stepped back into the crowded ballroom. "Now, where are our men?"

The men in question, being more than experienced enough not to stand still and invite others to approach them, had been idly strolling around the perimeter of the large room. They'd discussed this and that, but being such old friends, they were also comfortable sharing long silences.

Breaking one such silence, Charlie confided, "With Claudia, you know, I can see the path she and I are strolling amiably along, and I understand where that path inevitably leads. Yet despite that knowledge, to my astonishment, I don't feel like fleeing." He tipped his head to glance at Barnaby and met his eyes. "That's telling, isn't it? It says something, y'know?"

Barnaby had to work to mute his smile. "I do, indeed." Unable to resist, he clapped Charlie on the shoulder. "Good luck, old man, and I fully expect to shortly be saying 'Welcome to the club.'"

Charlie grinned rather foolishly. "Well, then. Onward we go."

Later, when he and Charlie had been found by their respective ladies just in time to join the couples on the dance floor in another waltz, Barnaby looked into his wife's shining eyes. "It seems Charlie and Claudia are inching toward a declaration."

Penelope's smile was reminiscent of a cat that had devoured an entire jug of cream. "They are." She sighed deeply. "And I couldn't be happier for them. I predict they'll make an excellent match."

Barnaby smiled and kept them whirling.

A few revolutions later, Penelope sighed again, this time with even deeper satisfaction.

Barnaby looked into her face and cocked an inquiring brow.

She smiled in obvious contentment. "It's so lovely when cases turn out just right."

Two days later, Barnaby and Penelope were enjoying a leisurely breakfast when the doorbell rang. Both tilted their heads, listening, and heard a familiar voice greet Mostyn, then, seconds later, Stokes walked in.

Smiling, he nodded to them both. "Good morning, you two."

Occupied with a mouthful of eggs, Barnaby nodded.

"And to you," Penelope returned and waved Stokes to the third chair at the table.

He drew out the chair and sat before the third place setting Mostyn had got into the habit of laying just in case Stokes turned up. Stokes eyed the platters, then helped himself.

Penelope waited, curious as to what had brought him there. If it had been a case, he'd have said by now, so...

After savoring his first mouthful and thanking Mostyn, who had hurried in to fill his coffee cup, Stokes turned his gaze on his hosts. "I cannot convey with sufficient emphasis how sincerely relieved and, indeed, happy the commissioner is with the outcome of the Sedbury case. Apparently, the marquess has heaped laurels on all our heads and impressed on the commissioner that, despite the case having more to do with those who live on the docks than those who inhabit Mayfair, the contributions made by the pair of you and your supporters were crucial to our joint success."

Stokes met their gazes. "When appealed to for my opinion, I echoed the marquess's accolades." His smile deepened. "You may now expect to be called upon with even greater frequency, and I've been informed that, henceforth, I should consider drawing you in as consultants even if the case has no connection to higher society."

Barnaby arched his brows. "Is that so?"

Stokes nodded.

"How intriguing," Penelope said, her tone indicating that she was already scheming.

Stokes waved his fork. "The commissioner suggested that any, in his words, twisty case would, in his view, be a candidate for your attention." Stokes looked across the table and smiled. "So how do you feel about making yourselves available on a wider basis?" He reached for his cup and took a sip, watching them over the rim.

Penelope looked at Barnaby, read the naked interest in his eyes, and let her very real enthusiasm show.

She turned her gaze on Stokes. "With the obvious contingency of family demands, I'm sure we can manage to make time should you have more twisty mysteries to solve."

Stokes lowered his cup, and his smile broke slow and deep. "Excellent." He set down the cup. "In that case..."

Dear Reader,

When writing a novel, occasionally, I have the title in mind from the start. More frequently, the title suggests itself as the story take shape as being the obvious description for that particular book. Such was the case here, with Dead Beside the Thames being the first point known about the murder, but also the crucial, critical clue to solving the murder.

Villains, I might add, take just as much, if not more, time to develop than the storyline. Indeed, you can't have one without the other, and quite often, learning the character of the villain requires deep diving into the psychology of the darker soul. Again, that was especially the case here, in creating a villain everyone who knew him despised.

I must admit I'm having a ball following the fresh cases that are arising—ore more accurately that my imagination dreams up—to confront and challenge Barnaby, Penelope, and Stokes. I hope you enjoyed the latest installment.

My next release will be another investigative foray with Barnaby, Penelope, and Stokes, when the trio are simultaneously called upon by Salisbury City Police and Henry, Lord Glossup, of Glossup Hall in Dorset, to solve the puzzling mystery of a lady who lives in a tiny village who has been discovered strangled in her own front parlor. Henry has been accused of the murder, but while the evidence is both weak and circumstantial, in this case more than any other, the local gossips will have their day.

Information about earlier volumes in THE CASEBOOK OF BARNABY ADAIR series—*Where the Heart Leads, The Peculiar Case of Lord Finsbury's Diamonds, The Masterful Mr. Montague, The Curious Case of Lady Latimer's Shoes, Loving Rose: The Redemption of Malcolm Sinclair, The Confounding Case of the Carisbrook Emeralds, The Murder at Mandeville Hall* and *The Meriwell Legacy*—can be found following, along with details of my other recent release.

Barnaby, Penelope, Stokes, Griselda, and their families, friends, and supporters continue to thrive. I hope they and their adventures solving mysteries and exposing villains will continue to entertain you in the future just as much as they do me.

Enjoy!

Stephanie.

For alerts as new books are released, plus information on upcoming books, exclusive sweepstakes and sneak peeks into upcoming novels, sign up for Stephanie's Private Email Newsletter http://www.stephanielaurens.com/newsletter-signup/

Or if you don't have time to chat and want a quick email alert, sign up and follow me at BookBub https://www.bookbub.com/authors/stephanie-laurens

The ultimate source for detailed information on all Stephanie's published books, including covers, descriptions, and excerpts, is Stephanie's Website www.stephanielaurens.com

You can also follow Stephanie via her Amazon Author Page at http://tinyurl.com/zc3e9mp

Goodreads members can follow Stephanie via her author page https://www.goodreads.com/author/show/9241.Stephanie_Laurens

You can email Stephanie at stephanie@stephanielaurens.com

Or find her on Facebook
https://www.facebook.com/AuthorStephanieLaurens/

COMING NEXT:
MARRIAGE AND MURDER
The Casebook of Barnaby Adair #10
To be released in March, 2025.

Five years ago, Henry, Lord Glossup, was suspected of murdering his late wife. Although he was exonerated and the true murderer caught, Henry has been accused of murdering a lady again, in the same fashion. He appeals to Barnaby and Penelope for help, as does Stokes who, having been the inspector in charge of the previous case, is tasked with solving the current one. The investigators soon establish that the evidence implicating Henry is flimsy and circumstantial, and his alibi is easily verified. But that leaves them, along with the sister of the deceased, to unravel the tangled puzzle of who strangled Viola Huntingdon and was it the secret admirer she referred to only as 'H?'

Available for pre-order by October, 2025.

RECENTLY RELEASED:
The eighth volume in
The Casebook of Barnaby Adair mystery-romances
THE MERIWELL LEGACY

#1 NYT-bestselling author Stephanie Laurens returns with her favorite sleuths to unravel a tangled web of family secrets and expose a murderer.

When Lord Meriwell collapses and dies at his dining table, Barnaby and Penelope Adair are summoned, along with Inspector Basil Stokes, to discover who, how, and most importantly why someone very close to his lordship saw fit to poison him.

When Lord Meriwell dies at his dining table, Nurse Veronica Haskell suspects foul play and notifies his lordship's doctor, eminent Harley Street specialist Dr. David Sanderson. In turn, compelled by a need to protect Veronica who is at Meriwell Hall as David's behest, David calls on his friends Barnaby and Penelope Adair for assistance.

However, as the fateful dinner was the first of a house party being attended by the local MP and his family, the Metropolitan Police commissioners also consider the Adairs' presence desirable, and consequently, Barnaby and Penelope accompany Stokes to Meriwell Hall.

There, they discover a gathering of the Meriwell family intended to impress the visiting Busseltons so that George Busselton, local MP, will agree to a marriage between his daughter and Lord Meriwell's eldest nephew, Stephen. But instead of any pleasant sojourn, the company find themselves confined to the hall and grounds while Stokes, Barnaby, and Penelope set about interviewing everyone and establishing facts, alibis, and the movements of those in the house.

To our investigators' frustration, while determining the means proves straightforward, and opportunity reduces their suspect list, motive remains elusive, and their list of suspects stays stubbornly long.

Then the killer strikes again, but even then, the investigators are left with the same suspects and too many potential reasons for the second death.

What did the killer hope to gain?

More importantly, will he kill again?

At last, the investigators stumble on a promising clue, yet following it requires sending to London for information, and their frustration builds.

As the clock ticks and they doggedly forge on, they uncover more and more facts, yet none allows them to identify which of their prime suspects is the murderer.

Will they get the breakthrough they need, one sufficient to exonerate the innocent?

When the answer arrives, they discover that the Meriwell family legacies are more far-reaching than anyone realized, and that the crimes involved and the motivation for the murders is far more heinous than anyone imagined.

A historical novel of 78,000 words interweaving mystery and murder with a touch of romance.

A FAMILY OF HIS OWN
Cynster Next Generation Novel #15

#1 New York Times bestselling author Stephanie Laurens returns to the quintessential question of what family means to a Cynster in this tale of the last unmarried member of the Cynster Next Generation and the final mission that opens his eyes.

Toby Cynster is not amused when informed that his new mission is to be his last in the shadowy service of Drake, Marquess of Winchelsea. Courtesy of Toby being the last unmarried Cynster of his generation and the consequent martial obsession of his female relatives, he will be given no more excuses to avoid society and, instead, expected to devote himself to finding a suitable bride. But Toby sees no point in marrying—thanks to his siblings, he has plenty of nephews and nieces with whom to play favorite uncle, and he has no thoughts of establishing a family of his own.

But then the mission takes an unexpected turn, leaving Toby to escort the irritatingly fascinating Diana Locke plus the three young children of a dying Englishman from Vienna to England.

Diana is no more enthused about their journey than Toby, but needs must, and forever practical, she bows to events and makes the best of things for her godchildren's sakes. She's determined to see them to safety in England and does her best to ignore her nonsensical and annoying awareness of Toby.

But then their journey becomes a flight from deadly pursuit, and their most effective disguise is to pass themselves off as a family—the sort of family Toby had been certain he would never want. Through a succession of fraught adventures, Toby, Diana, and the children lean on each other and grow and mature while furthering their ultimate aim of reaching England safely, and along the way, Toby and Diana both learn what having a family actually means to them, individually and together, and each discovers the until-then-missing foundation stone of their future lives.

A classic historical adventure romance that sprawls across Europe to end in the leafy depths of the English countryside. A Cynster Next Generation novel. A full-length historical romance of 108,000 words.

PREVIOUSLY RELEASED IN THE CASEBOOK OF BARNABY ADAIR NOVELS:

Read about Penelope's and Barnaby's romance, plus that of Stokes and Griselda, in
The first volume in
The Casebook of Barnaby Adair mystery-romances
WHERE THE HEART LEADS

Penelope Ashford, Portia Cynster's younger sister, has grown up with every advantage - wealth, position, and beauty. Yet Penelope is anything but a typical ton miss - forceful, willful and blunt to a fault, she has for years devoted her considerable energy and intelligence to directing an institution caring for the forgotten orphans of London's streets.

But now her charges are mysteriously disappearing. Desperate, Penelope turns to the one man she knows who might help her - Barnaby Adair.

Handsome scion of a noble house, Adair has made a name for himself in political and judicial circles. His powers of deduction and observation combined with his pedigree has seen him solve several serious crimes within the ton. Although he makes her irritatingly uncomfortable, Penelope throws caution to the wind and appears on his bachelor doorstep late one night, determined to recruit him to her cause.

Barnaby is intrigued—by her story, and her. Her bold beauty and undeniable brains make a striking contrast to the usual insipid ton misses. And as he's in dire need of an excuse to avoid said insipid misses, he accepts her challenge, never dreaming she and it will consume his every waking hour.

Enlisting the aid of Inspector Basil Stokes of the fledgling Scotland Yard, they infiltrate the streets of London's notorious East End. But as they unravel the mystery of the missing boys, they cross the trail of a criminal embedded in the very organization recently created to protect all Londoners. And that criminal knows of them and their efforts, and is only too ready to threaten all they hold dear, including their new-found knowledge of the intrigues of the human heart.

FURTHER CASES AND THE EVOLUTION OF RELATIONSHIPS CONTINUE IN:

The second volume in
The Casebook of Barnaby Adair mystery-romances
THE PECULIAR CASE OF LORD FINSBURY'S DIAMONDS

#1 New York Times *bestselling author Stephanie Laurens brings you a tale of murder, mystery, passion, and intrigue – and diamonds!*

Penelope Adair, wife and partner of amateur sleuth Barnaby Adair, is so hugely pregnant she cannot even waddle. When Barnaby is summoned to assist Inspector Stokes of Scotland Yard in investigating the violent murder of a gentleman at a house party, Penelope, frustrated that she cannot participate, insists that she and Griselda, Stokes's wife, be duly informed of their husbands' discoveries.

Yet what Barnaby and Stokes uncover only leads to more questions. The murdered gentleman had been thrown out of the house party days before, so why had he come back? And how and why did he come to have the fabulous Finsbury diamond necklace in his pocket, much to Lord Finsbury's consternation. Most peculiar of all, why had the murderer left the necklace, worth a stupendous fortune, on the body?

The conundrums compound as our intrepid investigators attempt to make sense of this baffling case. Meanwhile, the threat of scandal grows ever more tangible for all those attending the house party – and the stakes are highest for Lord Finsbury's daughter and the gentleman who has spent the last decade resurrecting his family fortune so he can aspire to her hand. Working parallel to Barnaby and Stokes, the would-be lovers hunt for a path through the maze of contradictory facts to expose the murderer, disperse the pall of scandal, and claim the love and the shared life they crave.

A pre-Victorian mystery with strong elements of romance. A short novel of 39,000 words.

The third volume in
The Casebook of Barnaby Adair mystery-romances
THE MASTERFUL MR. MONTAGUE

Montague has devoted his life to managing the wealth of London's elite, but at a huge cost: a family of his own. Then the enticing Miss Violet Matcham seeks his help, and in the puzzle she presents him, he finds an intriguing new challenge professionally...and personally.

Violet, devoted lady-companion to the aging Lady Halstead, turns to Montague to reassure her ladyship that her affairs are in order. But the famous Montague is not at all what she'd expected—this man is compelling, decisive, supportive, and strong—everything Violet needs in a champion, a position to which Montague rapidly lays claim.

But then Lady Halstead is murdered and Violet and Montague, aided by Barnaby Adair, Inspector Stokes, Penelope, and Griselda, race to expose a cunning and cold-blooded killer...who stalks closer and closer. Will Montague and Violet learn the shocking truth too late to seize their chance at enduring love?

A pre-Victorian tale of romance and mystery in the classic historical romance style. A novel of 120,000 words.

The fourth volume in
The Casebook of Barnaby Adair mystery-romances
THE CURIOUS CASE OF LADY LATIMER'S SHOES

#1 New York Times bestselling author Stephanie Laurens brings you a tale of mysterious death, feuding families, star-crossed lovers—and shoes to die for.

With her husband, amateur-sleuth the Honorable Barnaby Adair, decidedly eccentric fashionable matron Penelope Adair is attending the premier event opening the haut ton's Season when a body is discovered in the gardens. A lady has been struck down with a finial from the terrace balustrade. Her family is present, as are the cream of the haut ton—the shocked hosts turn to Barnaby and Penelope for help.

Barnaby calls in Inspector Basil Stokes and they begin their investigation. Penelope assists by learning all she can about the victim's family, and uncovers a feud between them and the Latimers over the fabulous shoes known as Lady Latimer's shoes, currently exclusive to the Latimers.

The deeper Penelope delves, the more convinced she becomes that the murder is somehow connected to the shoes. She conscripts Griselda, Stokes's wife, and Violet Montague, now Penelope's secretary, and the trio set out to learn all they can about the people involved and most importantly the shoes, a direction vindicated when unexpected witnesses report seeing a lady fleeing the scene—wearing Lady Latimer's shoes.

But nothing is as it seems, and the more Penelope and her friends learn about the shoes, conundrums abound, compounded by a Romeo-and-Juliet romance and escalating social pressure...until at last, the pieces fall into place, and finally understanding what has occurred, the six intrepid investigators race to prevent an even worse tragedy.

A pre-Victorian mystery with strong elements of romance. A novel of 76,000 words.

The fifth volume in
The Casebook of Barnaby Adair mystery-romances
LOVING ROSE: THE REDEMPTION OF MALCOLM SINCLAIR

#1 New York Times bestselling author Stephanie Laurens returns with another thrilling story from the Casebook of Barnaby Adair...

Miraculously spared from death, Malcolm Sinclair erases the notorious man he once was. Reinventing himself as Thomas Glendower, he strives to make amends for his past, yet he never imagines penance might come via a secretive lady he discovers living in his secluded manor.

Rose has a plausible explanation for why she and her children are residing in Thomas's house, but she quickly realizes he's far too intelligent to fool. Revealing the truth is impossibly dangerous, yet day by day, he wins her trust, and then her heart.

But then her enemy closes in, and Rose turns to Thomas as the only man who can protect her and the children. And when she asks for his help, Thomas finally understands his true purpose, and with unwavering commitment, he seeks his redemption in the only way he can—through living the reality of loving Rose.

A pre-Victorian tale of romance and mystery in the classic historical romance style. A novel of 105,000 words.

The sixth volume in
The Casebook of Barnaby Adair mystery-romances
THE CONFOUNDING CASE OF THE CARISBROOK
EMERALDS

#1 New York Times *bestselling author Stephanie Laurens brings you a tale of emerging and also established loves and the many facets of family, interwoven with mystery and murder.*
A young lady accused of theft and the gentleman who elects himself her champion enlist the aid of Stokes, Barnaby, Penelope, and friends in pursuing justice, only to find themselves tangled in a web of inter-family tensions and secrets.

When Miss Cara Di Abaccio is accused of stealing the Carisbrook emeralds by the infamously arrogant Lady Carisbrook and marched out of her guardian's house by Scotland Yard's finest, Hugo Adair, Barnaby Adair's cousin, takes umbrage and descends on Scotland Yard, breathing fire in Cara's defense.

Hugo discovers Inspector Stokes has been assigned to the case, and after surveying the evidence thus far, Stokes calls in his big guns when it comes to dealing with investigations in the ton—namely, the Honorable Barnaby Adair and his wife, Penelope.

Soon convinced of Cara's innocence and—given Hugo's apparent tendre for Cara—the need to clear her name, Penelope and Barnaby join Stokes and his team in pursuing the emeralds and, most importantly, who stole them.

But the deeper our intrepid investigators delve into the Carisbrook household, the more certain they become that all is not as it seems. Lady Carisbrook is a harpy, Franklin Carisbrook is secretive, Julia Carisbrook is overly timid, and Lord Carisbrook, otherwise a genial and honorable gentleman, holds himself distant from his family. More, his lordship attempts to shut down the investigation. And Stokes, Barnaby, and Penelope are convinced the Carisbrooks' staff are not sharing all they know.

Meanwhile, having been appointed Cara's watchdog until the mystery is resolved, Hugo, fascinated by Cara as he's been with no other young lady, seeks to entertain and amuse her...and, increasingly intently, to discover the way to her heart. Consequently, Penelope finds herself juggling the attractions of the investigation against the demands of the Adair family for her to actively encourage the budding romance.

What would her mentors advise? On that, Penelope is crystal clear.

Regardless, aided by Griselda, Violet, and Montague and calling on contacts in business, the underworld, and ton society, Penelope, Barnaby, and Stokes battle to peel back each layer of subterfuge and, step by step, eliminate the innocent and follow the emeralds' trail...

Yet instead of becoming clearer, the veils and shadows shrouding the Carisbrooks only grow murkier...until, abruptly, our investigators find themselves facing an inexplicable death, with a potential murderer whose conviction would shake society to its back teeth.

A historical novel of 78,000 words interweaving mystery, romance, and social intrigue.

The seventh volume in
The Casebook of Barnaby Adair mystery-romances
THE MURDER AT MANDEVILLE HALL

#1 NYT-bestselling author Stephanie Laurens brings you a tale of unexpected romance that blossoms against the backdrop of dastardly murder.
On discovering the lifeless body of an innocent ingénue, a peer attending a country house party joins forces with the lady-amazon sent to fetch the victim safely home in a race to expose the murderer before Stokes, assisted by Barnaby and Penelope, is forced to allow the guests, murderer included, to decamp.

Well-born rakehell and head of an ancient family, Alaric, Lord Carradale, has finally acknowledged reality and is preparing to find a bride. But loyalty to his childhood friend, Percy Mandeville, necessitates attending Percy's annual house party, held at neighboring Mandeville Hall. Yet despite deploying his legendary languid charm, by the second evening of the week-long event, Alaric is bored and restless.

Escaping from the soirée and the Hall, Alaric decides that as soon as he's free, he'll hie to London and find the mild-mannered, biddable lady he believes will ensure a peaceful life. But the following morning, on walking through the Mandeville Hall shrubbery on his way to join the other guests, he comes upon the corpse of a young lady-guest.

Constance Whittaker accepts that no gentleman will ever offer for her —she's too old, too tall, too buxom, too headstrong…too much in myriad ways. Now acting as her grandfather's agent, she arrives at Mandeville Hall to extricate her young cousin, Glynis, who unwisely accepted an invitation to the reputedly licentious house party.

But Glynis cannot be found.

A search is instituted. Venturing into the shrubbery, Constance discovers an outrageously handsome aristocrat crouched beside Glynis's lifeless form. Unsurprisingly, Constance leaps to the obvious conclusion.

Luckily, once the gentleman explains that he'd only just arrived, commonsense reasserts itself. More, as matters unfold and she and Carradale have to battle to get Glynis's death properly investigated, Constance discovers Alaric to be a worthy ally.

Yet even after Inspector Stokes of Scotland Yard arrives and takes charge of the case, along with his consultants, the Honorable Barnaby Adair and his wife, Penelope, the murderer's identity remains shrouded in mystery, and learning why Glynis was killed—all in the few days before the house party's guests will insist on leaving—tests the resolve of all concerned. Flung into each other's company, fiercely independent though Constance is, unsusceptible though Alaric is, neither can deny the connection that grows between them.

Then Constance vanishes.

Can Alaric unearth the one fact that will point to the murderer before the villain rips from the world the lady Alaric now craves for his own?

A historical novel of 75,000 words interweaving romance, mystery, and murder.

ABOUT THE AUTHOR

#1 *New York Times* bestselling author Stephanie Laurens began writing romances as an escape from the dry world of professional science. Her hobby quickly became a career when her first novel was accepted for publication, and with entirely becoming alacrity, she gave up writing about facts in favor of writing fiction.

All Laurens's works to date are historical romances, ranging from medieval times to the mid-1800s, and her settings range from Scotland to India. The majority of her works are set in the period of the British Regency. Laurens has published over 80 works of historical romance, including 40 *New York Times* bestsellers. Laurens has sold more than 20 million print, audio, and e-books globally. All her works are continuously available in print and e-book formats in English worldwide, and have been translated into many other languages. An international bestseller, among other accolades, Laurens has received the Romance Writers of America® prestigious RITA® Award for Best Romance Novella 2008 for *The Fall of Rogue Gerrard*.

Laurens's continuing novels featuring the Cynster family are widely regarded as classics of the historical romance genre. Other series include the *Bastion Club Novels*, the *Black Cobra Quartet*, the *Adventurers Quartet,* and the *Casebook of Barnaby Adair Novels*.

For information on all published novels and on upcoming releases and updates on novels yet to come, visit Stephanie's website: www. stephanielaurens.com

To sign up for Stephanie's Email Newsletter (a private list) for heads-up alerts as new books are released, exclusive sneak peeks into upcoming books, and exclusive sweepstakes contests, follow the prompts at http:// www.stephanielaurens.com/newsletter-signup/

To follow Stephanie on BookBub, head to her BookBub Author Page: https://www.bookbub.com/authors/stephanie-laurens

Stephanie lives with her husband and a goofy black labradoodle in the hills outside Melbourne, Australia. When she isn't writing, she's reading, and if she isn't reading, she'll be tending her garden.

www.stephanielaurens.com
stephanie@stephanielaurens.com

Printed in the USA
CPSIA information can be obtained
at www.ICGtesting.com
LVHW021231181024
794099LV00005B/1096